SMALL ACTS OF DECEIT

OTHER BOOKS BY THE AUTHOR

The Cat and The Corpse in The Old Barn

The Man Who Vanished and The Dog Who Waited

The Missing Wife and The Stone Fen Siamese

Murder and The Moggies of Magpie Row

SMALL ACTS OF DECEIT

KATE HIGH

First published in Great Britain in 2025 by
The Book Guild Ltd
Unit E2 Airfield Business Park,
Harrison Road, Market Harborough,
Leicestershire. LE16 7UL
Tel: 0116 2792299
www.bookguild.co.uk
Email: info@bookguild.co.uk
X: @bookguild

Copyright © 2025 Kate High

The right of Kate High to be identified as the author of this
work has been asserted by them in accordance with the
Copyright, Design and Patents Act 1988.

All rights reserved. No part of this publication may be
reproduced, transmitted, or stored in a retrieval system, in any form or by any means,
without permission in writing from the publisher, nor be otherwise circulated in
any form of binding or cover other than that in which it is published and without
a similar condition being imposed on the subsequent purchaser.

The manufacturer's authorised representative in the EU
for product safety is Authorised Rep Compliance Ltd,
71 Lower Baggot Street, Dublin D02 P593 Ireland
(www.arccompliance.com)

This work is entirely fictitious and bears no resemblance to any persons living or dead.

Typeset in 11pt Minion Pro

Printed and bound in Great Britain by CMP UK

ISBN 978 1835742 143

British Library Cataloguing in Publication Data.
A catalogue record for this book is available from the British Library.

Dedicated to
Hilary Johnson

1

Apart from the low buzz of distant traffic coming from the main carriageway, the avenue was quiet. It had begun to rain, a slow relentless drizzle, and Mauve held the rail, minding her footing to step cautiously down the curved narrow stairway leading to the basement flat, cursing each step, wishing she'd swapped her impractical four-inch heels for a pair of flat trainers.

It was as she'd remembered, with debris and leaves shed by the lime trees in the avenue gathering in the square concrete area at the bottom and on the wet metal steps of the stairs, adding a slippery hazard to her downward progress.

The front door was still yellow but now chipped and dirty, not as she recalled it from her visit over eight years earlier, freshly painted, clean and shiny. It was half-open and she felt a mix of fear and nausea, not knowing what might be waiting on the inside. Pushing it gently with her fingertips, it moved silently as the light entering through a window at the end of the hall spread to encompass her. A musical thumping beat started from above the basement flat, startling Mauve and breaking her concentration.

It was Friday. Less than an hour ago, she'd been in the kitchen when her mobile rang. The radio was turned up, and her short, straight, blonde hair bounced as she flicked her head to the retro 1960s music. Having kicked off her Louboutin heels, Mauve held up her favourite long-stemmed glass, pausing intermittently to sip cold white wine.

With business for the week finished, she anticipated the arrival of her partner, Zack. Tomorrow, Kit, her twenty-one-year-old son, would return from university for the summer break. She was looking forward to going with him to her Norfolk house for some special mother-and-son time.

As she danced around the kitchen, her only companion, Timothy, a scruffy, brown mongrel lying beneath the table, watched her with benign detachment. Having just eaten his dinner, he was content. The dancing woman was not his favourite person, that title belonged to Kit, but when the young master was away it was she who fed and walked him. He rewarded her by spreading himself to sleep overnight at the bottom of her bed. His allegiance and bed changed immediately on the return of the young master.

Looking at her watch – Mauve had taken her time to meander from the kitchen to the foot of the stairs, where her brown leather jacket was hanging and retrieve the phone from a pocket – she thought about Zack. He was late, but that had become the new norm. Recently, Zack was always late.

The mobile rang out before Mauve reached it, and playing back the message, she'd instantly recognised Lena's Irish lilt.

'*Help me, Mauve! I need you. Come now, please. I'm not messing, come now!*'

Automatically, Mauve returned the call before questioning why she was doing this. Lena, her teenage nemesis, was back. It hadn't taken much for her half-sister to jerk her strings.

Mauve's return call went instantly to messages. She didn't leave one. Lena's voice was already lodged inside her brain: '*Come now!*' She could feel the rising panic and her skin prickling with tension. The edge in the voice held genuine fear. She'd known Lena better than anybody – cool, commanding, someone who never begged – it wasn't her way. Then, it was more than eight years since they'd last spoken, things changed.

Draining her glass, she'd pushed her feet back into her heels and slid the jacket around her petite frame before grabbing her car keys and bag. Then, scribbling '*back soon*' on the back of an envelope for Zack, she headed to the door.

Her car, a pale-blue convertible Jaguar, contained the usual shit to indicate Zack had borrowed it earlier that day: an empty crisp packet, a used tissue and a chewing gum wrapper. Zack shed debris like a cat moulted hair. Starting, then gunning the engine, she swung the car out of the driveway into the road. As she gathered speed to cut into the outer lane, another driver honked, giving her the middle finger. Avoiding eye contact, Mauve ignored him.

The traffic on Friday evening was always the busiest of the week. Within ten minutes she was on the ring road, the most direct route to get to the flat. Although Lena had not said where she was, it was the most obvious option.

Outside the basement flat, Mauve glanced again at her watch before peering along the hall. It was 7.04p.m. Thirty-two minutes since she'd picked up the call and driven like a maniac, cutting and weaving through the traffic, the panic of the drive leaving her clammy and disorientated.

Lena's voice had taken her back to a reminder of things she'd believed to have left in the past. Lena was dangerous, but it worked both ways. If what Lena had on Mauve, what they'd done, became known to the police, it would destroy them both. It was how Mauve had convinced herself she was safe. They'd had a deal, one that had cost her a lot of money; it included buying her half-sister this flat. Out of curiosity, she'd visited it only once, after which Lena agreed to them never contacting each other again; the cleanest way to move on.

Then Mauve remembered the urgency in Lena's voice. She'd assumed it was genuine. But she knew her half-sister well enough to consider the possibility that Lena might be playing her.

Stepping across the threshold of the flat, Mauve saw the door lock had been broken before her attention was caught by a smeared line to the right, running along one wall. A daubed, wobbly red line broke the blank beige paintwork. With fear heightening, she took it in. The blood appeared like clumsy art from a child's painting that had dribbled downwards in places. Could it be from a hand, someone bleeding and trying to steady themselves to keep upright? Her strongest instinct was to run. Fearful that someone unseen was hiding, watching, the back of her neck itched. She looked about before moving cautiously into the hall, calling Lena's name.

'Lena, are you here?' Nothing. Silence. 'It's me, Mauve. I picked up your call.'

Mauve glanced to the left into the living room. It looked bare. Stepping inside, the blue Venetian blinds she remembered from her previous visit were pulled down with the slats open. The summer evening brightness spilt in, forming neat stripes of light and shadow. The carpet was a mottled blue with marks where furniture had once rested, and on the walls square and oblong shapes indicated the now absent shapes of prints and pictures. In the centre of the room hung a naked bulb; even the shade was missing.

Mauve fought with confusion. If Lena had already moved from here, why had she phoned to leave the message? Or had she expected Mauve to go somewhere else? The front door open, the lock broken and the blood on the walls suggested violence and someone making a hasty getaway. But when had it happened? An hour ago, yesterday, or days ago? Back in the hall and looking closely at the smeared wall, she could see the blood that had run down was still damp, so it was recent. Had someone attacked Lena after she'd left the message?

Crossing the hall, she entered the small room her half-sister used as an office. Again, it was empty. Returning to the hall, she realised the sounds from upstairs had stopped, and the silence, deep and oppressive, closed in like a cloak around her. It was a combination she feared: blood and silence. Over the last eight years, she had developed coping strategies for panic attacks, but until now she had not been truly tested. And after the silence, walking forward, the sound of her heels clicking on the wood floor seemed exaggerated and loud.

She stopped to examine the closed kitchen door, painted beige like the walls, but with red fingerprint smudges. Lena's blood, perhaps?

'Rich bitch, rich bitch.' Lena's shrill, singsong voice was in Mauve's head, using words she'd hurled after gatecrashing her life. While Mauve had been Daddy's official special girl, Lena was his dirty little secret.

A sudden gust of wind picked up the leaves, lifting them through the open front door to swirl and dance inside the hall. Mauve jerked, startled, turning back to stare. After a moment, gripped by fear, she moved her focus again to the kitchen and found she was trembling.

Hesitating for a moment longer, she came to a decision, and in one fluid movement threw open the door. The kitchen was darker, the light coming in through the glass kitchen door and window. Mauve automatically flicked the light switch, remembering the small lights fitted into the pine-clad ceiling that had brought the room to life on her previous visit. Nothing changed and, she realised, in an empty flat the electricity would have been disconnected.

It was, as with the other rooms, devoid of furniture, but there was blood, and so much of it. If the smear on the hall wall had been an entrée, this was the main course.

Red flecks patterned the walls, and blood, with small perfect pomegranate-seedlike bubbles, pooled to one side of the kitchen on the dark-brown quarry tiles. In an involuntary gesture, Mauve pushed her hand across her nose and mouth, trying to stem the metallic odour from the blood filling her nostrils. As her hand came to her face, a spasm, like a jolt of electricity, ran through her body and she returned, in her mind, to Cumbria as it had been over eight years earlier. The only difference was that today she was sober, and there was no corpse on the floor to fix her with blank, sightless eyes.

She moved her gaze up from the bloody floor. In the kitchen, devoid of any culinary items or furniture, a lone round hatbox with a lid sat incongruously on an otherwise empty shelf. The perfect, unsullied white of the box translated in her brain to virginal. Clean and pure amongst the surrounding mayhem that spoke and smelt of death. Lena loved her hats, but would that be what the box contained?

Mauve's thoughts again returned to the day over eight years earlier. Lena had grabbed her arm. 'Run,' she'd hissed. 'Run.' And Mauve, disorientated and drunk, had been dragged along on legs as heavy and immobile as concrete blocks, knowing her life depended on it.

On the threshold of the kitchen, Mauve turned to leave. With her heart racing and struggling to breathe, she tried to calm herself to banish the merging images of then and now. She pressed her hand against her chest and began a repetitive breathing exercise. Counting slowly to five, she inhaled and seven to exhale. Her eyes tightly shut as she tried to regain control, her instincts screamed for her to leave.

With what she intended as a final glance back to the box, she changed her mind. She had to see what was inside; if Lena had wanted her to come here, there must be a logical reason. It would take only a moment to look.

Skirting the pool of blood on the tiled floor, she quickly reached the waist-high shelf and pulled up the lid to stare hard at what it contained.

It was unnecessary to touch it to recognise the foot-high, chunky wooden doll. For hair, its head was painted jet black with a thin white line of damage across the painted hair. The cheeks and lips were as red as the blood on the walls and floor around her. The silk dress that adorned the doll, which once might have been bright, was a muted yellow, with a black ribbon interweaved into the hemline. The doll had been handmade and carved, dating around the mid-nineteenth century. The last time Mauve had seen it was in the house in Cumbria, in the Lake District, clasped in the arthritic, clawlike dead hands of eighty-two-year-old Paulette Franklin. Paulette's dyed hair, red cheeks and lipstick were a mirror reflection, mimicking the doll, the blackness of her hair and the brightness of the cosmetics an incongruity on the elderly lined face. The doll's wide-painted, expressionless eyes were a perfect match for Paulette's. Mauve's memory had gaps, like a jigsaw with key pieces missing. Her last recollection was of being in the passenger seat of Lena's car in a state of confusion and dishevelment.

Not touching the doll, Mauve quickly replaced the lid

and turned. Her fingerprints would be everywhere: the front and kitchen doors, light switches. It wasn't too late to change that. She could take the lid with her and wipe where she'd touched with her sleeve as she left.

With bile rising in her throat, she pressed her hands against her face, struggling not to vomit. Then the sudden flash of a swirling blue light passed the window and stopped, and Mauve straightened, fearful.

Going into panic mode, she shot forward with alacrity. She had to get out before the police found her. The thought filtered through her mind again that she should have replaced the heels she'd been wearing all day with flat trainers. As her feet encountered the bloody pool, she realised that, in her panic to leave, she'd forgotten the need to move around to the edge. Her high heels skidded out from under her, and she flailed her arms, hands open and outstretched in a failed attempt to grab something and save herself. Falling backwards, she crashed down.

When, a few moments later, two uniformed police officers appeared, they stopped short in the kitchen doorway as they looked on in silence, their eyes censorious.

Mauve, on hands and knees, still struggling to get to her feet, stared, her eyes fixed like a Shakespearean character, upon her blood-covered hands. It was the same as all those years ago. The only difference was that Paulette's body had been lying on the floor directly in front of her.

Now, like a pig after wallowing in mud, the fall and failed attempts to push herself upwards had left not only her hands but the whole of her body saturated in blood.

2

After being brought from the basement flat to the police station, Mauve experienced another panic attack. An officer called in the duty doctor. Once calm, she'd been allowed a shower, but the metallic stink of the blood still clung to her. The loose-fitting grey pants and top, given as temporary replacement for her clothes, swamped her tiny frame and also had an odd odour, and she speculated who might have worn them previously. Then, after a period of stillness, waiting for the arrival of her legal advisor and agreeing she was well enough to be interviewed, she was given a bag containing a pair of jeans, a sweater and trainers.

'Left by your husband,' a young, uniformed officer told her, unceremoniously dropping the supermarket carrier bag onto the table before her.

'Is he still here?' Mauve asked hopefully to the departing back. Zack was not her husband, he was her partner of five years, but she didn't correct the misunderstanding.

'No, after you spoke to your legal advisor, he phoned

your husband. Told him you needed clothes, and he came, left those, then went,' the officer replied, uninterested.

Changing into the clothes, relieved to be out of the smelly police garments, she cursed Zack. Why was he so dim that he couldn't have worked out that she might need a pair of knickers, a T-shirt for under the sweater and socks for the trainers? And worse, why had he not waited to find out when she might be released?

The interview room was small, and with four people around the table it felt closed in and claustrophobic. Mauve started at a disadvantage. After the shower, her face was without a scrap of make-up, and she hung her head, feeling naked, while imagining her damp hair unattractively flattened against her skull. Knowing the interview was being video recorded added to the tension. Every word she uttered and her every facial expression would be pored over, considered and pulled apart by unknown, possibly hostile, officers.

Detective Sergeant Sue Teller's small dark eyes set in a pallid face had been hardened by years of watching, waiting and listening. Mauve could feel cynicism leaching from the woman. Her accent was Scottish, her tone blunt. Mauve imagined herself observed, assessed and labelled by the DS as rich, shallow and deceitful. She had been judged and found wanting. The officer didn't believe her. Yet most of what she'd said was true.

Charlie Morrison, Mauve's friend and legal advisor, suggested Mauve might want to give 'no comment' responses. 'It's an option,' he'd added dryly. 'But if you've done nothing wrong and are telling the truth, then honesty is best.'

Mauve didn't like the word 'if'. Had he worked out that she was holding something back? He'd known her long enough to understand the way her mind worked. Pushing that thought aside, she agreed that honesty was the best policy. Anything connected to tricky, manipulative Lena, her father's other daughter, might come back later to bite her on the arse. And whatever had happened this evening in the basement flat was not her doing. She'd done nothing wrong. She felt a momentary sense of guilt talking to Charlie, knowing she might well have done nothing wrong tonight, but that eight years ago, she had. The doll in the box had been left to send her a message.

Unaware of her half-sister's existence until she was thirteen years old, Mauve had been shocked to discover that Lena was only six months younger, conceived while Celia, Mauve's own mother, had been pregnant. The discovery that she had a half-sister happened after Lena's Irish mother, Bonnie Kelly, arrived at their home with skinny, sour-faced Lena. After telling Henry Gilcrest, Mauve's father, 'It's your bloody turn with the annoying little bitch,' she'd left the girl. Bonnie had flounced out, driven away by her son, Robin. Five years later, Celia returned the favour. Lena, aged eighteen, had stolen money from Celia to travel to France with a boyfriend. On her return, after being dumped by the boyfriend, Celia, treating Lena like an unwanted parcel, arranged for her to be returned to sender and left on her mother's doorstep. Henry agreed with the decision taken by his wife.

Mauve detailed her sisterly connection with Lena to the DS, the phone call, and her reason for going to the flat.

She could never reveal the dark, murderous side of their relationship.

The bright, fluorescent lighting of the room made Mauve's eyes ache, and she'd had to steel herself to keep her gaze up to meet the scrutiny of DS Teller's unbroken stare. And with tension wracking her body, Mauve's thinking split into two directions. Part of her was answering questions, another part was trying to accept the likelihood that Lena was dead. How to explain her relationship with Lena? Love and hate in equal measure. Lena was wily, intemperate and never cared what anyone thought, an echo of Henry Gilcrest. Mauve had adored her father, and Henry's characteristics were alive in Lena. Mauve didn't want Lena to be dead, but it would close a chapter. The thought brought a wave of relief, then guilt. Did it mean she hoped Lena was dead? If she were, Mauve would never again have to be fearful of someone finding out what they'd done. Her deliberations kept returning to the doll; could it be a copy? The damage on the wooden head, the white line, was precisely placed as she'd remembered, but if it was the original, who had left it in the blood-drenched flat?

The detective sergeant played back Lena's message several times.

'So, when this sister, who you haven't seen for years, has a problem, you go running to find her?' It sounded like an accusation.

'I was worried about her,' Mauve said. 'She was clearly frightened.'

'It looks like there was reason. If the blood in the flat

turns out to be hers, the quantity of blood must lead to the conclusion that she's dead. Has Lena asked for help before? You said you'd not seen her for over eight years.'

'The last time I saw her was over eight years ago. After that we drifted apart.'

'Strange. You said you'd given the flat to Lena. Extended at the back, four bedrooms and garden. Even eight years ago, it must have cost a lot, and for someone you're not particularly close to.'

'My client has already explained that.' Charlie's cold East London drawl cut in. 'At that time, Lena needed support. My client helped her in a one-off gesture because of the link with their father. You're going in a loop, DS Teller.'

'You told me your father,' DS Teller looked at her notes, ignoring Charlie's intervention, 'the late Sir Henry Gilcrest, bequeathed on his death, a substantial amount to Lena White. It meant she should have had no further claims on your inheritance.'

'My client is a soft touch.' Charlie spoke before Mauve could respond. 'Lena, her half-sister, had not used her inheritance wisely, and she'd fallen on hard times. Ms Gilcrest kindly gave her the flat and a lump sum of money. It was a one-off gesture. Mauve's late father was Sir Henry Gilcrest, the property magnate. He left an equal amount to each of his daughters. The bulk of the estate went to his wife, Celia, which Mauve inherited on her mother's death. A blessing and a curse; Ms Gilcrest's wealth is a lure for gold-diggers.'

The DS's pursed lips and sour expression suggested

she knew the connection. Mauve directed her gaze to the grey table between her and the police officers. Knowing who Henry Gilcrest was and his reputation would never score any points. Most remembered the building scandal caused by the substandard work in a particular North London tower block and the court case brought about due to structural problems in houses.

Mauve kept her eyes focused on the table. It was bolted to the floor, with a metal bar on one side, presumably to handcuff those showing violent tendencies. Next to the DS was a detective constable, younger than his colleague. He remained mostly silent. Charlie was beside Mauve on one of the brown utility chairs fixed to the floor.

A momentary silence fell before DS Teller returned to the same question.

'Are you sure you hadn't seen the doll before?'

'I told you. I've never seen it before.'

'And you didn't take it out of the box?'

'I took the lid off the box to see what was inside.' Mauve remembered her concern about her fingerprints on the lid. 'But I didn't touch the doll; I put the lid back on.' She repeated what she had told the DS several times over.

'My client has already answered that.' Charlie pushed the subject aside before pausing to raise one of his bushy eyebrows meaningfully. Aged fifty-four, he was tall and gangly, and as he slowly unfurled himself to rise from the chair, he pushed a hand through his wiry brown hair threaded with grey. 'You've listened to the recording on Ms Gilcrest's phone; she has explained her every action and answered all your questions. Mauve Gilcrest went to the aid of her half-sister; she's a victim, not a murderer, and she's still in shock.' Charlie looked at Mauve. 'And even if you consider Ms Gilcrest to be a "person of interest", there is no evidence to suggest any wrongdoing on her part.'

DS Teller glowered at Charlie, giving a curt nod before directing her words to Mauve. 'Before you leave, we need fingerprints and a DNA sample. And don't plan any long trips. As we progress with our enquiries, we'll no doubt need to talk to you again.'

It was Mauve's turn to nod, and as she rose from her seat, she wobbled. Charlie extended his arm, his hand briefly cupping her elbow.

DS Teller's humourless, small dark eyes were on them, no doubt working some significance into the gesture.

In the darkness of Charlie's large dark-blue Mercedes, Mauve hunkered into the comfort of the beige leather upholstery. Leaving the station, she had trembled, and Charlie had taken off his tan-coloured cashmere coat to wrap it around her shoulders. Tough on the outside, his soft side with Mauve was just below the surface. It was nearly midnight, and the roads were quiet. The semi-darkness of the car made it feel like the safest she'd felt all evening.

'Tell me again what the doll looked like.' Charlie, concentrating on the road, did not look at her as he spoke.

'It was wooden, I think,' Mauve muttered. 'Painted hair and face, with a yellow dress. I don't want to think about it anymore.' She made her voice bland, unconcerned. 'What did Zack say? You phoned him?'

'After you called me and told me what'd happened, I

rang him to ask him to bring clothes and shoes over, which he did. Another thing: you won't get your car back until the police have given it a thorough going-over. If they find a speck of blood in there that matches that in the house, you'll be in the shit.'

'They won't,' Mauve said. She waited for Charlie to say something more about this, but his next question had moved on, taking her by surprise.

'Have you heard from Eliza Kelly recently, Lena's daughter? She came after you for money, didn't she? Or was that from Robin, Lena's brother?' Charlie glanced at her.

'It was about six months ago. I told Eliza to bog off. I've heard nothing from Robin; I told you he'd been struck off?'

'You'd mentioned he used to be a doctor. Drug smuggling was clearly more lucrative,' Charlie said.

Mauve shook her head.

'What about Damien, Lena and Robin's other brother?'

'You have got a good memory,' Mauve said. 'I only met him once, when I was a kid. I wouldn't even know what he looks like now. I understand he joined the army. A squaddie, I think.'

'OK.' Again, Charlie glanced at her briefly. 'Eliza is your only real link to Lena, and you've had no contact with her for six months?'

'I'd had enough of them leeching off me. Eliza is twenty-two or three. She needs to make her way. That goes for Zack as well. He's happy to take handouts but didn't bother to hang around at the police station to make sure I'd be OK.'

'Is there anything you should be telling me? Something I might be concerned about?' Charlie's voice was thoughtful as he stopped at a set of red lights.

'Like?'

'Like, apart from what happened tonight, are you and Zack on the way out?'

'That's not your business.' Mauve was tart.

'It is if he comes after you for money, like Thom... or the others.'

Mauve pulled a face in the semi-darkness as the lights turned green and the car moved forward. Charlie was a pain in the backside, constantly second-guessing situations, and even more irritating, he was usually spot-on. He was ten years older than her, and once, a very long time ago, there had been a spark between them. It had resulted in a sexual encounter, rough and hurried, late at night, on the floor of his office. Luckily, they'd been able to move on, neither wanting to lose the friendship. Both had been in relationships that would come to an end. Hers with Thom and Charlie's with Helen.

Charlie had negotiated a settlement for her with Thom, who'd always told her he hadn't married her for her money, but after only five years came up with an eye-watering figure that would take a big chunk of it. The amount Charlie got him to agree to was a fraction of what he'd asked for. Kit had been almost three when he left. Thom had never had time or shown any interest in the child and seemed relieved that part of the deal was never seeing Kit again. After Thom, Mauve had never remarried.

'Well?' Charlie pushed.

'It's not so much if, it's when,' Mauve admitted. 'Zack and I have been on the way down for months.'

'Do you need me to get involved… when he asks for money?'

'Zack and I never married. I learnt that lesson with Thom.' Mauve turned to look at Charlie's profile as he drove. 'Leave it for now. There's too much going on.'

'With what happened this evening?'

'Yes, that and Kit is coming home tomorrow from uni.'

'If that's what you want.' Charlie shrugged as he pulled up outside Mauve's home. 'Shall I go in with you?'

'No, I'll phone you tomorrow,' she said, dismissing him as she wriggled off his coat to leave it on the seat. She stood for a moment as he took her in. Without make-up she had lost a barrier of defence, and in that moment she saw herself through his eyes: small, pale and skinny with tousled hair, like a defenceless child who had just got out of bed. She ducked her head down to move away and then watched the car as it pulled away from the kerb, its tail lights disappearing into the night.

The light from the house spread to illuminate the front lawn. Parked at the side, a maroon-coloured Citroën Pallas blocked entry to the garage. Mauve knew if she were to measure distances, the car's bumper would be ninety centimetres from the garage door, and the same distance from the wall to the right. While not extreme, her son's OCD tendencies were recognisable to his mother. Kit was home.

3

'What the hell happened to you?' Mauve snapped as Zack came into the hall holding the half-filled chunky glass he favoured for whisky.

'I did what Charlie asked.' Zack sounded surly and his progress was unsteady. 'You phoned him, not me.'

'Charlie is my legal support. It had to be him,' Mauve said. 'You could have stayed to see how I was, or what time they'd let me leave.'

'You had Mr Perfect. What more could you want?' Zack slurred the words, clearly drunk.

Mauve looked him over. He hadn't asked what had happened and how she was after her ordeal. Then, they both knew, whatever happened, he'd stopped caring a long time ago. At thirty-eight, Zack was five years her junior. She'd once found him amusing and sexy, back when he had ambition and a six-pack. Now, most days he spent mooching around the house, leaving a trail of mess, and the sagging belly that drooped over his trouser belt indicated gym visits were no longer on his list of activities.

Was she the cause of the downward trajectory? Then, she reasoned, it wasn't so much her as what she represented. 'Rich bitch, rich bitch.' Lena's words were again in her head. While relationships always got off to a good start, the financial balance was weighted in her favour. She'd never achieved a long partnership with someone of equal economic stature. It seemed unfair that rich men could take up with penniless females and the women wouldn't feel lessened by the imbalance. All the men she'd had as part of her life eventually felt emasculated.

'Mother!'

As Zack staggered back in the direction he'd come from, Mauve caught sight of her son's bare feet and long skinny legs encased in lime-green jeans coming down the stairs, two steps then a pause, another two steps and a pause. The ritual when descending stairs had not been altered since early childhood. He was cradling Timothy, the dog, in his arms. Reaching the hall, Kit advanced rapidly towards her, dark-haired, slender and over six feet tall, his every movement fluid as water. Mauve braced herself. She was Mummy when Kit wanted something or was being affectionate, and Mum was for everyday encounters. Using the word Mother meant Kit was seriously pissed-off.

'Bloody *Auntie* Lena. What the hell has she got you into now?' Kit's emphasis on the word "auntie" was mocking. He raked her with his eyes.

'I wasn't expecting you home until tomorrow. Did Zack tell you what happened?' Mauve looked in the direction Zack had gone. 'Charlie told him the whole story and asked him to bring me some clothes and shoes to the station.'

'I changed my mind, decided to come home tonight, and as you might have noticed, Mother, Zack is pissed. He was like that when I arrived an hour ago.' Kit leaned towards his mother in full flow. 'What he said didn't make sense, and when I called Charlie, his phone kept going to messages.' He looked her up and down, as if seeing her properly for the first time. 'Mummy, you look like crap.'

Mauve ignored the comment on her appearance. 'An hour ago, we would have been in the police interview. He'd switched his phone off.'

'Shit for brains,' Kit nodded his head in the direction Zack had gone, 'told me Lena left a message, you went into meltdown panic mode and went to her flat and ended up covered in blood.'

'There's a bit more to it than that.' Mauve tried to placate him.

'So, tell me.'

Mauve touched his arm to guide him. 'Let's go to the kitchen. I could use a drink, and there's an open bottle of white in the fridge.'

As her son put Timothy down in the kitchen, Mauve smiled, taking in the royal-blue jacket with pink embroidery worn by the dog.

'You've got a new jacket for him.' Mauve bent to stroke the dog's head. He butted her legs in appreciation.

'A new *designer* jacket,' Kit corrected her. 'From the private collection of a yet-unrecognised, amazingly talented young designer.'

'What's their name?'

'You won't have heard of them,' Kit said haughtily.

'So funny that you and I are the only two people he likes in the whole world.'

'There are one or two others.' Kit raised his eyebrows.

'Veronica?'

'Of course.'

Perched high on leather-topped stools around the central kitchen island, Mauve poured them both a glass of wine before telling Kit what had happened, from the phone call to making a statement with Charlie.

'Shit, Mum, that was horrible for you. No wonder you look like crap. Do you think Lena's dead?'

'I don't know. The police think the amount of blood suggests the victim must be dead, but no body. Then again, it might be somebody else's blood.'

'That doesn't make sense.' Kit took a sip of his wine, his face serious. 'It must be something to do with Lena; otherwise, why would she have phoned you? She'll be in on whatever's happening and was banking on you going to the flat.' He searched her face. 'What was the doll all about? How is that connected?'

'I don't know.' Mauve stood up. 'I think I need to go to bed. I feel rubbish. But in the morning, I want to hear about your plans for the summer break.'

'Mm, you don't get off that lightly. I want to talk more about Lena tomorrow. I'm going to make you a camomile tea to help you sleep.'

'No tea, darling, thank you.' Mauve went to gently stroke his cheek before heading to the door. 'You know everything I do now; nothing else to know.'

'If Lena's involved, there's always got to be something else going on. Gather your thoughts, Mother dear.' Kit sounded arch as he fixed her through his long-lashed, dark-brown eyes with a long stare. 'You must have an opinion on what she's about, which undoubtedly involves screwing money out of you.'

'Yes, that's something we can agree on.'

Later, after taking another shower to further remove the smell of blood Mauve imagined still clung to her, she changed into peach-coloured silk pyjamas.

Sitting in the darkness, propped up by a bank of pillows, she allowed her eyes to wander around, taking in the familiar shapes in the room: a chest of drawers, a round walnut table, chairs, and against the wall, a pile of 1920s crocodile suitcases, making a triangle shape as each case went up, smaller than the one below it. A sweet smell came from pale-pink roses in a vase on the windowsill, flowers from her garden, not the forced, scentless variety from the florist.

Being here, amongst familiar things, was comforting, as was remembering Kit was in the house, which took on a different feel when he was home. Zack had long since been banished from her bedroom, keeping to his own, but tonight she missed the presence of Timothy on the bed and the funny, comforting noise of the dog's snuffles and his deep breathing. Four years earlier, the dog, of indeterminate age, had been a stray that followed her son to their Norfolk home from the beach. Kit loved everything about the scruffy animal, including his cross-eyes and crooked teeth. While her son was away, the dog would sleep contentedly on the end of her bed; once he returned home, she was abandoned. Kit was Timothy's first choice for companionship and as a bed mate.

Mauve tried closing her eyes to sleep, and each time an image of the basement kitchen came to her: the blood, her slipping and sliding and the association with the doll. She fumbled in the darkness on her bedside table to find ear tips, and with her eyes closed and an iPod on her chest, tried to lose herself in the familiar sounds that helped her relax. The movement of the sea, and the cry of dolphins, followed by Tibetan singing bowls and the Om chant of monks, and finally the tinkle of a solitary bell. It did not have the desired effect; if anything, she felt more tense. Putting the iPod aside, she switched her thoughts to Kit. The homecoming reunion had gone better than she'd imagined. They hadn't argued, which had something to do with what had happened this evening, blowing any other discussion out of the water. Trying to hide secrets from her beautiful boy was difficult; it felt as if he could look through flesh and bone to get inside her head and read her thoughts. Their relationship had been perfect when he was small, but not so good as he got older. When she complained about Kit's stubborn streak, he'd retort that he had inherited it. Starting university, it felt as if he'd had a personality transplant. Then, she supposed the change was natural, with him needing to find his way to negotiate the curve balls life threw at him.

Recently, their relationship had hit rock bottom. She'd

imagined he would become something exceptional, a financier or eventually a captain of industry. During his last break, he told her he was giving up after almost two years on an economics degree to follow his heart and become a make-up artist, to work in TV and film. His joy in sharing was challenging, imagining his mother would be thrilled with the new career choice, and Mauve found puncturing his enthusiasm painful. Their time together ended in sour discord. Before leaving, Kit's retaliation had been cruel, his words crushing. He'd informed her that she was a terrible mother with an unworkable relationship template.

It had taken every weapon in Mauve's armoury to get him to go back for the last term of that academic year. She'd cajoled, bullied, begged and blackmailed. Finally, he agreed to return and think more about it. They would talk further when the current academic year was complete.

Another sticking point was Kit's resentment that Mauve had made a deal for Thom not to contact them. Telling him that Thom had been a loser hadn't much helped. He'd said it had to be something he judged for himself. Mauve did not doubt that Kit would one day contact Thom and be bitterly disappointed by the person he found. And then there were so many other things Kit didn't want to talk to his mother about. It included his university friends and Veronica, who looked like she had done at twenty-one, with blonde shoulder-length hair and way too much lipstick. She had to welcome Veronica, but asking questions was off-limits.

Mauve imagined them going to the house in Norfolk

while he was home for the summer break. Staring into the darkness, she acknowledged that while she had been looking forward to it, in truth, it was no longer something Kit enjoyed.

The night dragged. Mauve tossed herself around the bed, feeling wretched. When sleep eventually came, it was not peaceful.

She was in a garden with a long pathway, a fallen tree to one side and a broken wooden bench to the other. It led to a grand house with a pantile roof and many bright sparkly windows encased within white-painted wooden frames. It was the home of Paulette Franklin. Her memory moved, as always, from one place to another; there was no flow or connection with the images. Her reflections flicked back to Lena's slim legs, walking in front of her along the pathway as she swigged from a bottle of whisky. She laughed as she passed it back to Mauve to take a swig. Then, taking her hand, Lena had swirled around dancing. Mauve followed, her legs, once in motion, moving like an automaton, up and down. It went on for a few moments – or forever – the two of them dancing in the dark.

Moving nearer the doorway of the house, a man waited in the shadow, and as she stepped forward, he turned to look down, more than a head taller than her. She recognised the square jaw and arched nose – the profile of Robin Kelly, Lena's older brother. The facial features indicated membership of the Kelly clan. He stepped out to hold her arm, and Lena's, and they became a circle – turning, dancing and swaying. A memory reawakened: Robin had been there. He must have followed them from

Lincoln. The memory faded and jumped, and now she was inside the house in a small room, hot and airless, with a lot of clutter, every surface piled with books, newspapers and boxes. And there it was again: the doll. Although the yellow dress looked soft and silky, it had, in parts, a rough texture, as if something sticky had once been spilt and the fabric had not been cleaned.

The texture of the silk was rough. The image had stopped. Like a video on repeat, endlessly rewound and replayed. *The silk between Mauve's fingers was rough.* Suddenly, she was awake, sitting upright. She had handled the doll; why had she not remembered that before? Perhaps the shock of what happened this evening had triggered the memory. It was one of the missing pieces of the jigsaw.

'And you didn't take it out of the box?' DS Teller's voice repeated the same question during the taped police interview.

'I didn't touch the doll.' How many times had Mauve given that response, three or four? She'd believed it to be true, but it wasn't.

Feeling hot and flustered, Mauve was suddenly wide awake, sliding out of bed. Remembering newspaper headlines in bold lettering. Murder Hunt: Police Seek Motive for Murder. She paced the bedroom. How long would it be before the police had the blood match results and the DNA from the doll's dress? Twenty-four hours, forty-eight, or perhaps sooner? One thing was for sure: if she were correct and had touched the dress's fabric, they would find her DNA, and she would have to explain how it got there. And if they had a record of Paulette's DNA from the investigation into her murder, it would match the doll's dress and easily connect the dots. Paulette's relationship with her sexually incontinent father and disagreement with him and her mother, Celia, was on record. And then there were the diamonds!

Closing her eyes tightly, she pushed herself to recall the feel of touching the fabric again, rubbing it gently between her thumb and forefinger. There was no doubt she remembered the sense of it, drifting through the alcoholic haze, knowing something spilt had dried to make the fabric feel coarse.

Mauve started to dress, hastily grabbing jeans, a sweater and trainers. Going to her wardrobe, she pulled an overnight bag from the back to quickly stuff clothes inside. In the bathroom, she threw in her toothbrush and cosmetics. There would be other things she needed already at the house in Norfolk. She had to get away before the police came to question her.

Over eight years earlier, she had been at the Norfolk house while Kit had been away, skiing in Switzerland with a school group. Lena had contacted her before arriving. They had gone together from Norfolk to Robin's house in Lincoln, then on to Cumbria. But Robin had not accompanied them. Why had she now remembered his presence in the doorway of Paulette's home? Had he and Lena scammed her, stealing the diamond necklace for themselves, and had Robin played a part in Paulette's murder?

4

Sitting on the bed, Mauve considered her options. She had to go. But with the knowledge that it would only take a short time for the police to find out about the Norfolk house, she couldn't hang about. Her memory of that night in Paulette's home was fractured, there were gaps, and she had only Lena's word on how it all ended. She'd always known Lena was tricky, but when, after Cumbria, she realised she was in a hole, she couldn't have done anything other than agree to buying her half-sister's silence and then try to put distance between them.

Her mind became set: she would follow the exact route taken then. Norfolk was the start of her journey, and importantly, she needed to collect something from the house before moving on. Next, to Robin's home in Lincoln and lastly to Cumbria. The doll connected the house and Paulette's death, which in turn was linked to what happened in Lena's basement flat. She would be at the Norfolk house for a few hours, hoping it might trigger fresh memories, but couldn't risk sticking around for long.

Mauve's stomach felt tight, twisting with anxiety as, pacing quietly around the bedroom, she formulated the plan. The house was silent, and her mind went again to the sudden silence earlier in the flat. Concentrating on counting her breathing, she kept her thoughts from Lena, and the blood.

Finding paper and a pen, she looked at the blank sheet, considering what to write. If she were to stay and talk to Kit, it would be impossible to explain why she was in a state of panic without giving him the whole story. An unlikely tale she didn't fully comprehend herself.

Darling Kit, I am so sorry to leave like this. I need to go away for a few days. I will be back soon. Please take care of Timothy while I'm gone. Love you always, Mummy xxxx

Mauve left the packed bag on the upstairs landing as she crept into her son's room to leave the note by his bedside.

Kit's long, skinny body was spreadeagled, face down, on the bed, wearing shiny blue boxer shorts. His head to one side on the pillow showed a five o'clock shadow, and long, dark eyelashes against a pale cheek. He looked peaceful and snored gently. Mauve resisted an urge to reach out and touch the floppy brown hair fanned over the pillow. Timothy opened his eyes momentarily, acknowledging her presence before returning to sleep.

As she put the note on the bedside table, Mauve spotted Kit's car keys and remembered the vehicle was blocking the garage doors. Picking them up soundlessly, she went downstairs.

It was nearly 6.00a.m and Mauve, feeling twitchy and unsettled, was suddenly desperate to get away before the roads became clogged with early morning traffic.

It was light outside. The sky, a cloudless blue, suggested the day would be dry and warm. After opening the garage doors, she dumped her bag into the boot of a black-and-white Range Rover. She would have preferred her blue Jaguar, but it was not an option, and anyway, the Range Rover would attract less attention in the Norfolk countryside.

Kit's car started noisily on the third attempt. Mauve cringed, knowing he would recognise the throaty sound, and hoped his slumber was as deep as it had appeared, to allow her to escape without waking him.

After backing the Citroën further along the drive out of her way, she dropped the keys through the letterbox.

The road was quiet and almost traffic-free. Pulling out, Mauve felt wretched, torn, leaving her precious boy behind, knowing her sudden departure would cause him anxiety. The bedside note should have contained more affection, and why write, 'Look after Timothy'? He would do that anyway. Timothy was his dog! Her hands felt clammy against the steering wheel as the internal dialogue continued, reasoning that her going would protect him. If she stayed, how to explain to him that his mother was a murderer?

Further along the road, Mauve instinctively glanced into the car's rear-view mirror. Behind, in the centre of the road, jumping up and down, making star shapes with his outstretched arms and legs, Kit was frantically trying to get her attention. Tall, gangly and barefooted, he wore nothing but his shiny blue boxer shorts. Beside him, serenely watching the action, was Timothy.

Mauve swiftly took a corner before putting her foot down.

The mobile phone rang incessantly throughout the time it took to get out of the city. Weaving to move back and forth across traffic lanes as it became busy, she joined the motorway with relief. It felt symbolic somehow that she had shed London like a creature shedding its skin to become something else.

With the start of a headache, she worked to focus solely on the road ahead. As the phone began tinkling again, she groped around in her large leather bag, open on the passenger seat behind her. The display showed it was Kit, and with a knot of sorrow like a tightening ball in her chest, she switched the phone off.

The image of Lena's kitchen was still in her mind: the long stretch of red on the kitchen floor. If it were Lena's blood, it did not seem possible, as the mean-eyed DS had pointed out, that she could still be alive.

Thinking about her Norfolk home, a haven of safety, brought forth a momentary sense of peace. The feeling was quickly swamped by panic. It had been where the problems began, with Lena's visit and her knowing where Paulette Franklin lived and when she would be alone. To go with Lena and confront Paulette had not felt unreasonable, especially after a few drinks. Now all these years later, she was to follow the same pattern and hoped to unlock the full memory of that night. And, in part, it had already begun. The blood in the flat yesterday had taken her back to the house in Cumbria. She did not have all the missing pieces of the jigsaw, but she'd remembered the touch and feel of the dress's fabric on the doll and Robin being at Paulette's house that night.

In Norfolk, driving through the familiar towns and countryside, she was reminded of times she'd passed through on this journey with Kit. There was the wedge of Cheese House; so named by Kit when he was five because of its shape. Long but narrow. A triangle, tall at one end, with a steeply slanting roof. Further on, the angel's tree, because of its shape. Then there was what Kit referred to as the spinach place, a village shop that stocked spinach in small tins. As a child, he'd hated fresh spinach but went through a phase of loving the odd taste of the tinned variety.

After entering Canston Village, Mauve drove along the familiar lanes that surrounded her Norfolk bolthole. As she reached the high street, ahead, walking a pair of beagles, she spotted the familiar short, stout shape of a woman wearing a red duffle coat, a rear view of village gossip Sophie Toft. The woman rarely missed anything, delving into the problems of others and getting joy from spreading news of their misery. If she were aware Mauve was visiting, even knowing she would never get beyond the front door, Sophie would still turn up unannounced on her doorstep. Mauve cursed, indicating left, making a detour to avoid passing her.

Cutting swiftly up the next side road, she drove along an attached lane surrounded by nothing but fields, and eventually, two miles out of the village, arrived at the extended low cottage with a wooden nameplate attached to the gate: 'Deeping End'.

After getting out of the car to open the gate, drive through, and getting out again to close it, she went to the back of the cottage, leaving the car in an old barn. The inside of the barn was dry and fusty. Outside, Mauve stretched her arms up to feel an ache run down her torso into her legs, and tension in her head, like a tight elastic band. Then, walking to the house, she took in the sense of peace and tranquillity.

The sky was now pale blue with pink candyfloss clouds. The farmer had ploughed the fields surrounding the house and garden, and the wind carried the odour of freshly turned earth, the bucolic smells replacing the car fumes of London.

Fishing in her bag for the keys, she looked at the house with an overwhelming sense of relief; she'd done it. The first leg of the journey.

Remembering DS Teller's small, mean eyes, Mauve shuddered. She'd sensed her wealth and lifestyle represented her as a type to the Scottish police officer, and guilty or not, there would be satisfaction in bringing Mauve down.

Between the barn and the house, she stood for a moment, reaching her hand out to touch one of the purple flowers of an old buddleia tree, the brightly coloured butterflies fluttering around, much like the thoughts in her mind, uncontrolled and random. She turned her attention to her country home.

Originally a trio of terrace cottages, these had been sympathetically expanded into one five-bedroomed dwelling. The roof swept gracefully downwards, and the windows were perfectly aligned and in character with the age of the original late-eighteenth century buildings.

Once inside, Mauve put the kettle on, wrinkling her nose as she took a jar of instant coffee from a cupboard. It was what she considered as builders' coffee, suitable to offer workmen. Still, with no better option, she made a cup, carrying it with her to meander from room to room. Back in the hall, an image of Lena filling the doorway came to Mauve. The excesses of her half-sister included not only her spending and gambling habits but also her need to dominate. On that visit, eight years earlier, Lena had worn a voluminous orange tentlike cotton top, with tight black leggings emerging from below the floating haze of orange. Lena talked with her voice and hands as if to strengthen her argument. She spoke incessantly without pause.

Mauve blinked, flicking away the image to climb the stairs. The familiarity of the rooms, which should have increased her sense of ease, had an odd disquieting effect. An old chair that sagged had been one Kit used to fall asleep in. It was well past its sell-by; she should have thrown it out years ago. As was the case with the piano banished to an unused room downstairs, enjoyed, used and abused by her son for practice when they were away from London.

With its familiar smells, furniture and furnishings, her Norfolk home took Mauve's reflections back to the past and then the future, with the possibility of her incarceration.

If her misdemeanours had finally caught up with her, the inevitable consequence was that she would be in prison for a very long time. Looking around, it felt as if she were saying goodbye, not to possessions but to herself and the lifestyle she so enjoyed.

From a cupboard, Mauve produced a navy overnight bag. She took clothes and shoes to push them into the bag. It would add to the one she'd packed in London, still in the boot of the car.

Walking across her bedroom, lost in her reflections, Mauve sat on the bed to finish the coffee. Then, drained of all emotion, she lay on the bed. She would not get undressed to get in the bed or pull the drapes; the light coming in through the windows would keep her awake. She could rest for half an hour before opening a tin in the kitchen downstairs, maybe tuna or salmon, and eating it with a second coffee. Then move on.

She woke with a start, sitting upright. There had been a sound. The afternoon had turned into evening, the room was dark, and she had been asleep for hours. Downstairs a door closed. She was suddenly fully awake and alert. It had to be the police. Light spread to illuminate the stairs and the landing outside the bedroom. It could only be the police. Not finding her in London, they had come here.

Rolling from the bed, Mauve looked around the room. It would take too long to open the window, and there was a long drop outside. Going out of the bedroom was not an option. She would meet the police coming up the stairs. The sour face of DS Teller again filled her mind. Frantically looking about, she pushed, with her foot, the overnight bag she had left on the floor under the bed. She reached her walk-in wardrobe in three strides and went inside, closing the door tightly behind her. A moment later, soft footsteps approached her hiding place. Then silence. Mauve held her breath.

'Mother!' The voice contained suppressed anger. 'That is the most pathetic hiding place. You managed better with hide-and-seek when I was five. Come out now. I'm beyond furious with you.'

Mauve opened the door slowly. Kit, his eyes burning with anger, stood motionless, his feet set apart and arms folded. Beside him, Timothy focused on her with a look of censoriousness, as if in full agreement with his master.

5

Watching Russ walk away brought Eliza a mixture of sadness and relief. Sadness recalling the niggling voice of doubt inside her head. It was one of the rare times she'd ignored her instincts. Her inner voice had told her they were not suited and she would never love him. Now, the tidal wave of relief, because there was no longer a need to keep up the pretence. The relationship was over.

Framed in the window of the second-floor flat, Eliza watched the tall man with broad shoulders and crew-cut blond hair until he disappeared. He didn't look back, then she hadn't expected anything else. He was not the emotional type. Their discussion, followed by him leaving the flat, was devoid of drama and rancour. He hadn't anticipated her being there on his return, and all trace of her seven-month occupancy would be gone. Russ had accepted the situation and moved on.

Examining her emotions, Eliza realised her annoyance was less with him; she'd known what she was getting into from day one. It was partly with herself for ignoring that inner voice, but she reserved the main ire for her mother, Lena. If she'd had somewhere else to go, might she have left sooner?

Eliza fetched the two large brown cases she'd arrived with from the hall cupboard. It didn't take long to empty the contents of the drawers and her toiletries from the bathroom and fill the cases. Then, there were books in the living area and her favourite cup in the kitchen, plain white porcelain. Russ had been Mr Magnanimous; it was his flat, but she was welcome to stay until she found alternative accommodation. She told him she'd contacted Beatrice, an old schoolfriend, not mentioning Beatrice did not have a spare room, but had agreed to let Eliza sleep on her couch until she found something permanent. Eliza feared if she stayed, he would talk her into reconsidering, and she might weaken.

Beatrice had not been her first choice. Eliza had phoned Lena three times, leaving messages; not because she'd had an overwhelming desire to return to the North London flat to live with her mother. Her reasons were mercenary. Lena owed her big time, so Eliza expected to stay rent-free.

Realising that her relationship with Russ felt more and more like a tick-box exercise made her departure inevitable. The first drink of the day – hot water with a squeeze of lemon – tick. Perfunctory sex – always with him on top – tick. Shower – tick. Muesli and orange juice – tick. In the evening, the routine reversed, starting with eating. Always some kind of salad. He was annoyed when she refused the predictable bedtime shag, which always ended with him muttering, 'Love ya, babe,' before rolling away to fall instantly into a deep sleep. It was the only time the L-word was used, and Eliza never said it back. To be fair, she couldn't forget the many good things about Russ. He was easy on the eye, never drank too much, was polite with her friends and took responsibility for his share of cleaning and washing-up. He would have been great material as a flatmate rather than a lover. That realisation had come too late to change their relationship into something more platonic.

An unpleasant encounter with a large drunken man, resulting in a broken finger, had spurred Eliza to take up not only judo but kickboxing. Two years later, having achieved her black belt, she'd moved, after a fall-out with Lena, to a flat share in South London and joined one of Russ Appleton's intermediate classes. Russ was a seventh-dan judo instructor. He sported his red-and-white belt with pride. Several weeks in, he'd invited her for a coffee, and their relationship away from the class progressed.

Looking at her suitcases, Eliza mused that she didn't have much to show in the way of possessions. There was still her sewing machine to fetch from the hall cupboard and the case that held her drawings, designs, fabrics and samples of work in progress. Her dream of attending college to train in stage and costume design had been within touching distance. It made her cringe to think she'd considered staying with Russ only to keep a roof over her head. She realised having to follow his daily rituals made the relationship time-limited. The irritation it provoked would eventually have made her scream.

Eliza was working two jobs: waitressing and bar work. Both jobs were poorly paid. She needed to make much more money to afford her own place, but that would not happen any time soon. Once settled at Beatrice's, she would start the search for a room to rent in someone's house. She had already investigated available bursaries and grants but needed to find part-time work that fitted with her studies.

Carrying the sewing machine out of the cupboard to leave it next to the front door, Eliza sat on the solid box containing the machine as she pondered her options. What would *he* have done? When deciding which road to take, an image of her dad always popped into her head; someone who'd shown unconditional love and trust, and whose opinion mattered to her. Then, she knew what he would have done – what he had done – planning in anticipation of her current circumstances. When Eliza was eleven years old, after the bitter separation followed by divorce from her mother, and before his sudden death four years later in a road traffic accident, Lazor Jaworski had set up a trust fund for his only child, one that he thought he'd put beyond the reach of his ex-wife. Earlier in the year, when she reached the age of twenty-one, Eliza had been able to access the fund, only to find that the money was gone. Lena had stolen her legacy.

A picture of a skinny woman with wavy brown hair came into Eliza's mind. Lena didn't converse, she held court. She had no interest in two-way discourse. Her appetites were expensive; always the best in food, wine and clothes. Then, there was the gambling. Although spending money brought her pleasure, the games involved in acquiring it brought the greatest joy.

Yesterday, the same day Eliza decided to dump Ross, she had visited her mother; it was payback time. Having not spoken to Lena since discovering the stolen legacy, she decided it shouldn't be a barrier to getting free accommodation. Why should she have to crash on a friend's sofa when her mother, with a four-bedroom, two-bath flat, owed her? That Lena did not respond to the three messages left on her phone made Eliza furious.

The money for the flat, which had been Eliza's home from the age of thirteen to twenty-one, had come from what Lena called 'the bank of Mauve'. It meant she had persuaded or conned her half-sister into paying for it.

The traffic in North London had been getting busy. It was after 5.00pm on Friday; the gap after the lunchtime cafes and bars had been emptied of office workers looking forward to the weekend was coming to an end. A little sozzled, they'd gone back in their places of employment, counting the minutes until home time. The road traffic was building.

Frustrated by the traffic stop-start, Eliza tried to stem her thoughts. Unless game-playing made it to her advantage to keep her distance, Lena tended to respond to calls quickly. Could she be smarting about her daughter's prolonged absence, or might she be all loved-up with a new man and out of the country? After revealing she'd stolen Eliza's inheritance, Lena had pleaded lack of funds. 'That money went years ago. I've got nothing, darling. I'm penniless.'

Two years earlier, after an argument, Eliza began referring to Lena by her first name. Lena always preferred to be called Mom over Mum or Mummy. One of her many affectations; she had no connection with America.

'You shouldn't call me Lena,' her mother had whined. 'Call me Mom.'

Turning into the quiet street, Lena remembered the first time, aged thirteen, that she'd arrived here. She hadn't wanted to relocate; all her friends were on the other side of London. They might say they'd keep in touch, but she knew the hole she left would soon be filled. And if she was quiet in the new flat after moving, Lena hadn't noticed.

Before the move, Eliza realised her mother had got herself into what she always described as 'temporary difficulties'. The warning signs were there: a pile of unopened invoices on the hall table and insufficient money to pay for school trips or replace shoes and PE kits.

Lena had done one of her disappearing acts. 'Away for a few days, darling,' she'd told her thirteen-year-old daughter. Later that day, after returning home from school, Eliza found a twenty-pound note on the kitchen table. True to her word, her mother had gone. The disappearances usually happened when Lena was besotted with the new man in her life, during what Eliza thought of as the relationship's honeymoon period. There hadn't been a new man this time, but she'd overheard Lena talking several times to Uncle Robin by phone the week before.

Three days later, Lena had returned, buzzing and gleeful.

'We're going to be moving,' Lena said. 'I've been visiting the bank of Mauve.'

Eliza was used to the name-calling. Lena also called Mauve the cash cow. She said nothing.

Lena returned bearing a gift – a chocolate egg – two weeks after Easter. The box had a reduced half-price sticker. Lena always brought small, insignificant gifts on her return. There was never any sign of remorse or an apology. Perhaps, Eliza had reasoned, Lena felt she hadn't anything to apologise for.

Stepping down the metal stairway to the flat, Eliza sensed something was wrong. The door lock was broken, and inside the flat was empty. Going from room to room, she felt her world shifting. Her home here no longer existed.

In a daze, she retraced her steps from the sitting room, her mother's office, kitchen, and the bedrooms. What had happened to all the things she had left in her bedroom: clothes, books, CDs and DVDs? It hadn't been possible to take everything when she'd left. Then, she had not imagined Lena up sticks and moving. Eliza felt suddenly hot, burning with anger. It had been foolish to imagine Lena would respect her property. It had undoubtedly ended up on some rubbish dump.

She left in a state of agitation to spend the night at Beatrice's flat. The following morning, Russ called to tell her the police had arrived looking for her, and he'd given them Beatrice's address. Half an hour later, she received a visit from two officers. An anonymous call had been made to the police, resulting in them going to Lena's Camden flat during the early evening of the previous day, where they discovered a large quantity of blood. There was, they informed her, a strong possibility her mother was dead and they requested that Eliza provide a DNA sample so that the blood found at the flat might be confirmed as being her mother's.

Having provided the sample, Eliza followed Lena's rule of giving only necessary information to the police. She did not tell them she had called by the flat and that, at that time, there had been no blood.

Eliza's mind had jumped back to eight years previously. The memory of Lena disappearing for several days. On her return, the chocolate egg in a box with a half-price sticker. And sufficient funds to buy a North London flat.

Had Lena pushed her luck too far this time, setting up some dodgy money-making plan that had gone awry, and was she dead?

6

The silence was short-lived.

'Leaving me to chase you halfway across the country, *and* with the police on your back. You are a great example of how *not* to behave.' Kit unfolded his arms to wave them as he raged at his mother.

'I didn't ask you to follow me.' Mauve lifted her head haughtily to march past her son and fish under the bed for her travel bag. 'You should go, get back to London. I'm sorry, Kit, but I need to go places alone.' She placed the bag on the top of the bed.

'When the police still want to speak to you,' Kit said. 'You told me what that snotty DS said. This makes no sense.'

'I have my reasons. Stay here or go back to London. It's your choice.'

'I'm not going back. Like it or not, I'm with you, Mother.'

Mauve allowed her gaze to travel around the bedroom before it settled on the dog. 'Why did you bring Timmy?'

she said, trying to steer the conversation in another direction.

'His name, as you well know, is *Timothy*, not Timmy, Timbo or Tim.' Kit's face was stony. 'Did you expect me to leave him behind in London with Zack, shit for brains? He'd die of starvation in less than a week. And don't change the subject.'

'I'm not.' Mauve turned to head for the lighted landing, with Kit following and long shadows attaching themselves to trail behind like lost souls.

'Why do the police want to speak to you again so soon?'

'Do they?' Stopping to turn and face her son, Mauve felt queasy.

'Stop it, please, Mother.' Kit's voice was reasoning. 'We both know the police are on to you for something you've done – or something they believe you're involved in. You know what it is, I don't. You need to tell me, fill me in – please?'

Mauve stayed silent.

'What happened last night in Auntie Lena's flat, it was her sending you a message, right?'

Mauve, deep in thought, considered how much to tell him.

'Don't think about it,' Kit said as though reading her mind. 'Just tell me. You know Lena is probably dead, but if you didn't kill her and the police can't connect you to it, why are you running away?'

If she gave Kit a little information, he wouldn't be satisfied, he'd want more. Like a determined rodent, chewing to make a hole big enough to get through, Kit would keep gnawing until he had demolished all her defences and he knew everything.

Instead of answering, she turned, going back to the bed to pick up her bag before going down the stairs into the kitchen to drop it on the floor. Kit and Timothy followed in silence.

'What happened after I left?' Mauve asked. 'You say the police are interested in me?'

It was Kit's turn not to answer; instead, once in the kitchen, he went to the cupboards to take out two dishes from one, and a tin of dog food from another. He filled one dish with water, the other food from a can. After he had put them on the floor, Timothy walked unbidden to the food dish and began to eat.

'Sit down.' Kit pulled out a chair tucked under an oblong beech table before sitting himself on another of the chairs. After a moment of hesitation, Mauve joined him.

'The police phoned to speak to you. I told them you were out shopping.' Kit looked at his mother, his eyes beady. 'They phoned back later, but I'd left to follow you by then.'

'How do you know they called again after you'd left?' Mauve looked down at her nails, shying from Kit's gaze.

'Charlie told me,' Kit said. 'When he rang, I pulled into a service station so I could have a good chat with him. After I'd left, the police phoned the house and spoke to your beloved partner, Zack. He told them you'd gone, probably done a runner. Then the police phoned Charlie. They said they'd spoken to Zack and what he'd told them. Charlie said he's sent you loads of messages.'

'I switched my phone off.' Mauve looked at the door leading back to the hall. 'It's in my bag. I haven't checked it since I arrived here.' Going out, she returned with her large leather shoulder bag and, once seated again at the table, took out the phone.

'Don't switch it on.' Kit put his hand out, taking the phone. 'Do you want the police to be able to trace you here?'

'Ah.' Mauve pulled away to put her hands into her lap as if she had touched something contaminated. 'I didn't think about that.' After another moment, she added, 'Did Zack really drop me in it like that?'

'It's what Charlie said.' Kit nodded.

'Bastard.' Mauve spat out the word. 'After everything I've done for him.'

'What, you mean undermining and stripping him of every ounce of self-confidence?' Kit held his head at an angle questioningly as he spoke.

'Don't be silly. That's not me at all!'

'I'm not his biggest fan, but I think if Zack did feel that way, I couldn't disagree. You're not an easy person to be in a relationship with.' Kit sounded matter-of-fact. 'Disrespectful and rude, and it's always your way or no way. Then, when a relationship goes into freefall, you go into your dippy *I don't understand* mode.' Kit linked his thumbs to lift his hands up and down like wings flapping.

'Does that apply to you and me?' Mauve's eyes were wide as she stared at him. 'I've always tried to make sure you have everything you could want or need.'

'Do you mean throwing money at problems?' Kit

waited, but Mauve again did not respond. 'What you say is not strictly true. I could cite many instances, but I'll remind you of my last visit home. You went into complete meltdown when I tried to discuss my future.'

'But you weren't serious, my darling, were you? A make-up artist? *Really!* It was just a silly whim.' Looking hopeful, Mauve put her hand out to touch his arm. Kit pulled it back, out of reach.

'You know it wasn't a whim. You're such a control freak.' Kit glowered, standing up to look down at his mother. 'But we are going off-piste. We can talk more about my plans once we've sorted the police issues. Why do the police want to talk to you?'

'What did Charlie say? You said you talked to him?'

'Answering a question with a question will get us nowhere fast.'

'Please,' Mauve pleaded.

'Charlie,' Kit gave an exaggerated sigh, 'said you had agreed to make yourself available when the police next needed to interview you. Mummy, he was furious. I've known Charlie forever and never heard him that angry. He didn't understand why you'd done a bunk and asked me if I knew anything more about what was behind it.'

'And you said you didn't,' Mauve said.

'Naturally.' Kit shrugged. 'Charlie did mention that as the police have tried to make contact numerous times since early this morning, if you still haven't got back to them by late afternoon, he says they will undoubtedly send someone to check and see if you're here.' Kit looked at his wristwatch. 'It's nearly ten; you're on borrowed time.'

'He didn't tell you if they'd found anything out?' Mauve got up abruptly. 'The reason they want to talk to me?'

'Like what?'

'Anything,' she said.

'No.'

'I have to go.' Mauve put the strap of her bag over her shoulder before picking up the holdall, then headed towards the door.

'You won't get far.' Kit assumed a casual attitude and leaned against the table.

'What?'

'The police have the details of the Range Rover's registration.'

'How do you know?'

'Charlie told me they'd asked Zack what car you'd use. In fairness, Charlie did point out it wouldn't take long for them to find that information anyway.'

'*Shit, shit, shit!*' Mauve screamed in frustration. 'Bloody Zack, I'll have to borrow yours; we can swap.'

'No, Mother.' Kit was firm. 'The car doesn't belong to me. I've sold it. The deal is I give it to Terry, a mate at uni, after the summer break. Terry is in Australia with his mum's family for the summer.'

'Kit, please, darling,' Mauve said. 'I'll look after it, or better still, I can buy Terry a new, more expensive car in replacement.'

Kit raised his eyes before lifting his arm in an exaggerated gesture to glance at his watch. 'Tick-tock, tick-tock,' he said, his face deadpan.

'Bugger it. Come on, then, let's go.' Mauve marched

out of the room. 'What do you need to take?'

'As always, I am far more organised than you.' Kit sounded smug as he pulled up the zip of his leather jacket to walk to the front door. Timothy followed, walking to heel. 'Everything Timothy and I require is in the car.'

'Wait.' Mauve dropped her bags on the floor to run up the stairs, returning a moment later.

'What did you forget?' Kit asked.

'It doesn't matter.' Mauve squeezed her hand, feeling the solid shape of a set of keys. Picking up her bag, she pushed them inside.

7

The warmth of the day carried into the evening. Following Kit to the car, Mauve paused to breathe in the sweet smell of the yellow honeysuckle attached to one wall of the house. It reminded her of laughter on pleasant evenings, sitting outside with friends, drinking wine, while Kit and the children of guests rocketed around the garden.

Behind the house was her rose garden. A direct copy of the one Paulette Franklin had created in Cumbria. As a child, Mauve's mother and Paulette were best buddies; Mauve had visited the house in Cumbria often. It was before Paulette had done the unforgivable and been found out. Celia had always known her husband was a philanderer, but he generally kept his women at a distance. In time, as always, she forgave Henry, but not Paulette. The betrayal by her best friend and confidante went too deep. Then, Henry had admitted to his love for Paulette, something he had never done with previous conquests, making the treachery unpardonable.

Walking away from her Norfolk home, Mauve's

feet crunched on the gravel. The feeling she was saying goodbye came again, rising in her like a startled bird, to bring a tightness to her throat.

At the car, Kit had opened the boot. Having collected her bag from the Land Rover, he laid it and the one she had packed since arriving inside, on top of the neatly organised lines of bags already there.

'You do have a lot of bags and boxes. Didn't you unpack your uni stuff at home?' Mauve asked.

'Yes, Mother, I left a lot in London. These are things Veronica, Timothy or I might need.' Kit looked pointedly at his mother's bags. 'I hope you haven't just doubled up on the same stuff you took from London. You'll need clean underwear daily. Then one pair of jeans, one pair of trousers and three tops should suffice.'

'Of course, darling.' Mauve, unable to remember how many pairs of trousers or tops she'd packed, didn't much like being told what was considered 'sufficient', by her son. She suspected, knowing she needed to find a way to make Kit return home to London as the journey progressed, their differences of opinion would grow.

The inside of the car smelt of wet dog, and she glanced at Timothy, stretched out on a thick blanket on the back seat. He ignored her, his loving gaze resting instead on the back of his master's head.

'Did he get wet?' Mauve asked.

'It was raining when we stopped at the service station. Timothy had a walk to break the journey.' Kit glanced from the dog to his mother. 'Don't make a thing of it. He sleeps on your bed when I'm not at home.'

'Only because he scratches outside my door. You spoiled him by letting him sleep on yours. He comes to me when you're not there.' Ignoring the memory of missing Timothy's presence on her bed the previous evening, Mauve sounded defensive.

Kit turned to rub his hand gently across Timothy's head.

'Should he not be strapped in? It's illegal not to,' Mauve said.

'I don't think you're in a position to lecture me about legalities, and no, I'm not doing that because Timothy doesn't like it.' Kit pulled his seat belt across his body to strap himself in.

'OK.' Mauve acquiesced, deciding that she would hold back to save heated discussions for the big arguments rather than wasting energy on small battles.

'It would be a good idea to give me the address.' Kit looked pointedly at the satnav.

For a moment, Mauve thought about suggesting again that she go on alone before remembering the urgency to leave. Delving into her bag, she brought out a sheet of paper with the name and address.

'Robin Kelly, Lena's brother?'

Mauve nodded. 'He might shed light on what happened yesterday at the flat.'

'Is it not easier to pick up a phone? The drive to Lincoln is over two and a half hours,' Kit grumbled.

'I don't have his current number,' Mauve said. 'He doesn't have a landline, and I remember, from what Lena told me, that he changes his mobile almost weekly.'

'Sounds slippery.'

'A perfect word to describe Robin.'

'Does he look much like his half-sister? You told me once the Kellys might have been made in a mould, they all look so much alike.'

'It's the Kelly features, the square jaw. Luckily for her, Lena missed out on the arched nose. Handsome in a man, less so with a woman; although her mother, Bonnie, had it. My mother said it worked for her, gave her a look of strength and arrogance.'

'Why have I never met him, or the other one, Damien? I know Auntie Lena and Eliza.'

'Why would you?' Mauve spoke as the car moved to leave the house behind. 'My connection to him is because of Lena. He's, as you say… slippery. I didn't want him anywhere near you. And I've only ever met the other one, Damien, once, when I was a child.'

'Then why are you going to find Robin now if you can't trust him? It's illogical. You must know that whatever it is you think he might know, he'll never tell you the truth?'

'Are you not putting his postcode into the satnav?' Mauve questioned.

'Let's just get away from the house,' Kit said. 'I know the direction; we're heading north. Unless you want to arrive at his house in the early morning, we first need to find somewhere to stay when we get to Lincoln.' Kit glanced briefly at his mother. 'I'm assuming you are not on some police wanted list at the hotels? We have the choice of booking a hotel, or if Robin is home and answering the door, expecting him to give us beds. That, or sleeping in the car.'

'I hadn't thought about it, but you're right. Robin putting us up is not an option.' Mauve sniffed as she glanced back at Timothy, who appeared to be asleep. 'And sleeping in the car's not a great idea.'

'You are so disorganised, Mother.'

'Not normally. It's after what happened at Lena's flat yesterday evening,' Mauve said. 'It's made me feel panicky.'

'Use my phone. We can't use yours in case the police are checking.'

Kit put his hand inside his jacket to take out and pass his phone and then pulled out a bank card. 'Find one of the large chain hotels and tell them to book us a double room with two beds, and we'll be there within three hours. Book it in Dad's surname, Bradley, not Gilcrest. The debit card is in that name.'

'I thought you always used Christopher Henry Gilcrest, not Bradley, Thom's surname?'

'Not always. And being double-barrelled doesn't suit.'

'You sound as slippery as Robin.' Mauve wondered what else he got up to that she didn't know about. And sharing a room would make it harder for her to give him the slip. It seemed that her son was a step ahead of her.

'Just say, "thank you, Kit," and make the call.' Kit cut short her ponderings.

'Are you sure you'd not prefer me to book two rooms?' Mauve said as she entered the number. 'You are a bit old to share with your mummy.'

'One room. I don't want you doing a bunk, thinking you can leave me there.' Kit spoke as if he'd read her thoughts. 'And don't forget to mention we have a dog;

most of them are dog-friendly these days.'

Mauve did not reply, instead googling to find a hotel, all the while wondering how her relationship with her only child had switched around, with him now being the one in charge. She hated it, but needed to go along with him until she could resolve what was happening with Lena.

'Can you put the hotel postcode in the satnav?' Kit asked.

Rain started to hit the windscreen, slowly at first, building into a squall.

After adding the postcode, she wrapped her jacket tight, like a comfort blanket, before becoming quiet. Into the silence there were distant faraway rumbles of thunder and the swish of the windscreen wipers. Mauve watched the rain while considering again how much to tell Kit. Going on a pointless drive would make no sense to him. If she'd said she was following the same route as last time, trying to remember things she'd prefer to leave in the past, while knowing the recollection, if it came, would be terrifying, how would she explain? And when they got to Lincoln, the need to work out how to safely get rid of Kit, leave him behind, or persuade him to return home. She didn't want him to meet Robin, and she was aware the more she told him the tighter he would cling on.

'I don't imagine Eliza would ever go there?' Kit broke into her thoughts.

'Lena's daughter? I doubt it. She lives in London, and I don't know how well she gets on with her uncle.' Mauve pulled a face in the darkness of the car. 'The police will have contacted her. She's Lena's next of kin.'

'If the blood actually was Lena's,' Kit said. 'Do you not still have a mobile number for Eliza?'

'Yes, she contacted me a few months ago asking for money; I told her to ask her mother.'

'Yes, I knew that, and then what?' Kit kept his eyes on the road as he talked.

'I've heard nothing else from her.'

Looking out into the darkness, Mauve remembered Eliza, after coming to the house to ask for money, had sent three text messages, her desperation palpable. But there was nothing to be gained by telling Kit about it. Mauve tried to focus on what had happened the first time she'd done this route with Lena.

Kit, silent beside her, concentrated on the road ahead. The car was warm, and she realised she'd stopped noticing the doggy smells. The beat of the rain and the swish of the windscreen wipers was comforting in the warmth and dryness of the car as the miles slid away.

There had been no silences during the drive with Lena. Constantly talking, rarely pausing for breath, she bounced from one subject to another. Despite him having been dead for years, Henry Gilcrest, their father, was always a hot topic. It was as if Lena needed constantly to return with venom to pick over the bones of Henry's life. Once a wealthy socialite, Paulette Franklin was a name on his long list of ex-lovers. He had promised to divorce Celia to marry her. Henry had possibly said the same to others; unlike them, Paulette had believed him and wanted revenge. And Henry made a foolish slip. He took Paulette to his home when Mauve, with her mother, Celia, were away for a weekend. Having, for many decades, been Celia's best friend, Paulette knew the house and Celia's lax habits well. The diamond necklace, known as The Queen's Diamonds, because it had once been owned by the French queen, Marie Antoinette, had not been locked away, as it should have been, in the safe. Celia had carelessly left it in her bedroom drawer, making easy pickings for Paulette. The reputation of the necklace for bringing bad luck to whoever owned it had increased rather than diminished the value of the stunning piece. When Paulette left, she took the necklace. After begging for its return and receiving a refusal, Henry had no choice but to confess all to his wife. But, as the police and insurance company agreed, Henry had no proof that she'd taken it. Paulette was rich in her own right and could afford the best legal team. In the end, it came down to his word against hers.

With both her parents dead and without an insurance payout, should the necklace ever resurface, Mauve believed that it should legally be hers. But it was all in the past, and she'd moved on. Or that was how it was, until Lena informed her that Robin had discovered from a shady friend that the diamond necklace was up for sale on the black market. A rich American had his eye on it for one of his lovers. Lena fired up Mauve's emotions to challenge Paulette with what she'd learnt and demand the return of the necklace. Paulette, she told Mauve, would be alone for the evening of the planned visit with no staff. The information had come from Robin. It was true that Paulette had been alone. Now, Mauve questioned how could he possibly have known.

Mauve had not told Lena how much she'd wanted to reconnect with Paulette. After Paulette's rift with Celia, she felt she had no other option than to take her mother's side. Celia had died when Mauve was thirty-one. There had been a four-year period when she might have contacted Paulette. It was the long lapse of time that stopped her. And, she reasoned, Paulette had made no attempt to get in touch with her. Going to Cumbria with Lena would break the ice. She questioned why Lena, who heartily detested Paulette – with the feeling being mutual – would want to go. Lena's greed at retrieving the necklace and splitting the proceeds on its sale appeared to be the logical reason.

Mauve knew Lena believed half of the value of the diamonds, once retrieved, was her due. While having had no intention of giving Lena anything, she'd played along, which was ironic. The visit to Paulette cost much more than she could ever have envisaged: the London flat, a lump sum, and, most importantly, a woman's life.

After Paulette's death, Mauve had pushed the whole experience out of her mind, wanting to dissociate all thought about what occurred that evening. Now she found herself dwelling on every aspect and questioning why she had not delved deeper to quiz Lena further at the time.

The overnight traffic was light. Mauve's reflections moved from one subject to another. Robin Rowley was dangerous, especially when working with Lena. They sparked against one another, each egging the other on to more outrageous behaviour. She didn't know Eliza well, having had little to do with her in recent years, but she would, Mauve presumed, be her mother's daughter. Mercenary and greedy.

She sat back deeper into her seat. The warmth in the car, combined with Timothy's regular low snore, made Mauve drowsy. The journey seemed endless.

'Wake up, Mother.' Kit spoke as he parked in the car park at the back of the hotel. 'We're here.'

Mauve realised she had fallen asleep again; it was becoming a habit. She watched Kit disappear into the hotel to register and collect the key. On his return, ten minutes later, they took their bags, followed by Timothy, to the room on the second floor.

'You can use the bathroom first,' Kit instructed, setting his bags side by side at the end of the bed nearest the door. 'After I've sorted out a water dish for Timothy.' He rummaged in his bag to find a small metal bowl which he filled in the bathroom with water. It was, Mauve noticed as her son put it onto the floor, perfectly positioned in the exact centre of one of the square floor tiles.

After washing and changing in the bathroom, Mauve slipped into her bed. On her bedside table was a cup with the name of the hotel chain, taken from the hospitality tray on the dressing table. Picking it up, she smelt the camomile tea before she tasted it. She smiled, knowing her son would have brought a box with him from home. Timothy had moved onto Kit's bed and eyed the bathroom door until his master returned.

'I told them when I registered that we might be here for a second night,' Kit said.

'You mean because Robin might not be home, he could be away?'

'Something like that. Let's think about that tomorrow.' Kit spoke gently. 'Get some sleep, Mum.'

8

The night-time hours dragged as Mauve moved restlessly around the bed. There were many questions fighting for attention. Should she phone Charlie in the morning, use the hotel phone? Would the police be monitoring the incoming calls on Charlie's number? Charlie might know if the police had new information about what had happened in the flat, but would they divulge that information to him? The big question was how to divert Kit and get him to return home. Giving him Robin's address had been a dumb decision. If she left him here, he would know where to go looking.

The bed next to hers was silent; even Timothy made no noise.

When her agitation became too much, fearing she might go into panic mode, she left her bed to tiptoe quietly to the bathroom. Not turning on the light, she sat on the bathroom floor.

With her arms wrapped around her knees, rocking gently, Mauve realised the last questions she would consider before falling asleep, and the first when waking, would be, was Lena dead, and if so, how had she died and who had killed her? Getting to the bottom of the mystery was urgent. Dead or alive, she needed to know what had happened. The realisation that eight years ago Robin had followed her and Lena to Paulette's house changed everything. Might Lena have lured her to the flat last Friday evening, using the doll as leverage for blackmail, only to have been killed by Robin? And could Robin be the one who'd killed Paulette? The dawning acceptance that she could not move on with her life until she got to the truth filled her with terror. Yesterday, her distress was centred entirely on ensuring her own preservation. Kit tagging along, and his dogged resistance to going home, was never part of her plan. The reality was that she didn't know what she was getting herself into; the last time she had tangled with Lena, a woman ended up dead. If Robin had killed Paulette and Lena, what might he do to Kit to get money from her? Mauve couldn't face the idea that her beloved boy might become enmeshed and be in danger.

The fear tightened her chest, and Mauve remained on the floor, reverting to the breathing exercises until the overwhelming sense of panic eased. Going back to bed, she finally succumbed to sleep.

Waking, she found Kit and Timothy gone. It was 7.12a.m. Knowing Timothy's routine, she knew that the dog would have woken expecting to be allowed outside at about 7.00a.m, especially when he was out of his comfort zone, not being at home.

On Kit's bedside table, in perfect symmetry: a hair

comb, brush, toothpaste and deodorant. The car keys were not there.

Ten minutes later, in the shower, Mauve considered her choices. The only real option was to reason again with Kit to make a deal. Then, what had she to bargain with? An offer to ensure his agreement to take the train home? Whether Robin was home or not, she would need Kit's car to get her to the Cumbrian house.

After dressing, Mauve sat on her bed to blow-dry her hair, wet from the shower.

'You're an early bird.' Kit came into the bedroom with Timothy at his heels. His hair was ruffled and windblown, and he brought a fresh blast of air from the outside world into the room with its stale overnight air.

'I thought you might still be in bed.' He carried two cardboard cups of coffee, a brown food bag and newspapers under his arm.

'Where did you get those?' Mauve asked.

'There's a garage at the end of the road. I noticed it last night when we arrived. I know you can't focus until you've had coffee, and you hate instant.' Kit let his eyes wander to the sachets of instant coffee and the electric kettle on a table beside leaflets giving local tourist information. 'And we have cheese rolls.'

'You are a star.' Mauve took a coffee from him.

'Mm,' Kit muttered, rolling his eyes as he dropped newspapers onto the bed. 'I'm not the cleaner, Mummy. You always call her "a star", usually just before you tell her she needs more elbow grease for cleaning the loo or kitchen sink. The *Mirror*, *Mail*, *Times* and *Express*.'

'*Hurrumph.*' Timothy looked studiously at his master, trying to get his attention.

'Yes,' Kit said, 'I hadn't forgotten.' He went to his bag to take out a dish and a tin of dog food. He put the food on the floor beside the dog's water bowl. Timothy went eagerly to eat his breakfast.

'That jacket is cute.' Mauve observed the black-and-cream creation that Timothy wore.

'All his outfits are cute,' Kit said.

'Is there anything in the papers?' Mauve pulled one towards her.

'Let's have a look.' Kit took the *Mail* to his bed, and each pored over the news pages while drinking their coffee.

'Nothing in this one.' Mauve gave a deep sigh after she'd scoured the newspaper.

'Nothing in any of them,' Kit concluded as he bit into his cheese-filled roll. 'Shall we pack up? There is no reason to hang around in here.'

'Kit,' Mauve began gently.

'Don't, Mother,' Kit reprimanded her. 'Please don't go there.'

'What? You don't know what I was going to say!'

'No! You weren't going to suggest me letting you take the car while I took a train back to London, were you?' Kit said, his tone sour.

'I don't want to involve you in anything… illegal.' Mauve looked at him over the rim of the cardboard carton.

'When did the panic attacks start again?'

'I don't know what you mean.' Mauve got up, flustered; clearly, her son was, again, ahead of her.

'You had one in Lena's flat, and you went in the bathroom last night to do your breathing exercises!' Kit's voice brooked no arguments.

'It might be easier, stress-wise, if I knew you were on a train back to London.'

'Don't twist it to make me the bad guy,' Kit huffed. 'You don't have the attacks because of me. It's about what happened, or is happening, with Lena, all the things you're keeping from me.' He stared at her. 'And I'm not going anywhere; you're stuck with me. It might make life easier to take me into your confidence.'

'Kit, sweetheart.' Mauve went about the room collecting her belongings to repack a bag while she talked. 'Lena and I did have problems, issues, but what you don't know can't hurt you. I need to get to the bottom of what happened in her flat; if I can see Robin, he might shed some light on it.'

'It isn't Lena's flat anymore.' Kit, sitting on the bed, watched to see her reaction.

'I thought with all her stuff gone, she might have sold it, but how would you know about that?' Mauve paused as she forced her make-up bag into the holdall, unable to stop her face giving away her surprise.

'Charlie told me. I phoned him when I was out with Timothy.' Kit waited for more of her questions; when they didn't come, he continued. 'Lena sold it to a housing association. The deal went through a few days before your visit. It's routine for the new owners to change the locks immediately. Lena must have broken the new lock to get in. That is, assuming it was her who'd broken the lock so you could go in and discover the blood and the doll. Charlie and I believe it couldn't have been anyone else.'

'Why? What else did Charlie say?'

'Charlie thinks running away is the worst possible thing because it makes you look guilty. He also asked about your panic attacks.'

'You didn't tell him?' Mauve said sharply.

'He told me you'd had one in Lena's flat, then again at the police station before your interview,' Kit said. 'I told him you had one here last night.'

'You shouldn't share private things with other people.'

'Charlie isn't other people; he's your brief, your legal adviser and probably your only real friend.' Kit stared her out. 'You can't count on the drinking buddies who hang around just to leech off you. They aren't friends. They'll only be there for the good times.'

'Let's get out of here.' Mauve picked up her bag and walked past him to the door, angry at his words.

In the car park, after packing the car and putting Robin's postcode into the satnav, Kit drove around the side of the hotel to the exit.

'Hope that's not for you, Mother.' Kit nodded towards a police car parked near the hotel entrance.

'Don't be silly.' Seeing the vehicle and having the same thought, Mauve looked for the police officers.

'They're probably inside.' Kit watched his mother's gaze wandering to the entrance. 'If we can't contact Robin and need to hang around for another night, we'll need to find somewhere else to stay. Or better still, follow Charlie's advice and head home?'

'Just go,' Mauve said.

On the ring road around the city, she tried to remember the last time she had come here. They had gone straight from Norfolk to Robin's home. Today they were coming in by a different route. Lena had been driving. Although she professed to visit her brother rarely, she knew the way without needing a roadmap or satnav.

Passing a supermarket, Mauve glanced to the right to a display of fruit and vegetables set out in front of a shop. Peterson. She remembered the old-fashioned green sign above the greengrocer's and a tobacconist and paper shop next door to it. It had, like today, been a Saturday. Lena had stopped to buy cigarettes. Mauve had waited in the car and watched an old man coming out of the shop with his *Daily Mirror* under one arm, the progress of a mother with a pram and a screeching toddler, and a young couple picking over the fruit and vegetables. It surprised her, thinking about it, that she could remember all those details and so precisely, while the time in Paulette's house was a mental jumble.

'We're in Canwick,' Lena had said when she returned, throwing packs of Benson and Hedges onto the back seat before getting into the car. 'Robin's place is just around the corner.'

'I thought he lived next to Bailgate, Steep Hill,' Mauve said, remembering the information from a conversation she'd had with Robin.

'Ha!' Lena laughed. 'Think of all the Londoners you know who live in Highgate or Hampstead.'

Mauve thought about it. 'No, I don't get that.'

'If you visit them, you'll find it's Crouch End or Tufnell Park.'

'I didn't know Robin was a snob.' Mauve remembered the man's arrogance and exaggerated pomposity, but she'd imagined him too intelligent for that level of petty snobbery.

'Not everyone has the money to give them choices,' Lena snapped.

Mauve wondered how the innocent conversation had somehow meandered into such dangerous territory.

'Still.' Lena's eyes were fixed on the road, her voice excited and greedy. 'We'll both be quids in once we get the diamond necklace. You just need to sell it to the highest bidder, all legal and above board. After all, it belonged to our dear departed father, Henry, not Paulette.'

My mother, not our father, owned it. Mauve smiled, not voicing her thoughts.

'Not far now.' Kit broke into her reflections.

'Yes, just around the corner.'

'You have been here before then?' His question was light, implying the answer was of no concern.

'Once, a long time ago.' Mauve looked along the narrow road as the car turned in from the main street.

On the left, a long low building named Dallow and Sons, a printing company, in the front of which was an expanse of concrete space. On the opposite side of the road, cars were parked outside a tyre company. Outside the two buildings used to change tyres, trucks and cars appeared to be in a queue, and to one side, a small office. A grubby, wind-battered sign gave the opening times, which included Saturday morning until noon. Cars were inside the service areas, and the vehicles on the forecourt had customers sitting inside awaiting their turn. A lanky man in his early fifties stood propped against a wall, smoking. The peak of his cap and wraparound sunglasses covered the top half of his face. His grey shirt matched grey chinos, and below that once-white trainers – dirty and grey – one of Mauve's pet hates.

'Why do men wear white trainers and let them get so dirty?' she muttered. 'They could try cleaning them.'

'Who cares?' Kit glanced from the dirty shoes to his mother. 'You're thinking of Zack?'

Mauve shrugged. 'As you say, who cares?'

As they reached the end of the road, the satnav voice informed them they had arrived at their destination. Kit pulled alongside the two detached one-storey houses forming an end to the cul-de-sac.

'Which one?' Kit asked.

'On the left.' Mauve nodded towards the mid-twentieth century bungalow.

'Not what I was expecting.' Kit looked from the house to his mother.

'Lena said few people knew of this address. I think it's a bolthole,' Mauve said. 'He spends most of his time in either Leeds or London. He comes here when he wants to get away.'

'To hide away?'

'I don't know him that well.' Mauve shrugged.

'Shall we go and see if he's here?' Kit suggested.

'Wait a few minutes.' Mauve kept her eyes on Robin's

home, breathing slowly in, counting silently the breath out.

The property had a look of sad abandonment. Dandelions sprouted between cracks in the paving in the small area of the garden to the front of the property. The wooden window frames were rotting, and behind the unclean glass, net curtains, yellowed with age, sagged. Her heart sank, taking in the signs of neglect, sensing she would not find Robin. Why had she come, and what had she believed was achievable? Kit, beside her, looked straight ahead. Having cut the engine, his hands relaxed in his lap. Behind, Timothy had sat up, waiting as he looked about with interest.

9

After about ten minutes, Mauve climbed from the car and Kit followed. Timothy, realising he was not going with his master, spread himself to stretch back across his blanket.

The sun was high in a clear blue sky. Noise from the tyre company spilt like leakage along the road. The sharp whirling of equipment used to change tyres and a radio tuned to a pop programme merged with the raised voices and banter from visitors to the office.

The hinged gate creaked as they entered the small front garden. Mauve used the metal knocker to bang on the door. The sound seemed to vibrate through the house, and she shuddered, tingling with fear, as with the basement flat, anxious about what she might discover inside.

After waiting a few minutes, Kit went to peer in through the window.

'I don't think we'll see anything of Robin,' he said. 'Looks like it's been a long time since anyone has been here.'

'I'm going to look around the back.' Mauve moved to the corner of the house before turning into the backyard area. 'Why not wait in the car?' She threw the words into the air over her shoulder.

'It's a waste of time, Mum.' Kit followed, ignoring the suggestion.

The yard was small, an enclosed area of cracked concrete. The only form of decoration was a collection of old plastic pots of varying sizes. Each was full of dried hard earth and dead weeds, lined in a row under the back window. Mauve stood on tiptoe on the doorstep, looking into the kitchen through the top glass part of the door.

On her previous visit, Robin had also been absent when they'd arrived. Lena hadn't bothered to knock on the front door, instead immediately leading Mauve around to the back. Once there, Lena had reached up to run her fingers along the top of the door frame until she found a key.

'Shall we go back to the car?' Kit said. 'He's not here.'

'I just need a moment to gather my thoughts,' Mauve said. 'Why not go and check on Timothy? I won't be a minute.'

Kit hovered at the corner, uncertain for a moment. 'Don't be long,' he said.

Mauve trailed behind, watching him until he reached the car, then swiftly darted back to the rear door to copy Lena's actions from eight years earlier. Her fingers encountered the metal of the key and, bringing it down, she quickly opened the door and stepped inside. Her thoughts returned again to her Friday evening visit to

Lena's flat before flitting to all those years ago when she had followed Lena inside this house. She hesitated, breathing slowly, and concentrated on the noise coming from the tyre company.

Gathering her courage, she scurried, like a skittish cat, through the small property, glancing nervously this way and that, mentally counting the rooms, the kitchen, bathroom, and bedroom. She reached the living room at the front. It contained a brown two-seat sofa, two matching armchairs, a side table, and a sideboard. Through the window, she could see Kit talking on his phone. Would it be Charlie? It must be him.

Little had changed inside the house since her last visit. In the kitchen, the floor was covered by worn, cracked brown lino. There was a kettle, mugs and a few utensils. Apart from the updated television in the lounge, the new one being larger with a flat screen, everything was as she remembered. The most critical items – the folder with paperwork and Robin's desktop computer – were no longer on the table. The information was part of the scam relating to the diamond necklace. Robin talked a good talk, the lists of contacts, and messages about its availability and opportunity for buyers. Mauve knew now that it had been part of a set-up.

Lena had poured whisky while they waited for Robin.

Before checking at the window to observe Kit, his face taut with concentration, still using his phone, Mauve went to sit in the armchair she had used the last time.

What had she expected to find or achieve here? All she could feel was tiredness and tension. It had been futile coming, a wasted journey. Back in the hall, she went about opening doors. The bathroom, with its avocado-green bath. Grubby and uncared for, a lone toothbrush and tube of toothpaste in a glass by the sink, and then to the room she had not entered last time, Robin's bedroom. The bed, with its blue throw, was neat, a dressing table with a can of deodorant, and there, on a table against one wall, was a desktop computer. *Is it*, she wondered, *the same one, or like the TV, might it have been updated?* It seemed unusual not to use a laptop, but Robin had both, bringing the laptop with him when he arrived.

Mauve pressed the start switch on the computer and was surprised when the light came on, bringing it to life. Odd, considering his visits were probably so infrequent, that he had not cut the electricity. A password was required, and without much thought, she pressed the switch again and watched as the screen went back to darkness. On the table directly in front of the computer was a USB memory stick. If it had been protruding from the computer, she might have missed it, but in the expanse of empty table in front she couldn't fail to see it. It was like the 'eat me' cake in one of Mauve's favourite childhood books, *Alice in Wonderland*. The memory stick was saying, 'Take me.'

'Mother!' Kit's angry voice reached her from the back door. 'What the hell are you playing at?'

Coming to an instant decision, Mauve picked up the black USB memory stick to push it into the pocket of her jeans, then went swiftly to find Kit standing in the kitchen.

'How did you get in?' Kit was red-faced with annoyance.

'Let's talk about it in the car.' Mauve shooed him along until they were outside. After locking the door, while her son stood grimly watching, she returned the key to where she had found it.

Back inside the car, Kit turned on her.

'You knew the key was there but didn't let on when I was with you. And you had every intention of going in. You thought you could do it without my catching you.'

'What if I did?' Mauve sounded weary. 'I didn't ask you to come, and I keep telling you that I don't want you here. I don't want to involve you in anything illegal.'

'Do as I say, not as I do. Is that what you mean?' Kit snapped, pushing his hand through his hair with agitation.

'I'm trying to keep you out of what might be a bad situation. Why can't you just listen?'

'I am listening, Mother.' Kit was not backing down. 'When are you going to start telling me what the hell you've got yourself into?'

A rap on the window of the car startled them both. Surprised, Timothy let out a low warning growl. A short, wizened man, with sparse hair stuck to his scalp with something shiny so that it resembled a row of fat black slugs, and wearing a crumpled jacket, leaned in on the driver's side, his gaze going from Kit to Mauve and back.

'Good boy,' Kit reassured Timothy.

'Are you here to see me?' He shouted the words at the windscreen, then jerked his thumb back to the bungalows.

'You live here?' Kit asked after he'd lowered the window.

'There.' The man pointed to the property next to Robin's.

'We hoped to catch your neighbour,' Kit said.

'Ah.' The stranger stared at Kit. 'That's Robin's house; he comes and goes. I don't see much of him.' As he talked he stared ahead towards the tyre garage as if unable to focus.

'Is he due this weekend?' Kit asked hopefully.

'He might; then again, who knows?' He held up a plastic bag before changing the subject. 'I've been shopping.'

'Yes.' Kit smiled.

The man nodded before shuffling away along the path to his home. After opening his front door, he went inside without a backward glance.

Mauve looked away from her son, her face twisting with dejection. The stranger's interruption had silenced their argument, but the tension was still heavy between them.

'He smelt like he's been on the booze.' Kit started the car to drive back along the road past the tyre centre onto the main road.

'At the end of the road, turn left.' The anonymous tone of the satnav gave instructions.

'Where are we going?' Mauve asked.

'To find somewhere to stay,' Kit said. 'I assume you still want to talk to Robin?'

'Yes,' Mauve agreed. 'Back to the hotel?'

'That is no longer an option.' Kit glanced at her as he spoke before returning to the road.

'What do you mean?' Mauve watched his profile. When he didn't immediately reply, she repeated the question. 'Kit, who were you speaking to on the phone? Why is it no longer an option?'

'It's more than twenty-four hours since you did a runner. Charlie says that the police are now *actively* seeking you. You are the number one person of interest in the possible murder of Lena Kelly.'

'But they haven't found a body.' With a rising feeling of panic, Mauve felt as if her lungs had been emptied of breath, and she realised her nails were digging into her hand as she squeezed hard around the seat belt. Heading through Lincoln, the buildings flashed past.

'A friend's managed to book a house for me. It's a holiday let cancellation, in a village near Sleaford.'

'Have they found a body then?' Mauve's voice was hostile. 'And what friend? Who have you talked to besides Charlie?'

As he exited the roundabout, following the sign for Sleaford, Boston and King's Lynn, Kit glanced again briefly at his mother. 'No, they have not found a body yet. And does it matter who I've spoken to? If someone is good enough to do me a favour and book the holiday property in their name so as not to give our name, count your blessings, Mother.'

'How could it have been booked that quickly? You were only on the phone ten minutes ago.'

'I asked my friend yesterday evening if they could try to find something, somewhere around here to stay. Not a hotel,' Kit said. 'Ten minutes ago I was given the directions to the property, paid for online yesterday.'

'You didn't mention it to me yesterday.' Mauve's voice wobbled with emotion. How many people had he blabbed to about her problems?

'Strange that we can both keep secrets; might it be in the genes?' Kit said coldly, his eyes fixed on the road.

Mauve stared straight ahead and remained silent for the rest of the journey.

10

The village was quiet. Its amenities included a mini supermarket, baker's, corner paper shop, and one pub. Kit parked the car outside 10 George Road, one of a row of 1950s terrace houses facing an identical line on the opposite side of the road. Unlike some of the properties, updated with white UPVC window frames, number 10 had wooden frames painted a dark bottle green, to contrast with the cream paint of the brickwork.

Why, Mauve silently pondered, *would anyone want to rent a holiday property here?* In Norfolk, she enjoyed the countryside and being near the beaches and sea. This place had little attraction.

'Stay here while I collect the key.' Kit was curt.

Mauve, resisting a sharp retort, remained silent. He was addressing her, but he might also have been including the dog in the command. She watched him walk along the row checking door numbers, and after knocking at one of the houses, he spoke to a woman in her early fifties wearing loose pants and flip-flops, who'd come out onto the doorstep. After a short conversation, she led Kit back to number 10, her eyes never leaving his face.

There was nothing, Mauve decided, as deluded as a coquettish woman of mature years flirting with a boy young enough to be her son. Then, had she not done the same? Mauve considered the thought, her mind flashing to loud, drunken evenings in bars with girlfriends, where the male bar staff had been young and beautiful, their bodies slim and taut. She winced inwardly; the woman flirting with Kit was only a few years older than herself. What had appeared wildly funny after a few drinks felt embarrassing and sad in the cold light of day.

Passing the car, Kit engaged the woman in conversation as, behind her back, he raised and waved his hand as if to shoo his mother away.

What did he want her to do, put a bag over her head, or hide on the floor?

Once the pair had entered the house, Mauve found Timothy's lead and, after attaching it to his collar to bring him out of the car, walked to the opposite pavement. How far away would Kit expect her to go? It was clear he did not want the woman to see or engage with her.

Timothy pulled as she led him away, looking back to where his beloved master had gone.

Later, watching the front door open, Mauve turned up the collar of her jacket, crouching to feign interest in Timothy. When she looked up a few moments later, the woman had returned along the street and was re-entering her home. Kit became busy taking bags from the back of the car into the house.

Mauve walked back with Timothy. Inside the house, the dog greeted his master effusively, rumbling with affection and pressing his head into Kit's legs as if their separation had been weeks.

'I didn't want Mrs Johnson – the property owner – to see you,' he explained. 'I said I was here with my elder sister.' Kit dumped the bags onto the floor.

'Ha. I'd have to be a fantasist to believe I could get away with that,' Mauve snorted.

'She didn't see your face,' Kit said. 'If the police are looking for a mother and son it might blur the picture if people think we're siblings having a holiday together. And you bending down helped; she wouldn't be able to see your height, how small you are.'

'Oh, I did do something right today then,' Mauve retorted.

Kit glowered.

'Whoever would want go on a holiday to Sleaford!' Mauve shrugged, her incomprehension clear. 'I'd be surprised if Mrs Johnson made money out of this place.'

'Mother, you are the limit. Such a snob,' Kit said. 'There is nothing wrong with a small country market town. People living in a city would enjoy the change and find a cottage like this had charm.'

'No, I don't get it…'

Ignoring her, Kit continued back and forth from the car until he had unloaded all the bags into the living room. After he left again, Mauve heard the car start. She imagined Mrs Johnson might have told him to move it once he had unloaded.

The front door had opened straight into the open-plan living room with a kitchen/diner; a typical two-up, two-down, modernised and extended at the back. The living room, wallpapered in dark purple, matched a three-seater sofa and armchair. Mauve wandered through, passing the narrow staircase with open, uncarpeted pine treads. Standing in the kitchen area, she looked out the window onto a small garden with a lawn. A footpath to one side led to picket fencing and a back gate.

'The garden at the back is enclosed,' Mauve said as Kit returned. 'You can let Timothy outside without him wandering away.'

'Yes, I know.' Kit filled a bowl with water and put it on the kitchen floor, then threw himself onto the sofa. 'It was on my list of requirements, although Timothy is not generally a wanderer.'

'Wasn't that how you got him?' Mauve, still feeling the sting of Kit's command when he left her in the car, felt argumentative. 'He wasn't left on the beach by aliens. He must have had a home before he attached himself to you and followed you home.'

'Obviously,' Kit said. 'But nobody came forward to claim him. We put enough notices up, if you remember.'

'Your list of requirements?' Mauve picking up on what he had said, raised her eyebrows questioningly. 'It sounds like you had a very long call with your "friend".'

'Do you think we should trade information? I'll show you mine once you've shown me yours.'

'Will you tell me what Charlie said, *please*.' Mauve felt the anger dissipate as she lowered herself into the armchair to sit opposite her son.

'First, he said he wants to speak to you himself. He will call on my number later, at about 12.30p.m.'

Mauve nodded.

'Next, the police are actively seeking you as a person of interest. They've been to the London house and spoken to Zack. Charlie called him and asked what information they wanted, it was what he'd expected.'

'Was Zack polite? He isn't one of Charlie's biggest fans.'

'Polite and sober apparently,' Kit said. 'Charlie said he believed Zack was genuinely upset and concerned about you. He asked that you call him.'

'Really?' Mauve said. She bit back the bitter words that had immediately formed in her mind. 'That is a surprise.'

'Mummy.' Kit leaned forward. 'We're all worried; it's not a joke. You must know you're in deep shit. Up to your neck in it.'

'What else did Charlie tell you?'

'Apart from the fact that they have also had the Norfolk police check to see if you were there. They found your Land Rover in the barn.'

'Oh.' Mauve's hand went involuntarily to cover her mouth. She had realised things would move forward quickly, but not quite this fast.

'The police have all the DNA results. You already know it was Lena's blood,' Kit said. 'They haven't found a body *yet*, but because of the quantity of blood are working on the basis that it's a murder case. Charlie thinks they must have something linking you to Lena or what happened in the flat. The police are keeping schtum; they aren't telling Charlie what they have.'

The DNA from the doll. The thought brought a rising panic, making Mauve catch her breath. *Have they*, she wondered, *already made the link to Paulette?* She started to gasp for air.

'Are you all right, Mum?' Kit asked, watching her.

'I'm fine,' Mauve lied. She began breathing in and holding her breath for five and out on a count of seven. 'Keep talking,' she instructed. 'Tell me everything.'

'Zack told the police that I went after you. They know I followed you to Norfolk and am with you now. Zack wouldn't have been able to give them the details of my car; he was too pissed to notice. But, with the amount of CCTV in London, it will be a doddle to find me driving from the house and getting the registration. Although it's no longer registered in my name, they could link it to me in a flash. I've moved it to the back alley. Mrs Johnson had asked me to move it from out front anyway. She won't think it odd that I put it around the back.'

'You can't use your car now, I suppose?' Mauve said.

'That's it.' Kit nodded.

'What have I got you into?' Mauve, her eyes wandering over the deep purple of the walls, felt overwhelmed and queasy as she clasped her hands to her head.

'I don't know, Mummy.' He leaned forward to put his hand over hers to draw them gently away down. 'This might be a good time to tell me.'

11

Half an hour later, Mauve, having taken the largest bedroom, stretched out on the double bed. The ground-floor extension to the back of the house continued upstairs, with two double, one single bedroom and a bathroom.

The conversation with Kit had got no further, Mauve having made her escape by telling him she needed time alone. Kit, his face fixed in a scowl, moved the bags upstairs into the bedrooms.

Mauve lay completely still, looking up at the ceiling. The room's walls were painted in a dark yellow, matching the bedspread, a slightly more calming choice than the purple downstairs, but the room had an oddly sweet, artificial odour. Having tried to open the window to let in some air and finding it wouldn't budge, she considered calling downstairs for Kit's help, eventually deciding against it. She needed her space; if he came to her aid, they would have to talk.

With the beginning of a headache and upset by the

prospect of Kit accompanying her on the journey, Mauve was further annoyed at the speed with which her plans were unravelling. She owned two cars but could use neither, and it seemed Kit's car was now on the police radar.

She heard Kit place his phone on the kitchen table. 'Remember, Charlie will phone at 12.30p.m,' he called up.

'I haven't forgotten.'

It had crossed her mind to take the phone to contact friends. Talking would feel normal, a form of escapism for a short time. Then, which friend would she call? Her address book was filled with names and numbers, but who to trust? Mauve mentally worked through a list. Her thoughts settled on one of her drinking buddies, Jade Simms. Tall and skeletally thin, with a short bob of auburn hair that always made her think of shiny conkers fresh out of their spiky green shells. Or Becky, recently returned from a trip to Turkey, her appearance transformed with super-white teeth. The almost fluorescent whiteness made them look more prominent, giving her a rodentlike appearance. Mauve, who'd long considered subservient Becky as Jade's pet mouse, remembered Jade wallowing in schadenfreude at the unexpected gift of Becky's new awful look. Then, Mauve had joined in the laughter. Perhaps Kit had not been too far out when he told her she had no real friends. She knew if her current situation was revealed, the reaction of many to her misery would follow a similar course. She had not always been the best or kindest of friends. Many might find pleasure in her misfortune.

Mauve's mind went to what had happened at Robin's house and the memory stick in the back pocket of her jeans. Glancing at her laptop, which was now on the bedside table, she lifted herself as her hand went to her back pocket, then froze. There had to be no possibility of Kit coming in and catching her. He would go out at some point to walk Timothy; she could wait. The memory stick might contain details of some of Robin's nefarious dealings, which Mauve might be able to use as leverage for information on Lena.

She rolled over onto her side; she needed to think. Charlie would ask her a lot of questions. How to answer them? The primary consideration was whether Robin, if found, would tell her what was going on. If he had killed Lena, he would hardly admit to it. In London, her plan to visit him had made sense, but finding a way to explain that to either Charlie or Kit was impossible. She couldn't reveal what had happened to Paulette in Cumbria. Robin would deny any involvement, and it was her DNA on the doll, not his.

Mauve felt a wave of anger and, getting up from the bed, paced around the bedroom. How would she explain her planned visit to Cumbria? It was reasonable that she'd wanted to talk to Robin. Charlie might get that. He wouldn't understand her need to visit an empty house in Cumbria where a woman with a complicated connection to her parents had been found murdered eight years earlier.

Hearing laughter, she stopped at the window to watch, on the opposite side of the street, a pretty child around about five years of age running in front of a young woman who was pretending to chase her. Both were enjoying the game, the shrill laughter filtering back. That had been her. It felt like a million years ago when, chased by Paulette in the Cumbrian rose garden, Mauve had laughed with delight as Auntie Paulette pursued her, brandishing a pair of rose cutters. Returning to that moment, the memory brought a smile. Paulette had made her feel special. Her mother's love of her best friend filtered down through the daughter. There had been no other woman, friend or relative, given the honorary title of 'Auntie'. Remembering, Mauve could almost feel the moment, with the warmth of the sun on her back and the true childhood feeling of adoration for Auntie Paulette. Things turned around after her mother discovered the reality of the relationship between her friend and husband. The title 'Auntie' was soon replaced by the word 'bitch', and Mauve was never again allowed to mention Paulette's name. It was the first significant loss in her life. As if her adored Auntie had died.

'Mother.'

Having disappeared into her thoughts, Mauve jolted back to the present as Kit knocked on, then opened, the door. He extended his hand holding the phone.

'Charlie,' he said. After passing the phone to Mauve, he closed the door and left.

'Charlie.' Mauve went to sit on the bed, waiting for an explosive outpouring of words. It didn't come.

'Are you OK?' Charlie's voice was gentle.

'Yes,' Mauve said. 'I'm so sorry if I put you in a difficult position. I needed to try to speak to Robin. He's the person most likely to know what happened to Lena. Perhaps whom she'd seen recently and if she felt in any danger.'

'Wanting a conversation with Lena's half-brother isn't going to get you off the hook with the police.' Charlie sounded calm. 'You shouldn't have disappeared, it makes you appear guilty.'

'Charlie, I didn't kill Lena, if that is what the police are saying.'

'Kit told you it's Lena's blood?' Charlie didn't wait for an answer. 'That is a one hundred per cent certainty. They did a crossmatch with Eliza. Lena is dead!'

'They didn't try to match it with Robin?'

'No, Eliza is her daughter. She agreed to having a DNA test. What is this obsession with Robin?' Charlie asked, now not quite so calm. 'Why would he know about Lena? You always told me they weren't especially close.'

'I know, but if something dubious is going on, it would seem probable they'd both be involved, trust me.'

'Why?'

'What's that supposed to mean?' Mauve said, becoming tetchy herself.

'Mauve, I know there's something you're not telling me.' Charlie spoke as though explaining to a child. 'I am trying to help you, but you're making it impossible. You need to open up before it's too late and come back and speak to the police.'

'I can't, Charlie,' Mauve said. 'Not yet. Once I've got to the bottom of what's going on, I'll return, I promise.'

'It's not enough, Mauve.' Charlie returned to his former calm. '*Please* come back and speak to the police. I'd be there with you. They have something on you that they're not telling me about.'

Mauve, listening to Charlie's plea, had a mental image of the doll in the white hatbox in a room covered in blood. The jolt of shock coursing through her body felt like an electric current.

'If you don't return, at least give me the true reason,' Charlie added.

'I'm sorry, Charlie.' Mauve felt large fat tears roll down her cheeks. 'I have to go.'

'You know I'm here for you,' Charlie said.

Mauve cut the call before throwing herself face down on the bed and pressing her face into the bedspread to diminish the sound of her sobs.

12

Downstairs, Mauve found Kit in the kitchen grating carrots. She placed his phone on the table before pulling out a chair to sit. After her conversation with Charlie, she'd lain on her bed for more than two hours and now knew every mark and shadow on the ceiling, including a cobweb in one corner, and while her headache had subsided, she felt neither rested nor relaxed. Her thoughts again went in endless circles. Was there the slightest hope that Lena could still be alive? Was Robin a murderer, and could going to what had once been Paulette's house in Cumbria really help her to remember? She came back to the conclusion that the doll had been left for her to find, to implicate her in Paulette's murder. From the first moment she had heard the panic-laden voice, she'd wondered if Lena was setting her up in some way but, ignoring that inner voice of caution, had hot-footed it to the basement flat. Then, it seemed, the danger to Lena had been genuine. There was all that blood, Lena's blood. She was now dead, and if not killed by her half-brother, then who else could it be?

Remembering DS Teller's menacing eyes, Mauve thought about the lies recorded by the police. How would it pan out if she returned to London and tried to set the record straight? 'Sorry, DS Teller, I was lying then, but I'm not lying now. Lena set me up eight years ago. And I killed Paulette Franklin – or I think I did – but the truth is, I can't remember. Lena is dead, so she can't tell us. But I believe her murderer might be Robin Kelly.' She couldn't see DS Teller being convinced by that.

Because it had gone on for too long, Charlie couldn't help. She didn't know how to tell him. If only she'd explained everything to him eight years ago. Yet another loop; buying Lena off at the time should have resolved the problem. She had a feeling of claustrophobia, not trapped in a physical space but in her mind. Ensnared in an endless nightmare with no exit.

'Did you have a sleep?' Kit asked over his shoulder.

She observed in front of him on the kitchen counter, in a perfect line, two carrots, a lemon and a lime, a jar of Dijon mustard, a peppermill, a bottle of Worchester sauce, the triangular shape of a pack of parmesan cheese, one egg and a tin of anchovies. To one side was a bowl containing shredded lettuce and croutons.

'No, I tried,' Mauve said. 'I've given up.'

'Reach any agreement with Charlie?' Kit picked up another carrot and continued grating.

'No,' Mauve said. 'What are you making?'

'A Caesar salad. We've got to eat.'

'Caesar salad doesn't have carrot, let alone half a ton of the stuff,' Mauve said, belligerent.

'Mine does, and if you don't like it, then don't eat it.' Kit looked at Timothy sitting patiently near the back door.

'Can you just walk him around the back garden, please? I think he needs a pee.'

'If you open the door, he can walk and pee all by himself! I always do that in London. I never faff around with him while you're away at uni.'

'Just as well I'm back then.' Kit turned, and the expression of annoyance disappeared from his face the moment he looked at his mother. 'Mummy, you've been crying. Has Charlie been horrible to you?' He stopped grating the carrot.

'Even on his worst days, Charlie is never horrible to me,' Mauve said. 'I think it would be impossible.'

'That's true.' Kit was thoughtful. 'Charlie has been in love with you forever, he's so protective.'

'In love? I don't know where that came from.' Mauve raised her eyes. 'He's my legal advisor, and we get on most of the time, but *love…*'

'Mother, you really believe yourself to be so worldly wise, but you never see what's under your nose. *Please…* Charlie's been carrying a torch for you for as long as I've known him, which is…' Kit held his fingers up and pretended to count on them 'Oh yes, all my life.'

'That's too silly.' Mauve felt her face growing hot.

'He's told you that you must go back and speak to the police?' Kit said gently. 'And Charlie knows, as I do, that Lena has always been jealous of you. You had your dad and your mum all the time. Lena only had your dad for a few years, and it's clear that her mother never wanted her. Charlie says Lena is your Achilles heel.'

Mauve shrugged, not wanting to be drawn. 'I'll take Timothy outside.' She turned the key in the back door as she spoke.

The sky had turned grey, which suggested rain was on its way. The garden was simple. The smell from the lawn indicated it had been cut recently, and around it was a border of yellow and white chrysanthemums. Practical rather than beautiful. Mauve turned her lips down; Mrs Johnson had probably chosen them because they were cheap, resilient and would last a long time. The narrow grey paving slab pathway she'd noticed earlier when looking out of the window edged its way to the picket fencing back gate.

Charlie in love with her, ridiculous! It was true he had a soft spot for her, but it wasn't love, or was Kit seeing something she couldn't? Mauve put her hands to her face; she felt flushed and giddy. Was it the menopause? She was far too young. Then, reality kicked in: she was forty-four! It was the L-word that had made her feel strangely warm and light-headed. As a teenager, she'd had a secret crush on the son of the school caretaker, Martin, a large boy with ginger hair, enormous hands and feet and freckles. He'd never even noticed her. Being diminutive, she always looked like the child she was. She'd been envious of the tall, well-developed girls who could pass for being years older. The feeling now was how she'd felt all those years ago when her secret crush was Martin, warm and secretive. Then, it wasn't her who was supposedly in love. If her son were correct, Charlie was in love with her. Mauve smiled. For some odd reason, even knowing Kit was way out in his judgement, the idea warmed her heart.

While Timothy decided which of the many spots he'd carefully examined to urinate upon, Mauve strolled to the gate. Kit's car was parked further along the back lane, between other vehicles, none new or expensive. They doubtless belonged to the people occupying the properties on George Road. She watched a woman walking a trio of long-haired harlequin dachshunds along the lane. A ginger cat spread along the top of a high wall was also observing them, his tail twitching. She stared at the cat. Eighty per cent of ginger cats were male, only twenty per cent female. Why had that statistic suddenly popped into her head, and why now? Was she going mad. *Lena was dead!*

Moving her attention upward, she focused on counting eight pigeons on a telegraph wire in a row. *Lena was dead, and she would be blamed for both her murder and Paulette's.*

Having urinated in several parts of the garden, Timothy yawned before working his way back inside through the open door. Mauve felt the first rain spots just as she noticed a man wearing a black raincoat. Having stopped at Zack's car, he walked around to peer inside. Automatically, she drew back while continuing to watch. It was probably a nosy neighbour who'd spotted the unknown car. As the man came from behind to walk on the gravel next to the vehicle and look in from the other side, Mauve saw, below the raincoat, the emergence of grey trousers and dirty white trainers. He no longer wore the wraparound sunglasses, but the peak of his cap hid the upper part of his face. For a fraction of a second, as he turned, she caught sight of his square jaw.

'Mother, you are just being paranoid.' Kit, having finished his salad, waved his fork like a schoolteacher flourishing a ruler, trying to put his points across as he talked. 'It might be the same man you spotted near Robin's house; everyone must live somewhere! He could have been at the tyre centre with his car and happens to live further along this street.'

'It's too big a coincidence.' Mauve poked the salad around the plate with her fork; she had lost her appetite. 'I'm not certain, but I think it could be Robin.'

'OK, Mother, so we go to Robin's house, and he is lurking watching us. That makes no sense.'

Mauve stayed silent. *It does make sense*, she pondered, *if he was watching to see if I went inside and could find the memory stick.* She couldn't tell her son. He would want to view it with her.

'You did say you didn't get a proper look at him, and lots of men have dirty trainers. You're always saying that.'

'Whoever it was, he was looking into your car, Kit,' Mauve said.

'I'll check the car when I take Timothy out for a walk,' Kit said.

'Don't put yourself in danger.' Mauve looked at the dog. 'Timothy can go in the garden tonight.'

'Don't be silly.' Kit frowned. 'We both commit ourselves to giving him his daily walks. You take him when I'm away, and I do it when I'm home; he loves his walkies.'

'*Arooooo!*' Timothy had heard the magic word. He came with alacrity to the table to stare at Kit, his tail moving side to side rhythmically.

'Now look what you've done.' Mauve stood up and started to clear the table, most of the salad still on her plate. 'One day without a walk won't hurt.'

'If that's all you're going to eat, I'll leave the dinner to you tomorrow.' Kit took his plate to the sink. 'You can choose something you like… without carrots!'

'I'll wash up,' Mauve said, contrite. Kit never hung back, he got on with things: cooking, cleaning, washing-up. He was the rare type who washed up while he was preparing the meal. He couldn't bear mess. Maybe part of his OCD condition. She should recognise her good luck.

'Good.' Kit picked up a dog lead and jacket from where they'd been draped across a spare pine kitchen chair and headed for the door, followed by Timothy. 'Lock me out, Mum,' he said. 'I'll only be about twenty minutes and will bash on the door when we get back.'

'Take the key,' Mauve said.

'No, lock me out, and remember I can't get in. The back door is also locked, so neither can anyone else. It'll make you feel safe.'

'I'd feel *you* were safer if you didn't go out.' Mauve spoke to the closing door before reluctantly locking it. Then, after hovering to glance at the plates in the sink, she came to a decision and sprinted up the stairs to her bedroom. With her laptop open on the bed, she turned it on and put in the memory stick taken from Robin's bungalow.

There was only one item on the stick, titled 'File One'. Mauve clicked to open it.

The years rolled back.

There was no sound to the video. It was dark, but the moon was full and lit the garden. It opened with Mauve's face too close to the camera, her eyes unfocused and her lips parted in a vacuous half-smile, like an unhappy chimpanzee being filmed by her keeper. She appeared dishevelled, her hair flattened and eye make-up smeared. The blouse she wore had a torn sleeve hanging down from her bare shoulder. She remembered the aqua-blue blouse, the name of the shop she'd bought it from and that it had been new, worn only once. After returning home from Cumbria, she had destroyed it in the garden burner, along with the trousers and shoes she'd worn that evening, all covered in Paulette's blood. Now her chin moved upwards in the video, making her appear to be gurning. Did she always look so ridiculous when drunk? Worse still, apart from the messy make-up, there were the marks on her face, something dark, earthy or blood-streaked in matching lines on each cheek, like a Native American in old 1950s films remembered from childhood; she needed only a headband with a feather to complete the image. Had she, on that fateful night, taken part in some ritual? The only comparison was a friend who had once shown her a photograph of himself after his first foxhunt, when he'd been 'blooded'. Fortunately, while her parents appreciated Ascot and horse racing, both considered the foxhunting fraternity boorish. The video moved on disjointedly. She was dancing on a lawn in the moonlight; someone out of shot had her right hand. She knew from her dreams that it was Lena pulling, swirling her around. Her free left arm was thrown outwards, and sometimes the camera came close to her face when it was lit up as if by torchlight. It could only be Robin behind the camera, filming.

Then Mauve was inside the house, sitting in a deep leather armchair. Paulette was sitting opposite, her lips moving, her expression gentle. She talked as she poured coffee from a percolator into a white mug and passed it to her. Suddenly, Mauve could hardly breathe; there was a pain in her ribs as she recalled how sweet Paulette had been. She tried lip-reading, longing to know what was said. In this section, Mauve's face was no longer painted, her blouse not torn. She raised her coffee mug to the camera as though making a toast. Her eyes were blank; she was there in body, but not in mind. Was Paulette trying to sober her up with the coffee? The filming jumped again, and Mauve was in a junk room with furniture and empty boxes. A memory came to her of the smell of decay. Tables were piled with old newspapers, and she was carrying the wooden doll with its painted face and yellow dress. She held it near the camera, as she had earlier with the mug, before staggering forward to the door, tottering like a newborn foal taking its first leggy steps.

Then the scene changed again, back to her blouse torn and the streaks on her cheeks. The way the recording was edited did not show the correct timeline of how things had occurred. In the last part, Mauve was on her hands and knees on the floor with a long-bladed knife in her right hand. She was revisiting the scene that recurred in nightmares, when she'd wake up in a panic, unable to catch her breath. The image she had carried in her mind throughout the past eight years. Paulette laid in a pool of blood, her arms and hands stretched out beseechingly. Had she been pleading, begging for her life before her death? Her throat slit and her dead eyes open wide, staring.

As the video ended, there was a sudden bang from downstairs. Hurriedly switching the computer off, she pulled out the memory stick to return it to her pocket before running downstairs to let Kit in.

13

The time dragged before Kit eventually went to bed.

Back from his walk, he'd immediately noticed the neglected washing-up. 'Mother!' He looked at the sink, his voice petulant.

'I'll do it now,' Mauve said. 'I went upstairs to unpack.'

'You were up there all afternoon. How long does it take to unpack a couple of bags?'

'I'm sorry,' Mauve said, flustered.

'No.' He looked up after unhooking Timothy's lead. 'You look terrible. I'm sorry, Mummy. It's only a couple of plates. Why don't you go to bed? We can make plans tomorrow.'

'We haven't got a car.' Mauve felt on the verge of tears, jittery and confused, the images from the video still fresh in her mind.

'Let's talk about it in the morning.' Kit steered her gently to the staircase. 'Go to bed, Mummy.'

Mauve did not undress. Instead, she returned to the bed and assumed her previous position, lying on her back to stare at the ceiling, waiting to hear sounds indicating Kit had gone to bed. She could not watch the video again until she was sure there was no chance of him catching her.

The sound of his voice filtering up from downstairs made her wonder who he was speaking to, presumably on his phone. The next sound was of the television. At last, after hearing the closing music to the late news, she heard his footsteps on the stairs. He went first to the bathroom and then his bedroom.

Mauve checked the bathroom to be sure that he really had gone to bed before she returned to her own room, and after placing a chair in from the door as a precaution, played the video.

It was a short sequence, and she played it again and again. She had already determined that the sections were not in chronological order. The first part in the garden, with her blouse torn and the marks on her face, must have been recorded at the end of the evening, after Paulette's death. The semi-darkness made it impossible to see if the blouse was blood-soaked. The more she watched it, the greater her sense became that she was not dancing in the moonlit garden. Her original observation that she was complicit in the dance was incorrect. After several viewings, it seemed more likely that she had been in bewilderment, and had Lena let her go she might have fallen over. The editing seemed odd; it could only have been done this way to confuse. If DS Teller watched it, might she not believe that Mauve was a willing participant in the dance? Each viewing of Paulette pouring coffee and passing it to her made Mauve feel wretched. Paulette's smile was gentle as she attempted to make eye contact with the drunken Mauve and touching her hand when she passed the coffee. It had been impossible to work out what she was saying. Then there was the betrayal after Paulette had seemingly been so solicitous. Why had Mauve killed her?

Putting the laptop away and removing the chair from the door, Mauve sat on the bed with her arms wrapped around her legs. It was Lena who'd told her she'd murdered Paulette. Mauve's four solid memories of the time at Paulette's house had been of walking along the path on their arrival, and Lena passing a bottle which she'd swigged from before dancing in the garden with Lena. Then Paulette was dead and she was kneeling in the blood. The fourth memory was looking back at the house as Lena drove them away. It was the third recall, Paulette's body, and the blood, from which her panic attacks stemmed, and her belief in Lena's version of the events to be true. Then, watching the recording, the thought had come to her that her kneeling in blood by Paulette's body could have been a set-up. Why had it not shown her killing Paulette? That would seem logical if the intention had been to blackmail her.

If they'd left the memory stick for her to find, who was she calling 'they'? With Lena dead, it surely had to be Robin alone. When he'd returned to his home eight years earlier, she and Lena were inside the bungalow drinking whisky. Robin knew she was aware of the location of the key. If it were part of his plan, there could only be one possible motive. To get her to hand over more money.

As the night crept by, Mauve felt she could never wind

down sufficiently to sleep. When, finally, she'd succumbed, it was curled on her side in a foetal ball. She awoke to find her mouth dry and the pillow damp where she had been dribbling. On the table next to the bed was a cold mug of tea, and she was thankful that she had remembered to remove the chair from the door. Kit would have considered the need to barricade herself in to be odd. Almost next to the mug was the black memory stick. Mauve felt a sensation of shock followed by breathlessness, as if something physical was moving towards her. Sitting still, she counted as she breathed in and out. Kit might have seen and picked up the memory stick when he'd left the tea. Where to put it? If she left it in the back pocket of her jeans, might it fall out? Working around the room, she looked high and low for a place. In the computer or make-up bags, on top of the wardrobe, or in one of the two bags she had brought with her? Eventually, her eyes rested on the hem at the bottom of the floral curtains, a darker shade of yellow than the walls. After examining it, she found her nail scissors and, cutting a few stiches to make an opening, slid the memory stick inside.

Picking up her watch, Mauve saw it was after ten. There were voices from the street outside, possibly neighbours chatting. She flopped onto the bed again. The feeling of nausea seemed to have been with her forever. Her back and legs ached, and her head felt thick as if starting with a cold, but it was more likely that having so little sleep was catching up with her.

The voices outside continued. One of them was Kit's. Why was he talking to the neighbours? There was a girlish laugh. Probably Mrs Johnson batting her eyelashes at him. Silly woman! Mauve groaned, thinking again of drunken evenings in clubs and bars with girlfriends and the handsome young male members of staff. It was too awful, and she didn't need that memory just now.

Mauve went to the bathroom with her towel and washbag. Returning to the bedroom after her shower, she dressed and put on her make-up. Time to face the world. She went out onto the landing and looked down. Timothy had come to the bottom step.

'*Hurrumph*,' Timothy called up to her in excitement, then disappeared toward the front door. Whoever was there was of interest to the dog.

The door was beyond Mauve's view. She heard it close and wondered if Kit was leaving or returning. The talking outside in the street began again, and while she could not hear what was being said, she recognised Kit's voice. Timothy set up a whining, wanting to be with Kit.

Returning to the bedroom, Mauve went to the window to peek from behind the curtain. Kit was standing next to a woman whose back was turned towards the window. The woman was of medium height. Probably young, with an athletic build. A jogger, maybe. She had shoulder-length brown hair and wore tight jeans and a brown leather jacket. *She has good taste*, Mauve thought; the jacket was identical to the one she owned. In front of them was Mrs Johnson. How long had the bloody woman been there? Had she no shame?

At last, Mrs Johnson turned and walked off along the street to her own home.

Kit walked back to the door. The young woman moved to follow him and then Mauve saw that it was Eliza Kelly, Lena's daughter, and the jacket she was wearing was Mauve's.

14

Mauve went slowly down the stairs, pausing on the bottom tread to watch Eliza coming in. Tall, slender and perfectly proportioned, she had the Kelly features, the square jaw complemented by chiselled high cheekbones, wide, dark-brown eyes and creamy, flawless skin. Where Lena had been merely good-looking, her daughter was beautiful. Lena, at the same age, had possessed the most amazing self-confidence. Her demeanour suggested she owned the world. Although she'd never met him, Mauve had seen photographs of Lazor, Eliza's Polish father. He had been tall and extremely handsome. She imagined Eliza had inherited her striking looks from his side of the family.

Timothy, wearing a purple jacket with red hearts, pressed himself against the young woman's legs, his excitement palpable.

'Timothy, Timothy, Timothy!' Eliza almost sang the name. 'You're a lovely boy, and I'm so happy to see you.' She took Mauve's jacket to hang it where it had been, on a hook by the front door. Then she went down on her knees to hug the dog. 'I've missed you too.'

Kit's words came back to Mauve in the kitchen of the London house after she'd commented that Timothy only cared about herself and him.

'*There are one or two others.*'

This must be one of the others! Mauve looked from Eliza to Kit. How long had the relationship between the cousins been going on, and when and where had they been meeting up without her knowledge?

'No need for an introduction,' Kit said, his attitude casual, as though Eliza was no longer the enemy but accepted as a much-loved buddy.

'Indeed.' Mauve was haughty.

'Hi, Aunt Mauve.' Eliza's smile seemed genuine. 'Sounds like Mum's been at it again; a complete pain in the arse, causing trouble.'

Mauve found herself speechless. How much about her private problems had Kit divulged to this woman? Going into the kitchen, she switched on the kettle.

'Coffee,' Kit said. 'Just what I was thinking.' He gave his mother a hard stare. Mauve read this as, 'Behave, Mother. Do not kick off.'

'What gives us the unexpected pleasure of your company?' Mauve's tone was frosty.

'Not so unexpected,' Kit answered before Eliza could speak. 'It was Eliza who organised this house rental for us. We were talking to Mrs Johnson. Eliza spoke to her by phone to make sure we could come straight in yesterday, not wait until four, the usual time she allows holiday renters to move in.'

'I didn't know that,' Mauve said. 'Why was she wearing my jacket?'

'Mrs Johnson only got your back view yesterday, bending over Timothy and your jacket collar was up. Eliza was pretending to be you. And she has been kind enough, in our hour of need, to bring us a hire car,' Kit added. 'It's in her name with me as the named second driver. She's going to leave it with us.' He smiled at Eliza. 'I'll run her back to Lincoln station later today so she can get a train straight to London.'

'Thank you,' Mauve said. 'That is so kind. You must tell me what I owe you. I wouldn't want you to be out of pocket.'

'It's all sorted, Mother,' Kit said. 'No need to worry about that.'

'I've brought the phones.' Eliza passed a plastic carrier to Kit. 'There are two.'

'Phones?'

'With new numbers the police don't have. There's one for you and one for me,' Kit said. 'Are they set up?'

'Yes, all ready to go,' Eliza said.

'You have been busy,' Mauve acknowledged.

'Timothy's jacket matches the décor.' Eliza laughed as she took in the purple walls.

'Yes, Timothy,' Kit said to the dog, 'don't stand too near the walls, or we might lose you!'

Eliza joined in with his laughter, and Timothy, not wanting to be left out, affectionately headbutted her legs again. Mauve busied herself making coffee.

'Designer jackets,' Mauve said. 'Kit has several.

Nothing is too good for Timothy, he adores him.'

Eliza nodded, smiling.

'Mummy, Eliza *is* the designer,' Kit said. 'You know she wants to go to college for a fashion degree course?'

'Oh...' Mauve looked from Timothy to Eliza.

'She did tell you when she visited about six months ago,' Kit said.

A recollection stirred. A conversation, something about college. 'Yes, yes, I remember.'

'Eliza designed and made all Timothy's jackets,' Kit said. He sounded proud, showing off on his cousin's behalf.

Mauve looked at them, dumbstruck.

'Are you OK, Auntie Mauve?' Eliza asked. 'From what the police told me, it all sounds hellish.'

'You appear to be pretty blasé.' Mauve found her voice. 'For someone whose mother is *dead*.' She banged three mugs onto the kitchen work surface.

'Lena – *my mother* – dead?' Eliza put her head back to laugh, showing her perfect pretty teeth. 'Please, Auntie Mauve, don't worry yourself. My mother will be behind all this shit. Have you not put it together yet? Mum is the master manipulator; she won't be dead. Never in a million years. Although,' Eliza gave a long look through half-closed eyes, 'if I know Mum, it's you whose being set up for the chop. She wants your money, and you in jail would put the cherry on the cake.'

Mauve poured the coffee before bringing out a plastic carton of skimmed milk and placing it on the dining table. She took one mug and sat at the table, setting it down in front of her. Kit and Eliza followed her example, joining her.

'And please stop calling me Aunt or Auntie; it makes me feel 103.' Mauve blew on her coffee. 'Aren't you being just a little disloyal to your mother?'

'Mm,' Eliza mumbled. 'Maybe. But Lena and I have gone beyond that. We went past the point of no return a while back. I've been giving her a wide berth.'

'It's since she got into your trust fund,' Kit added. 'The one set up for you by your dad. Dear, sweet Aunt Lena left you penniless.'

'Yup,' Eliza said. 'Not something you would expect from a normal mother; then, Lena has never claimed to be one of those.'

'She stole from you, *her own daughter*?'

'Why are you surprised?' Kit asked, sipping his coffee. 'You are her sister, half-sister,' he corrected. 'How many times has she screwed you over?'

Mauve nodded thoughtfully. It was true that Lena had pulled some shocking stunts, but with her daughter! Could she believe Eliza, or was it possible that Eliza, after falling out with her mother, was working with Robin to cause her and Kit grief?

'I didn't realise your dad had set up a trust fund before he died,' Mauve said.

'Yes,' Eliza said, her face serious. 'Dad was wealthy, so my mother married him. She would never have married a pauper. The wheels soon dropped off that relationship, and Lena – I've got out of the habit of calling her Mom – took him for every penny she could get. Dad set up a trust fund for me to cover college or university costs and enough money for my first flat.'

'How did she manage to get at it?' Mauve put her mug down to stare at Eliza. 'It should have been secure.'

'I believe that Dad thought it was. When Dad died I was told about the legacy, but I couldn't touch it until I was twenty-one,' Eliza said. 'Two days after my twenty-first birthday, when I approached the solicitors, they said there had been a codicil in my father's will that in the event of his death, my mother would take charge of my legacy until I was of age. Of course, there was nothing left. Lena goes through money, both her own and other people's – it makes no difference – like a whirlwind. She has no morals.'

'Do you think your father would have put in such a codicil?' Mauve asked.

'Never.' Eliza was firm. 'Before he died, the relationship between them was toxic. He didn't trust her. I think someone at the solicitors, perhaps the solicitor himself, was bent, or maybe took a percentage. Lena would have made it worth his while. The problem is that I can't prove it.'

Kit shook his head as if in agreement. Clearly, he already knew the story. Mother and daughter were alike. Lena had the ability to twist men to do her bidding. Eliza had Kit in her pocket.

'Why have you not challenged your mother?' Mauve asked. 'What Lena did is surely illegal, she can't just spend your legacy.'

'Two problems,' Eliza said. 'First, I need money to go

to court. The police were not interested. It's a civil matter. Lena says she invested the money in my best interest, but the company went bankrupt. It might take years to go through the courts. Second, what would be the point in me going down that route? Lena doesn't have the money. She's spent every penny. All the energy needed to go through the legal system would be wasted. I won't get it back. Once Lena gets her paws into something, it's gone.'

'Is she still gambling?' Mauve wanted to know.

'Is the pope still catholic?' Eliza laughed. 'Yes, of course she's still gambling. And it's no good telling me it's an illness; it won't get my money back.'

'I am sorry to hear that,' Mauve said.

Eliza nodded, stroking a finger down the coffee mug.

'You said hellish – from what the police told you – about my situation, that is,' Mauve said. 'What did they tell you?'

'That you went to Lena's flat. It was empty, but there was a lot of blood. The police found you there. They checked the blood in the flat against my DNA and blood type, and it's a familial match. So it was Lena's blood in that flat,' Eliza said. 'Why did you do a runner, Auntie… sorry, Mauve? The police said they are looking for you as a person of interest.'

Mauve looked broodingly from Kit to Eliza. How much to trust her? Could she be so different from her mother? Then, the information would only be what Kit had already told her.

'I wanted to check with Robin, your mother's brother, if he might know where Lena was,' she said eventually. 'I thought if Lena were up to something, Robin would know and probably be in on it.'

'Might be difficult,' Eliza said. 'I understand what you mean about Uncle Robin. He's slippery, just as rotten as his mother. He takes after Grandmother Bonnie. But Uncle Robin's been off the radar for a while. He got his fingers burnt in a deal that went pear-shaped; he's been out of the country for months.'

Mauve's mind went to the man she'd seen twice the previous day. 'How do you know that?'

'After the police contacted me about Lena, the blood and the flat, I did phone around the few people who Lena had contact with... nothing. I did the same with Robin. The information that I got comes from Grace, Damien's wife.'

'Is Damien married then?' Mauve asked.

'Yes, married and he has two kids,' Eliza said.

'I'd forgotten about Damien. I only met him once as a child.' Mauve wondered what he was like as an adult.

'Bonnie had a habit of dumping her offspring onto their fathers, as she did with Lena and your dad. Damien got lucky; he never went back to Bonnie, he stayed and grew up with his dad and stepmother,' Eliza told her.

'He was a squaddie, wasn't he?' Mauve asked. 'Joined the army.'

'He was in the army,' Eliza agreed, not expanding further.

'It looks like the trip up here has been a waste of time, Mum,' Kit said. 'If Robin is abroad, he won't know what's happening with Lena.'

'If,' Mauve said. 'I need to be sure.'

'I went to the supermarket while you were asleep.' Kit changed the subject. 'You've had no breakfast, and Eliza's had a long drive to get here. I'll make us all a sandwich.' He wandered to the kitchen. 'Have a think, Mummy.' He looked back at Mauve. 'With what you've learnt from Eliza, maybe it's time to drive back to London; meet up with Charlie and see the police. We could all go together rather than me taking Eliza to the station.'

Eliza nodded in agreement. 'There doesn't seem any point now in searching for Robin.'

15

Mauve ate her sandwich in silence while listening to the pair's chatter. It was clear they'd been seeing a lot of each other and had friends in common. Eliza had stayed in Nottingham with Kit while he was at university, and he had been to her flat and knew her ex-boyfriend, Russ.

During the drive to Lincoln, Mauve recalled that Kit had asked her about hearing from Eliza, and she'd lied to him. He must have already known the truth and that she'd been lying. That he had not corrected or challenged her made it somehow feel worse.

Two hours later, after Kit and Eliza had taken Timothy for a walk, Kit returned to the question of Robin.

'So, Mum, what have you decided?' Kit asked. 'There doesn't seem much point in going back to the bungalow. Robin won't be there. Do you want to drive back to London, the three of us?'

'No, I'm not ready,' Mauve snapped.

Kit and Eliza exchanged a glance.

Mauve imagined they had decided their plan of action while walking Timothy and viewed her as a recalcitrant child, which made her feel belittled and annoyed. How could she get them to agree to return to London together and leave her alone to move on to Cumbria?

She was no longer entirely committed to continuing the journey to Cumbria. What was the point? After viewing the video, one memory had returned – the smell of decay in the room with the newspapers – but other sections, rather than answering questions, only brought forth more. She'd known only what Lena had told her about the evening. After a falling-out with Paulette about the diamond necklace, she had, apparently, gone on to kill her. She puzzled, after watching the recording, how it could have gone from Paulette being so kind to the murder? Also, the expression in her eyes was weird; she had been in another world. The possibility that she had been drugged was now a recurring thought. In London, it had seemed sensible to go to Norfolk, Lincoln and then Cumbria, following the same route that preceded Paulette's death. Now she wasn't sure there was any point. Then, if she could get Kit and Eliza to agree to leave, it would give her time to think clearly. Their presence increased her sense of claustrophobia.

'I could drop the pair of you at the station,' Mauve said. 'You'd be in London by this evening. Why not leave the car with me, and I'll drive down tomorrow? Being by myself overnight will allow me to go over everything.'

'Mother, what is there to think about? It's obvious you can't keep running. You need to go back and face the police. And after what happened to you yesterday,' Kit huffed, 'you didn't even want me to walk the dog last night after you thought the man you saw at the tyre place was the same person you spotted looking into my car.' He glanced at Eliza. 'She even said it might be Robin!'

'What happened?' Eliza asked.

Kit explained in detail. When he finished, he and Eliza looked at Mauve as if expecting her to add to the conversation. When she didn't respond, Eliza spoke.

'If you're not coming, I can go back to London on my own, and if you run me to the station, why don't we all call at Robin's house on the way, one last time? It might put your mind at rest, Mauve, that he's not been there. If we get caught inside, I can say I'm his niece, and I was worried about him.'

'That is a kind thought,' Mauve said. Why was her niece being so bloody helpful? What was she expecting to get out of it?

'Why don't we all look in at Robin's and then come back here for the night?' Kit looked at his cousin. 'It's a three-bedroom house; there's a spare room. Then you won't need to get the train. We can all go back to London together tomorrow. If you don't mind staying over, Eliza. You've no plans for tonight?'

'No.' Eliza smiled. 'No problem.'

'I'll pick up a curry on the way back. I owe you one.'

'Sounds even better.'

In the bedroom by herself, Mauve pondered. After taking the computer bag from the bottom of the wardrobe, she opened it to stare at her laptop. Would it be safe here?

Then, why would anyone break in? It would be challenging for anyone other than an expert to get into her accounts, past her passwords and encryption. She put it back into the wardrobe, and after a glance around the bedroom, returned downstairs.

Eliza pointed out that the restaurants would not be open for a takeaway until later. After hanging around until six, she drove them to Robin's house.

'You've been here before?' Mauve asked. She was sitting in the back of the Toyota 4x4 with Timothy next to her.

'When I was younger. I came here with Mum twice,' Eliza said. 'We didn't visit Uncle Robin much. Mum said he moved around, but I always felt they weren't close.'

'What about your Uncle Damien?' Kit asked. 'Or Grandmother Bonnie?'

'I can't even remember the last time I saw Uncle Damien and Grandma died of lung cancer when I was little. Lena said she smoked sixty a day. I was too young to remember her.' Eliza spoke thoughtfully. 'We lived in Clapham when I was younger, then Mum got the basement flat. I was thirteen. I hated moving to the other side of London, switching school and leaving all my mates behind.'

'Thirteen is a tricky age to move,' Kit said.

Mauve sat quietly, listening to them chatting. They were relaxed together, and it was as though they'd forgotten she was there. Kit had once asked why he could not have a sister or brother. He had been six when the subject came up. These two could be siblings rather than cousins;

they appeared to have a bond. But could it be real? She considered again what Eliza might be up to. She had not asked for money. Still, if she were around until tomorrow, there would be plenty of time for that. Perhaps Kit and Charlie were right about returning to London. It would have been different if she could have spoken to Robin, asked him about Lena. Going to the flat now seemed a pointless exercise. On the other hand, if what Eliza had told them was true, and Robin was away, who else could have left the memory stick for her to find?

Reaching the cul-de-sac, the tyre company was closed, and the road was silent apart from the distant hum of traffic. Driving past to the bungalow, Mauve looked to where the man with the grubby trainers had been standing, remembering his grey trousers that she had also seen later that day, below the rain mac he'd worn while looking over Kit's car. She'd only got a glimpse of him and her mind was so addled by stress. She conceded that it might be as Kit had suggested, a coincidence that someone who had used the tyre centre lived in the village where they were staying.

Parking as they had done yesterday, Kit led the way to the front door and knocked.

'Nope,' he said after a few moments of silence. He wandered around to the back with Mauve and Eliza following. He put his hand above the back door to find the key and let them in.

'God, it's been years since Mum brought me here, and it's not changed a bit.' Eliza went into the living room, turning in a circle to look about.

Why did we bother? Mauve wondered. It was like something set. Nothing had altered.

'It's like a bolthole for your Uncle Robin, isn't it?' Kit said.

'Yup,' Eliza agreed. 'From what Lena used to tell me, he would come here to lick his wounds after some illegal shit went belly-up.'

Mauve left them talking as she wandered away to the bedroom. *Yackety-yack*. Eliza, with her big brown eyes and upbeat girly voice, was getting into her brain. She was becoming irritating.

Inside the bedroom, she froze.

The computer was not on the table. It was now on the floor next to the bed. In the centre of the worn wooden table was another memory stick. The twin, an identical brand, to the first one. Had the computer been moved so the memory stick seemed more prominent? '*Eat me*,' she thought again, her brain going into panic mode. She held onto the edge of the table, her chest tightening. Her breathing came in slow hard gasps.

'What's that room?' Kit asked from the hall.

'It's the bedroom,' Eliza said.

Mauve grabbed the USB stick to push it, as she had done on the first occasion, into the pocket of her jeans.

As Kit and Eliza entered the room, Mauve found her knees buckling, and suddenly she was kneeling on the floor. She tried to focus on the carpet, which had become a moving blur.

'Mum!' Kit said. 'What happened? Why are you down there?'

Mauve started counting, measuring her breathing in and out. She waved her son back, pushing his supportive hand away from her.

'What's happening?' Eliza asked, bewildered.

'She's having a panic attack.' Kit knelt on the floor beside his mother.

They kept their positions on the ground for an eternity while Mauve slowly regained control. Kit, waiting patiently by her side, rubbed his hand in a circle around her back.

'Breath slowly and deeply, Mummy.' He spoke soothingly.

When Mauve eventually stood up, Eliza gave her a glass of water she had brought from the kitchen. After she'd taken a few sips, Kit took her arm and she allowed him to guide her outside the house. Having locked up and returned the key to where they had found it, they walked around to the front gate.

'What brought that on, Mother?' Kit asked quietly.

'I don't know.' Mauve shrugged. 'It just happened.' She was still quivering and noticed Kit's look of concern. Her head felt thick and confused; Robin had been here. Her mind went longingly to the bed in the rented house and then the ceiling. She wanted to get back there, to do nothing but lie on the bed looking up and counting the cracks.

'Hello again.' It was the elderly man with the plastered-down hair who had been there on the last visit.

'Hello,' Kit said. 'We popped back to see if Robin might be back.'

'My Uncle Robin,' Eliza added.

'Ah.' The man looked sneakily from one to the other.

Mauve caught the smell of alcohol and noticed he was holding tightly onto his gate.

'Robin's not been back,' he said. 'Like I said yesterday, I haven't seen him for a long time. Did you want to leave a number or address? I'll pass it on if I see him.' He slurred the word address.

'No, not a problem.' Kit smiled charmingly. 'Thank you anyway.'

The man stayed at his gate to observe them returning to the car.

Timothy welcomed Mauve into the back seat. As Mauve took her position next to him, the dog rested his head on her lap. Absentmindedly, she stroked his head.

The man had been lying. Robin must have put him up to it. Mauve's face twisted in concentration. His reward had no doubt been a bottle of something alcoholic. And who had been the one to suggest that they come here tonight? Eliza.

16

The car stopped and Mauve resurfaced from her dark thoughts, realising they'd parked outside an Indian restaurant. It had been raining, and below the brightly lit restaurant sign, the street was shiny wet.

'Are you sure you don't mind us stopping for a takeaway?' Kit asked.

'No, you both go and choose,' Mauve said.

'What would you like, Mummy?' He put his hand back to touch hers.

'I'm not hungry.' Mauve saw the look of disappointment on her son's face. 'You know what I like.' She forced a smile. 'Something with prawns and pilau rice.' They went inside.

'It's you and me.' Mauve spoke to Timothy while stroking his back. He yawned with contentment while keeping his eyes fixed on his master as he disappeared into the restaurant, still chatting and smiling to Eliza as though he didn't have a care in the world.

Robin must have returned to the house to find Mauve had taken the USB stick. The next-door neighbour would have been able to describe her. He was playing cat and mouse; he would know she'd done as he'd anticipated. Was she so predictable? Of course, Lena knew how her mind worked and everything that she knew must have been passed on, repeated, to her half-brother.

Back at the house, Kit insisted on checking the street to ensure nobody would see Mauve before bundling her indoors.

'I'll be back down in a minute.' Mauve left them in the kitchen unpacking the food.

Once upstairs, she closed the bedroom door and, without switching on the light, pulled off her shoes to lie on the bed in the darkened room. It had become her place of safety. She returned to her feeling in Charlie's warm car after leaving the police station, his coat wrapped around her. That felt much safer, like the relief of going home.

Music was playing, mingled with voices drifting up from below. This feeling of safety could only be for a few minutes, she knew. She had to fix an affable face to go down and pretend to eat and be friendly with her niece, the woman she was now convinced was complicit and working with her uncle. She thought about Henry, her father, Eliza's grandfather. When she and Lena were teenagers, he'd caught Lena out. Mauve had asked to borrow one of her father's unique books; old and of great value. She'd been allowed to take it after promising to take great care it was not damaged. She'd overheard her father explaining to her mother what he'd seen and said. In Mauve's bedroom, Henry had come upon Lena tearing the book, a page at a time, into pieces and immediately realised that Lena was setting Mauve up to take the blame for the destruction. 'All your small acts of deceit will turn you into a very ugly human being,' he had said.

It wasn't until she was much older that Mauve questioned the hypocrisy of his words. Had Henry not spent his whole life deceiving? He'd often made money fraudulently, and the poorly constructed flats and houses caused a public scandal. Then, while maintaining his love for his wife, there was an endless list of his female conquests. Both Charlie and Kit had questioned why Mauve demonstrated loyalty to a half-sister who had continuously betrayed her. The answer had always been because Lena was like Henry, Mauve's adored father. Mauve closed her eyes to put her face in her hands. Why, as an adult, knowing Henry had been rotten to the core, had she been in thrall to her equally nasty half-sister? So much so that when she had taken the phone call on Friday evening, despite every instinct telling her to ignore it, she had walked into a trap. One undoubtedly set in motion by Lena. She took her hands from her face as she vowed silently to be strong and not make the same mistake with Eliza, her mother's daughter in every sense.

She rolled to her side to touch the jeans pocket, feeling the USB stick. She was desperate to play it, wondering what it could show that had not been on the other one. Perhaps there was a message? She would wait until Kit and Eliza were in bed.

Ten minutes later, Kit called to her and Mauve moved from the bed.

Putting her feet onto the carpet on the opposite side of

the floor, she encountered an odd shape under her left foot. Switching on the bedside light brought a gentle glow to the room and she found the item her feet had encountered, an eye pencil. The throw from the bed almost touched the ground and had partially hidden it.

Going around the room, Mauve could find nothing that had changed, and there was nothing else on the floor. The computer was where she had left it; her clothes were still in the wardrobe and drawers. The make-up bag was still on a chair. But she had not used that eye pencil. How would she have dropped it from the bag? After putting on the main room light and picking up the bag, she kneeled and closely examined the carpet where she'd found the pencil. There were faint traces of blue eye powder on the grey carpet, and further back, a lipstick lay under the bed, possibly having rolled there. Someone had been in the room searching. Running her hand inside the bag, Mauve found the same trace of blue matching that speckled on the carpet. It was an eye shadow that must have accidentally opened, scattering particles.

She put the bag back on the chair. Whoever had been in the room was looking for something. They must have emptied the contents of the make-up bag onto the floor and, perhaps, being in a hurry to get in and out of the house, had not noticed leaving the trace of powder and the two items hidden by the draped bedspread. The intruder must have been searching for something small enough to go inside a make-up bag. Mauve went to the curtain. The lump in the hem signifying the USB stick was where she'd hidden it was gone. She sat on the floor to work with her fingers from one end of the hem to the other, repeating the search several times. Nothing.

'Are you coming?' Kit's voice from downstairs came up to her. 'We're waiting for you.'

'I'm coming,' Mauve shouted. Then, bringing herself up to her knees, she did the counting exercise, followed by deep breathing.

'There you are, Mummy,' Kit said as she came down the stairs. 'I was just coming to look for you.'

Mauve joined the young pair at the table, her mind buzzing with questions. It had to be Robin, but why did he want the memory stick back? It made no sense. Had he taken anything else, and should she tell Kit? It would be difficult with Eliza being there; she didn't want to let her know that she was aware her uncle had been inside the house searching her belongings.

It was clear that Kit had laid the kitchen table. Every item of cutlery was precisely placed. Paper napkins had perfect knife folds. Placemats formed a square in the centre, and the foil trays on top at an exact distance from one another.

'Dig in, Mum, there's loads,' Kit encouraged when she put a small amount of rice and prawn masala on her plate.

'I'm not desperately hungry.' Mauve attempted a weak smile. She should tell him that someone had been searching her room – it would put Kit on his guard – but then he would want to know what she had that the intruder had been looking for. She decided to change tack.

'Tell me about the design course you hope to do,' Mauve asked Eliza.

Eliza and Kit exchanged a look of surprise. Kit nodded his encouragement.

'Well,' Eliza said. She spoke eloquently to explain the type of course, duration and what she hoped to achieve once she'd completed it. Kit remained silent throughout.

With Eliza's passionate response, Mauve felt like something was being sold to her, but couldn't help but feel impressed by the amount of research her niece had put into finding the best college and course to suit her requirements.

'You've put in an application?' Mauve asked.

'I've been accepted –provisionally,' Eliza said. 'They've seen my designs and the work I've produced from them.'

'She's just trying to get all her ducks in a row.' Kit put his fork down to look from his mother to his cousin.

'You mean funding and accommodation?' Mauve asked.

'Yes,' Eliza agreed. 'There is a small grant that I might qualify for, and I will need to find an evening job in a bar maybe, or restaurant.'

'Accommodation is the most expensive area to consider,' Kit added.

'And an evening job is good,' Mauve said. She considered what she would say if it were Kit in the same situation. 'But you don't want to work seven nights a week; you would be completely knackered. Maybe just two or three evenings.'

'That's easy to say,' Kit butted in. 'It's a matter of needs must. Even renting a room in someone's home is expensive. Eliza must have enough income to keep a roof over her head and put food on the table.'

'Yes…' Mauve agreed.

'Thanks for asking,' Eliza said. 'It's bad timing, me waffling on about college when you have so much hanging over you.'

'We can talk about it again, can't we, Mummy?' Kit's eyes implored her. 'After we have put all this trouble behind us.'

'Yes,' Mauve said. She forced false sincerity into her voice. She didn't mean it. Eliza wanted her financial support. If, as she suspected, Eliza was working with her uncle to scam her, there was no way she would get a penny, added to which, if she found it were true, Mauve would work to destroy the relationship between her scheming niece and her son.

Timothy came to headbutt Eliza's knee.

'Sweetheart, he wants to go outside.' Eliza stood up. 'I am the chosen one!' she announced dramatically.

'You certainly are.' Kit laughed as she went out, taking Timothy into the back garden.

'Are you sure you're all right?' Kit asked Mauve, his voice low. 'You look so pale, Mummy.'

'I'm fine. Don't worry about me.' Mauve pushed the food around her plate as she spoke.

'My turn now.' Eliza returned to the kitchen before going up the stairs.

'I'll go up after Eliza finishes in the bathroom,' Mauve said.

'Are you *sure* you're OK, Mummy?' Kit pressed.

'Don't fuss.' Mauve patted his hand.

'I'll do the walk with Eliza. The door will be locked while we are out.'

When Eliza returned, Mauve told them she would sleep on the decision about what she would do the following day.

In the darkness of the bedroom, she mulled over why Eliza was being so helpful, bringing the car and the new phones. That Timothy had chosen her to take him outside for a pee irked; it was she who looked after the dog for most of the time. It seemed her niece could not do enough to please.

It was strange how she'd begun to feel she could work out Robin's motivation and actions, just as Lena could with her. Then, her belief that Robin had ingested so much knowledge from Lena on how Mauve's mind worked might be a sign of madness. And she couldn't comprehend this new twist. Why would Robin want the memory stick back? It was not logical.

It might be that witnessing the close relationship between Kit and Eliza was tipping her mental state into a downward spiral. They made her feel shut out, lonely.

Mauve went to the window to peek out at the night between the curtains. It was raining again, the rain running gently down the windowpane. She had made her mind up. Tomorrow, with or without Kit, she was going on to Cumbria.

Resting against the windowsill, she shuddered. That someone had been in this room to take the USB stick removed her sense of security. Her personal space had been invaded. She stared at the curtain. Could she have missed it? She had checked three or four times. Returning to the place on the floor, she sat down to again pick up the hem of the curtain and run her fingers along where the stick had been hidden. And there it was! Pulling it out, it lay in the centre of her trembling palm. How had she missed it before? She was losing her mind.

A few minutes later, Mauve took the phone Eliza had given her out of her bag to dial a number she knew by heart. It was answered on the second ring.

'Hello, Charlie,' Mauve said.

17

Eliza smiled ruefully as she removed her boots before sitting on the narrow single bed in the smallest bedroom.

If Mauve had realised someone had been in her room while they were out, she hadn't let on. It had been an easy task to follow instructions before leaving and put the back door on the latch. Eliza hadn't known what might be taken; everything was on a strictly need-to-know basis. Then, just before Mauve came down to join them, she'd received the text. A memory stick left at the back door needed to be sneaked back up to Mauve's bedroom. Timothy, unwittingly, had given her the perfect excuse to go outside.

Eliza leaned back to prop herself against the pillows and deliberated. In Robin's house Mauve had gone into meltdown, leading to a panic attack. Kit was now more stressed than she'd ever seen him. Disturbed because his mother was desperately trying to dump him to move forward alone, and the harder she pushed him away, the more determined he became to hang on with her. For her own part, Eliza felt she'd have no other choice than to return to London the following morning.

The evening had gone as well as could be hoped. Mauve's antagonism had been less noticeable during dinner but still lurked below the surface. Mauve, when asking about Eliza's hopes and dreams of going to art college and becoming a designer, had drawn her into a conversation. The talk had seemed natural, the most normal conversation she'd had ever had with her aunt. Kit as always had been adorable, adding his support with words of encouragement.

Because Mauve had been a hot topic during her childhood, Eliza was aware, from Lena's point of view, of all her aunt's foibles. Her mother's opinions were never wishy-washy; everything was full-on. Love or hate, she was good at extremes. Her biggest love was for the card table at the casino. The buzz it gave her, she'd said, was a hundred times better than sex.

Lena's fervent hatred of her half-sibling came from two issues she'd perceived as being unfair. She had been taught by her mother, Bonnie, that money, above all else, was king. Mauve's monetary advantages irked Lena. Then, there was the time each had spent with the father they'd shared. That neither matter was of Mauve's making was irrelevant. The sum of money settled on Lena after the death of Henry Gilcrest, available to her from the age of twenty-one, was eye-watering. It removed any need for Bonnie to seek legal redress to ensure her daughter's financial security.

Eliza got up to pace around the bedroom, ending by

the window. It was dark outside, and, as Mauve had done earlier, she perched on the windowsill to stare blankly into the darkness. She didn't want to go back to London tomorrow, not knowing what was going on. She was aware it was dangerous. It was like reading half a book and not knowing how it ended. Still, she would find out later.

Going back to the bed, Eliza brooded as she slowly undressed. Following instructions, she had assured her aunt that Lena was alive, making light of the situation. That she could not muster more emotion for her dead mother worried her. Like an annoying itch she couldn't reach to scratch. Their relationship had been complicated, unlike that with her adoring affectionate father. Lena had never been tactile, neither had she expressed any form of affection. Being with Mauve made her aware how in certain ways the half-siblings were alike, while in other ways they were polar opposites. Putting her head back to stare out of the window from the lower advantage point of the bed, she could see the stars lighting up an otherwise black sky. The moment she stopped thinking about what was bothering, her the answer came. Her aunt's distress about Lena's presumed death was greater than her own!

The theatrical game being played out, starting with the London flat, had got into Mauve's head. She must realise it wasn't just about the money. Though Auntie Mauve didn't always spot the obvious. She wouldn't or couldn't accept that her half-sister thoroughly detested her.

Growing up, Eliza had listened to Lena's tales of the tricks she'd played on 'the rich bitch'. The ugly, unkind things she had said and done, both as a child and an adult.

She'd thought it hilarious, especially after a few drinks, to regale her only child with the tawdry tales. It was something she couldn't talk to Kit about. She loved that they had bonded so well, enjoying a close relationship. Then, as much as Mauve annoyed Kit, his love for her was unquestionable and he was intensely protective of her well-being. Repeating the bile Lena had spewed forth about Mauve would hurt him and compromise their friendship.

But what about the horrible things Lena had done to her own daughter? When Eliza confronted her mother about her stolen inheritance, she'd laughed. 'All's fair in love and war,' she'd said. 'Treat it like a learning curve, my darling. When money is involved, it's everyone for themselves.'

As well as the disappearing acts when Eliza was a child, left alone for days, Lena often brought men home. Some of her mother's guests were kind; others less so. At fourteen, there had been one who'd paid her a night-time visit, with Eliza woken from sleep to sense a presence. Instinct told her to remain silent, pretending in the darkness of the bedroom to be asleep. She'd felt the movement on her bed as the man, for a while, had sat beside her. She could feel her skin prickle with fear, imagining his eyes resting on her. Then she heard Lena's voice calling for him. He had stood up and hastily skedaddled, closing the door quietly behind him. In the morning, he had gone. She wondered if it had been imagined, or was it a dream? Then, reliving the panic she'd felt, the need to suppress it would not go away. 'Get over it,' Lena had said. 'Nothing happened.' Eliza experienced an overpowering sense of wretchedness and anger. She realised how things could have become much worse. From that time onward, when going to bed, Eliza positioned a chair with its back wedged under and against the door handle. It caused her mother to complain if she wanted to get into the room. Eliza would repeat her mother's phrase back to her. 'Get over it.'

As sleep evaded her, Eliza tried to push thoughts about Lena from her mind. The amount of blood found at the flat suggested Lena had met with a violent death. However horrible her childhood had been, she would not have wished that on her mother.

18

The following morning, Mauve was up early and made herself tea and toast before returning to her bedroom. Later, after hearing movements from downstairs, she assumed Kit was about and would take Timothy out for a walk. After waiting for his return, she joined him in the kitchen and told him her decision. She would not return to London with him and Eliza. She needed to move on, alone. She'd prepared for a volatile reaction, but he shrugged. 'It's what I've been expecting.'

'You don't know where I plan to go,' Mauve said.

'You can tell me when I return from taking Eliza to the Lincoln station,' Kit said. He looked upstairs to smile at Eliza coming down. 'Are you ready?'

'Yes.' Eliza passed the red leather carrying bag to Kit. 'Are you and Kit not coming, Mauve?' she asked.

'No,' Kit interrupted before Mauve could answer. 'Mother is moving on, so when I've dropped you I'll come back to collect her.'

Mauve bit back angry words. She did not want him

with her, but better to discuss it on his return after her niece had left.

'Ah,' Eliza said.

'*Ahhrah.*' Timothy rubbed his head joyfully across Eliza's legs.

'See you again soon, sweetie pie.' Eliza bent to hug the dog.

'Did you have something to say?' Kit, waspish, addressed the question to his mother. 'To Eliza before she leaves?'

'Yes, of course.' Mauve smiled. It was easier than she'd imagined. No awkward questions. 'Have a good journey.'

'Thank you.' Eliza nodded.

'*And?*' Kit stared hard at his mother.

'And… And…' Mauve ferreted around, trying to come up with what was expected. 'Thank you for the car and the phone,' she said eventually. 'You have been a godsend.'

'Says the biggest atheist on the planet.' Kit rolled his eyes upward. 'Lock the door behind me, Mother, and do not let Timothy out. He's been for his walk and had breakfast,' Kit instructed her as he followed his cousin outside, slamming the front door behind him.

Mauve resisted the anger rising like bile to respond with a biting retort. Being taught good manners by her son was beyond annoying. Still, Eliza was gone; on her way at last.

She'd felt odd this morning, more lost than ever. The memory stick could not have simply vanished, then returned. The only logical answer was that she'd missed it in the first search. It made her question her sanity.

Having made herself a coffee, she brought the laptop and phone downstairs with the two memory sticks to set up at the kitchen table. Turning the computer on, she thought about her conversation with Charlie the previous evening. She had told him she intended to go to Cumbria but had not given the reason.

'I wish you'd stop drip-feeding me. Just tell me everything, and we can move on to the next page,' he'd said.

'It's not that simple, and I'm protecting you and Kit,' she replied. 'What you don't know can't hurt you.'

'So that means it can hurt *you*?' Charlie retorted.

'Don't make me regret phoning.' Sitting on the bed, Mauve plucked, agitated, at the bed throw. She had already told him more than intended.

'Why did you phone?'

'A friendly voice,' Mauve said after a moment's hesitation.

'I'll always be that, but I would prefer you to trust me.' Charlie sounded sad. 'I feel hurt that you don't.'

'No emotional blackmail, Charlie.' Mauve became brisk as she told him that Eliza had arrived, about her surprising closeness to Kit, and that she'd brought the hire car and new phones.

'Is Eliza being close to Kit a problem?' Charlie asked. 'They are cousins.'

'She twists him around her little finger,' Mauve said. 'I don't trust her motives. Like mother, like daughter!'

'That's just silly,' Charlie said. 'Kit is young, but he has great instincts. Even if you don't trust her, you should trust him. Nothing gets past Kit.'

Mauve remembered her son's words. 'Charlie's been in love with you forever.' Did it mean she should trust Kit's instincts about Charlie's feelings? She again felt the flush of heat on her neck and face and was glad Charlie couldn't see her.

'I'm not sure I'd agree,' Mauve mumbled.

'Just because Lena has you wrapped around *her* little finger, it doesn't follow Eliza can do the same with Kit.'

'Me!' Mauve said.

'Yes, you!' Charlie spoke quietly. 'You always said it was because she reminded you so much of your father – that Lena had inherited his personality and eyes – but that's rubbish. You were always a pushover. Why, when you knew she was so dangerous, did you ever allow yourself time and again to become involved? DS Teller said during the interview that Lena only had to snap her fingers and you'd go running.'

'Yes,' Mauve agreed weakly.

Before finishing the call, Charlie told her he would phone her the next day. Lying on the bed, Mauve had listened to the drone of voices from downstairs before drifting into slumber.

With her coffee at hand and the laptop open, Mauve switched on. As she did so, the new mobile rang. It was Charlie. 'He said he'd phone later,' Mauve mumbled, looking at the time on her wristwatch. It had taken a while to build herself up to view whatever was on the latest memory stick. After a moment's hesitation, she pressed the button to take the call.

'Hi, Charlie.'

'Mauve, has Kit been out for the newspapers yet?'

'No.' Mauve froze, a feeling of fear tightening her chest. She closed her eyes, forcing herself to regulate her breathing. 'He left with Liza ten minutes ago. He's dropping her at Lincoln station.'

'The police have released a photograph of you with Kit; it's in all the papers. Wanted in connection with the disappearance of Lena Kelly and the unresolved murder of Paulette Franklin.' Charlie's words came out slowly, as if he was speaking in a courtroom with a witness. Mauve realised at that moment how well she knew him. He was being truthful, but at the same time trying not to panic her. It was not working.

'What have you got to do with Paulette Franklin's murder? You told me last night you were going to Cumbria. Where the murder took place.' Charlie's voice was taut, and Mauve realised he was fighting to hold back his anger. She should have told him. It was inevitable he'd find out anyway and, finding out this way, he might not be on her side.

'It's the same photo in all the papers and with many references to your "infamous" father,' Charlie continued.

'Where the hell would they get the photo?' Mauve gasped.

'Where do you think they got it?' Charlie said. 'It was probably given to them by your loving partner.'

'Bloody Zack!' Mauve said.

'When some of your buddies see the papers, you might find a lot more pictures out there. The gutter press pays top dollar for the stories and pictures from *friends*,' Charlie said. 'Some will be tempted to grab the money.'

Charlie dragged out the word 'friends' and Mauve's thoughts went to Jade and Becky, and her own amusement at Jade's awful new teeth. If they did go to the press, who could blame them?

'Kit looks about ten in the photo. I wouldn't recognise him, the man he is now. No one else will.'

'Read it to me,' Mauve said. 'What exactly does it accuse me of?'

'They,' Charlie said. 'It's in all the papers, and you even made it onto TV breakfast news.'

'Give me the gist,' Mauve pushed.

'I've already told you,' Charlie said. 'The police are seeking information leading to the whereabouts of Mauve Gilcrest and her son Christopher in connection with the disappearance of Lena White and the unsolved murder, eight years ago, of Paulette Franklin. There are references to your father and his connection to the dodgy flats scandal. Also, Paulette's relationship with your mother and a bit about the disappearance of The Queen's Diamonds.'

'Shit,' Mauve said. 'Shit, shit, shit.'

'Mauve, if you don't come back to London, then I'm coming up there to you,' Charlie said. 'We can talk things through, but you need to get it into your head that you can't keep running. You are going to have to come back and face the music.'

'I can't,' Mauve said. The words were little more than a whisper.

'Mauve, can you hear me?' Charlie's tone gave away his alarm. '*Mauve…*'

Charlie's voice, as with the carpet and the purple walls, were all entangled and blurred. Her chest hurt and there was a banging in her ears, but that didn't matter. Next thing, Mauve was on the floor, clutching the front of her blouse. A momentary chill turned into a wave of heat. Her legs felt numb. Had the panic attacks been this bad before or was this the end? She couldn't catch her breath. Trying to breathe was making her chest ache, while all around the walls were closing in on her.

19

The banging had stopped, but after a few minutes she heard a voice. Mauve curled on her side for a while, trying to ignore it to concentrate on her breathing. Then focusing on the front door, she saw the letterbox flap was open. A familiar voice was speaking through the gap.

'*Ywoow!*' Timothy sat directly in front of the door, shouting at the open flap.

'Mummy,' Kit said. 'Please get up and open the bloody door. It's locked.'

Mauve, even in her muddled state, knew Kit couldn't have gone to Lincoln and back. She pulled herself into a sitting position as she continued to count her breaths in and out. Had the police stopped him? Concentrating on the carpet, she found the phone and, going on all fours, crawled to the table to pull herself up. Putting the phone on the table next to the two USB sticks, she scooped them up and returned them to the back pocket of her jeans. Staggering, she reached the door, unlocked it and pulled it open, bracing herself for the arrival of the police, but it was just Kit followed by Eliza. Kit put his arm around his mother to lead her back, Timothy followed, and Eliza closed the door.

'Who was it on the phone?' Kit asked.

'Charlie.' Mauve gasped as she allowed him to guide her to the sofa. Flopping down, she noticed the bundle of newspapers her niece carried under one arm.

Kit picked up the phone. 'He's gone.' He pressed to redial. 'Charlie?' Kit walked away, holding the phone against his ear. 'I know, I've seen them. We just collected the papers from the newsagent's and looked at them in the car. We didn't get to Lincoln, just came straight back.' Kit looked at his mother listening to the one-sided conversation. 'Yes, she had another panic attack. It's OK. We're here now. I'll ask her to phone you later.' Finishing the call, he came to sit next to Mauve.

'Charlie said he told you what was in the newspapers.'

'Yes. You've seen it?' Mauve found she was tearful.

'It brought on the panic attack. I'm going to make you a camomile.' Kit squeezed his mother's hand before getting up to go and fill the kettle.

'Camomile! How much stuff did you pack? And Eliza will miss her train,' Mauve huffed.

'It's OK, I can get a later one,' Eliza said. 'Don't worry about it.' She took a place next to her aunt on the sofa. 'It must have given you an awful shock.'

'Let me look at them.' Mauve held out her hands for the newspapers.

Eliza looked at Kit, who nodded.

As Mauve went through each of the papers, Kit made

the tea and brought her the mug before perching on the arm of the sofa near her.

'Thank goodness Eliza pretended to be you when she arrived,' Kit said. 'I suspect Mrs Johnson is a bit of a gossip. It's just as well she doesn't know you're here.'

'Yes,' Mauve said. She looked from one to the other. 'That is something, but then!'

The young pair waited.

'What about that strange man?' Mauve said. 'Robin's next-door neighbour. He saw me.'

'Do you think he reads newspapers?' Kit said.

'He must have a television,' Eliza pointed out. 'It would be unlikely that he didn't have a TV.'

'I thought he was a bit shifty,' Kit said.

'Mm.' Eliza nodded her agreement.

'If he's a mate of Robin's, he won't want to get involved with the police,' Kit said hopefully.

'If he's a mate of Robin's, easily bribed with a bottle of booze, there might be something the police could offer to get him to talk to them.' Mauve's voice rose uncontrollably.

'Why do you think Robin bribed him with booze?' Kit put his hands on his hips. His eyes raked over Mauve. 'Is there something you're keeping quiet about that we should know?'

Mauve thought guiltily of the memory sticks in her back pocket. 'What could I know that you don't? You've been with me all the time and the only person I've spoken to since I got the new phone has been Charlie. The man stank of booze; I thought Robin might have given it… so he'd keep an eye on the place.'

'That makes no sense if Robin's not been there. How could he give him a bottle of booze? What do you want to do?' Kit asked, his voice heavy with forced patience. 'We could drive directly back to London, the three of us.'

'No, I'd rather you stick to the plan,' Mauve said. 'Take Eliza to the station. I'll be fine waiting here.'

'After seeing what's in the papers?' Kit asked.

'I can only go forward.' Mauve stood up decisively.

Kit stroked his chin, pondering as he watched his mother pacing the room like a caged panther.

'We'll need to alter your appearance.' Kit looked at Eliza as he spoke. She nodded in agreement. 'Get her away from here, move on today. If Mummy doesn't return to London, we'll go on with her…'

'You don't know where I'm going!' Mauve cried, exasperated. 'How many times do I need to tell you? I don't want you involved.'

'You haven't told me where you're going, but I'm guessing it's Flookburgh, Cumbria.' Kit gave his mother a wry smile. 'Not too hard to work out.'

'Where Paulette Franklin was murdered.' Eliza tidied the scattered newspapers unhurriedly into a pile before taking them to the kitchen table.

Mauve found Eliza's calmness extraordinary. It wasn't one of Lena's traits. Perhaps she'd inherited that from her father's side.

'Why would you connect me to Cumbria?' Mauve snapped.

'Mother, you went to the cottage in Norfolk. I know Auntie Lena had been there years ago, and then you needed to come here to see Robin,' Kit said. 'It seems logical if the police want to talk to you about Paulette's murder, you are thinking about it and might want to go to where it happened. I don't yet know how, but this road trip is all tied into something that's happened with Lena and Robin.'

Mauve mentally dredged around, trying to think of a reason to draw her son away from the idea. She could not come up with one.

'Make-up first, then hair,' Eliza said, looking over her shoulder as she continued to straighten the papers on the table.

'You'll need to go through what she's going to wear,' Kit told Eliza.

'It'll have to be pretty much what she has with her. We can't go clothes shopping,' Eliza said. 'And with her being so small, there's not much I have with me small enough to fit her.'

Mauve found them both staring hard at her, looking her up and down.

'Make-up, hair, clothes, what do you mean?'

'Mummy, dear, your image is plastered all over the press and TV,' Kit said. 'Mauve Gilcrest must simply disappear.' He snapped his fingers in the air.

'Get your stuff,' Eliza urged him.

Kit went upstairs to return a few moments later with a blue suitcase Mauve had noticed in the car boot.

'Can she borrow a wig from Veronica?' Eliza asked as she leaned in close, appearing to examine Mauve's head. 'Although they might swamp her!'

'I am still here!' Mauve snapped. 'I can hear the two of you.'

'There is one that's a bit tight for Veronica, it's brunette and slightly wavy with some volume.' Kit ignored his mother's interruption.

Mauve looked from one to the other.

'Perfect,' Eliza said.

With her eyes fixed on Mauve's head, Eliza brought the tips of her fingers together silently, pretending to clap.

'If you don't mind, I'll be the one to decide what's perfect.' Mauve realised that neither her son nor niece was listening. It seemed they had gone into another world. Physically they were present, but mentally they were lost to her. The worst of it was that the two were in complete harmony; it was she who was the outsider!

Over an hour later, Kit and Eliza stopped working on Mauve. They stood back with a collective sigh, Kit knitting his fingers together to examine their work.

Kit had tied back her hair, cleaning all the make-up she'd been wearing away with a cleanser and cotton wool. At first, Mauve, as she had done in the police station and when Charlie scrutinised her as she climbed out of his car, felt vulnerable and naked. At a certain point, though, she'd realised the pair were not seeing her as a woman without make-up but rather as a blank canvas that required their artistic input.

After moisturising her face, Kit applied a foundation before the concealer. When Mauve queried why, saying, 'It should be the other way around. And you've only used a whisper of concealer!' Kit put his finger to his lips.

'Trust me on which way around to use it, Mummy,' he said. 'And why would you need much concealer? It's not as if we're trying to hide a five o'clock shadow!'

Mauve, ignoring the twitch of amusement in Eliza's lips, found herself remembering the remarks made by Charlie about trusting Kit's judgement. She relaxed and asked no more questions.

The application of eye make-up was the most fascinating part of the process. With gentle but firm fingers, Kit spread white eyeliner over her eyelids before using a dessert spoon as a guide to apply a hazel-coloured eye shadow. He shaped the eyebrows using a mascara wand. Then, bringing out a kohl eyeliner pencil, he warmed the tip under the flickering flame of a cigarette lighter. After testing it twice on the back of his hand, he applied it in one coat.

Looking on, Eliza heated an eyelash curler with a hairdryer.

'Think the fake eyelashes might be too much,' Eliza said. She wrinkled her nose as she looked at Kit. They both took a step back to examine their canvas.

'Yes,' Kit said. 'I agree. Too much.'

Eliza switched off the hairdryer and, after folding its cable, put it back into the case, along with the eyelash curler.

'They curl better,' Eliza said, as if reading her aunt's thoughts, 'if the eyelash curler is warm.'

'We'll make up for the lack of fake lashes with the mascara.' Kit smiled as he applied a layer of mascara with the dessert spoon to stop it from making contact anywhere other than the lashes. He followed by combing in a translucent powder before another layer of mascara. He rubbed her lips with a suede stick.

'To exfoliate,' Kit said.

'Do you want me to mix a colour for the lips?' Eliza held out a small white dish she'd taken from the case.

'No,' Kit said. 'Think a shop-bought will be better than mixing a unique colour, easier when she needs to do it herself or top-up.'

'Mm.' Kit examined Mauve's face. 'Perhaps a little contouring, though, to bring out those cheekbones.'

Eliza nodded and passed him two brown gel pencils.

While Kit was applying the gel, Eliza disappeared upstairs to come down a moment later with a wig. Brown and wavy with a hint of auburn.

'This one,' she said.

Going over Mauve's short blonde bob, it felt like a hat. Kit and Eliza both fiddled and brushed. The exercise seemed interminable. Then, at last, they were finished, and Mauve tried to assess from the expressions on their faces examining her whether they considered the transformation a success.

'Can I see?' Mauve asked plaintively.

'Yes,' Kit said. 'Let me get a mirror.'

With the mirror in her hand, Mauve worked on her poker face, trying to suppress the question of how to tell the poor boy that his work was awful without hurting his feelings. Their last serious row had been about his desire to become a make-up artist. The passion went deep, all the way to his heart. Raising the mirror, she looked at the woman. Who the hell was she? A youngish, stunning brunette looked back at her.

Mauve took a sharp intake of breath.

'You're not going to have another panic attack?' Kit said.

'No...' Mauve found it hard to speak. 'I look... so different, transformed. It's amazing.'

'Is that as in "amazing good" or "amazing bad"?' Eliza asked, her face tense.

'Good,' Mauve said. 'Good, very good. The things you can do with make-up! I never thought I could look like this. You've brought out my eyes, and my face looks much thinner.'

'That's the contouring,' Kit said.

'Wow!' Mauve held the mirror at different angles. 'I thought I was pretty clued up with make-up techniques. I've got a lot to learn.' She looked at her son and niece with tears in her eyes. 'Thank you.'

'Don't you dare cry, Mummy,' Kit scolded. 'The mascara is supposed to be waterproof, but I'd rather you didn't test it.'

20

Upstairs in Mauve's bedroom, Eliza sat on the bed rooting through a pile of T-shirts and blouses as Mauve pushed clothes into her bags.

'Wear things that are low key; plain jeans and T-shirts. And bear in mind that your make-up will need doing every morning. Kit will teach you,' Eliza said.

Mauve restrained herself from retorting that she had forgotten more about dress and fashion than her niece ever knew. 'Yes, putting on the make-up will be the boring bit if it takes over an hour,' Mauve said. She could not help herself. Each time she passed the mirror, she stopped to admire her reflection. 'Nobody I know would recognise me looking like this, let alone a stranger. The hair makes a big difference.'

'That's it.' Eliza smiled. 'And you must be so proud of him.'

'Of course,' Mauve said. 'I've always been proud of Kit. When he sets his mind to something, he achieves so much. He makes friends easily, and everyone loves him.'

'I was thinking of the TV Talents Make-up Awards,' Eliza said. 'It's perfect for him. The competition's only been going on for four years for new people coming into the business and wanting to showcase their abilities and flair. Last year's winner has gone a long way. She's been taken on by one of the big film companies, to work alongside established artists. She'll learn so much.'

Eliza was relaxed and bubbly after the success of the make-over. *What the hell does she know about Kit that I don't?* Mauve thought.

'He's in the final three, so exciting,' Eliza continued. 'It's only a few days before the final.'

'It's Friday next week, isn't it?' Mauve asked.

'No, Thursday of this week,' Eliza corrected her. 'In fairness, with everything that's been going on, it's not his top priority. He said if he pulls out the organisers have a reserve list and there's always next year.'

'Yes,' Mauve agreed. 'There is that.' She fought a sinking feeling in the pit of her gut and tried to keep the concern from showing in her voice.

'I'd better go and see if there's anything to clear or tidy in the kitchen.' Eliza stood up, stretching. 'Don't want Mrs Johnson complaining.'

After she'd left, Mauve slumped on the bed. Kit had told her nothing about the competition, yet he had made the final, and if she couldn't resolve her situation within the next three days, he would miss it.

'*Bloody hell!*' Mauve uttered the words out loud. As if there wasn't enough going on. Apart from the probability that Lena was dead and she was trying to avoid spending the rest of her life in prison. Compared with these worries, the award was only some silly competition; she couldn't let that bother her. But it did, and she knew why her son had said nothing. He'd arrived home to discover that after being found by the police, on her hands and knees, saturated in blood; his mother had been taken for questioning, and things had worsened by the day. There had been little opportunity for a proper conversation about anything normal. Yet she still felt irrationally hurt that Eliza knew all about it, that Kit had not confided in her.

Mauve went about clearing the room of her clothes. With her bags packed, she walked back and forth in the small room, suddenly back to being a caged beast. Being polite and smiley didn't come easy when all she wanted to do was scream. The problem was that if she started to scream, would she be able to stop? Not knowing what was on the second USB stick was driving her nuts. Once they were together in the car, there would be no opportunity to watch what was on it. Coming to a decision, she found her laptop and went out onto the landing to lock herself in the bathroom.

Putting the loo seat down, she opened the computer and took out the two identical memory sticks. The first stick had been a silent video, but just in case this one wasn't, she put in her connected earpieces before switching the laptop on. The first attempt showed it was the recording she had already seen. She swapped it for the second stick.

There was only one file; incongruously, as with the first, it was called 'File One'.

'A tad lacking in imagination, Robin.' Mauve's voice was a whisper.

This one opened on a teenage birthday party – Mauve at fifteen – with sound. There were many familiar faces, including schoolfriends she had not seen for many years. Everyone sang 'Happy Birthday' as she blew out candles. Then Lena was behind Mauve, watching her open presents. Mummy and Daddy were watching, and Auntie Paulette. There was lots of laughter and smiling faces. Lena came to stand close after Mauve had finished unwrapping her presents and put her arm around Mauve's shoulders for the camera. The next piece was Mauve and Lena side by side on the hammock in the garden of the Hampstead house. Bono, her small black-and-tan coloured cocker spaniel, ran back and forth beneath them. Both wearing shorts and T-shirts, they were head to head, deep in conversation as the camera swept over their tanned limbs. They both waved to the camera. Next, Lena was sitting on a leather couch in their father's study. Henry Gilcrest had his arm around his daughter's shoulders. Mauve, looking at them so close together, felt a tug of jealousy; he was her daddy! She recalled how hard it had been accepting Lena into her life. Then, as she looked back and forth from one face to another, she remembered how much Lena looked like him. His eyes, the upturn of the lips in the smile. And the mannerism of absentmindedly pushing fingers through their hair when they were deep in thought. The clips continued. They were of happy times, and Mauve recognised that she had copies of most at her London home, although she had not viewed them for years.

'Are you OK, Mauve?' There was a tap on the door. Eliza was on the landing outside the bathroom.

'Yes, I'm fine. I'll be down in a minute,' Mauve called before listening to Eliza's footsteps going down the stairs.

Then, the image was of someone moving in the darkness. Mauve in the garden of Paulette's home, staggering as the camera moved from her to another figure.

'Don't hurt me!' The voice was Lena's. 'Please don't hurt me, Mauve,' Lena repeated.

'Why would she say that?' Mauve whispered.

The camera went back to Mauve, catching a glint of metal. It must have been Robin again with a torch. How else would the shot of the knife she was carrying be so precise? Back and forth, with Lena repeating the words again and again. 'Don't hurt me.'

Then, the final image again was of Mauve on hands and knees, covered in blood and holding the knife as she leaned over Paulette's body. The image froze on her face as she stared into the camera, her eyes again blank. She sat for a minute, staring at the black screen before removing the USB stick and turning the computer off before slipping quietly out of the bathroom to return to her bedroom.

After stacking the pillows up on the bed, feeling trembly and nauseous, she rested back into them and regulated her breathing. What had been the point of the video? She had seen all the shots of her and Lena as children many times. Although the clips were selective, they only showed Lena's good side. Part of the action on her fifteenth birthday had been Lena misbehaving. Caught stamping on a camera bought as a birthday present by Mauve's mother. After being caught out, Lena had gone into hissy-fit meltdown. The only section of the recordings that was puzzling was Lena appearing fearful while repeatedly saying, 'Don't hurt me, Mauve.' There was no evidence to prove Mauve had ever hurt her half-sister. She questioned the date of the filming. The part with her in the garden with the knife was from eight years ago, but when did the part with Lena wandering around in the darkness saying those words happen? Was that eight years ago, or had it been filmed recently? It wasn't even possible to be sure that it was Paulette's garden. Although it was Lena's voice, the images showed a moving figure in the darkness that might have been filmed more recently, and elsewhere. There was no hint of moonlight, as with the other night-time recording. Had the film been spliced together to give the impression that Lena was frightened of Mauve, because she was dangerous? If so, who might Lena be planning to share the images with?

Mauve groaned. Rather than answering questions, the footage had again brought more issues to bear. Why did someone come into her room to try to find the first USB stick? That someone had been in her bedroom was a definite; her not being able to immediately find it was due to her state of mind. It seemed clear that it had been left for her to find at Robin's house and it was intended to frighten her. In both cases, it had succeeded. Why, then, had they wanted to get it back? It made no sense. Lost in thought, she put the computer into her bag.

The sound of Kit's footsteps on the stairs caught

Mauve's attention. Two steps up, then a pause, two more steps then another pause. Only her son would walk up and down stairs in such a manner. Her mind moved momentarily to OCD and the previous evening with the perfectly aligned cutlery, and the sharp edge to the fold of the neatly placed paper napkins. She crossed the room to pick up her bags as the door opened.

'Veronica,' Mauve said.

The glossy, blonde, straight hair of Veronica's wig fell to finish just above the shoulders of her black T-shirt. Below that, dark denim jeans so tight they appeared to have been sprayed on and dark-brown biker's boots, with three straps on each boot, ending in shiny gold-coloured buckles. Over six feet tall and slim, her height added dramatic effect to Veronica's appearance. The bright-red and glossy lipstick reminded Mauve again of herself, aged twenty-one. The make-up on the perfect, youthful skin was immaculate, without hinting at the five o'clock shadow. Veronica had used the concealer to good effect.

21

'Have you packed, Mauve?'

'Yes, everything's done.' Mauve spoke as her mind went back to the image and the voice of Lena in the dark garden. '*Don't hurt me, Mauve.*'

'Make sure you've not left anything behind.' Veronica glanced around the room before taking the larger of the two cases.

She had taken on the role of mother hen, which should be Mauve's job. She didn't voice the thought. Instead, she said, 'I haven't phoned Charlie. I was going to call him back.'

'Do it now then.' Veronica took the second bag from Mauve. 'We're loading the car. Phone Charlie, then come and join us and we'll make a move.' She went down the stairs with both bags: one step, two, then a pause.

Mauve noted the use of the words 'join us.'

'Hi, Charlie.' Mauve sat on the bed for the last time.

'How are you feeling?' Charlie sounded concerned. 'I'm so glad you've called. Are you OK?'

'I'm fine. Just about to leave the house here in Sleaford.'

'I guess that means you're moving on to Cumbria,' he said.

'Everyone's worked that out,' Mauve said, peevish.

'It was you who told me, remember! And Kit and I talked about it after we'd seen the newspapers. We've both joined the dots. The road trip is connected to Lena, and to Paulette and her death, I take it?'

Mauve didn't respond. Kit had phoned Charlie yet again. All her attempts to manage the situation had failed. She had not realised how quickly the wheels would drop off, with all her attempts not to involve Kit or Charlie counting for nothing.

'Have you followed the same route before?' Charlie's voice was low and kind.

'Yes,' Mauve said. 'Not from London to Norfolk. I was already at the cottage in Norfolk and Lena came to me.'

'So… It was from Norfolk to Lincoln to see Robin, and then to Cumbria to see Paulette?'

'Yes,' Mauve agreed. There seemed little point in not admitting it or lying.

'I'm assuming Kit showed you the newspapers?'

'It was awful. A shock,' Mauve said.

There was a silence, when Mauve listened to Charlie breathing.

'Veronica has put in an appearance,' Mauve said.

'That's a positive,' Charlie said. 'And I'm guessing after seeing your picture in the papers that your appearance has changed somewhat.'

'Kit told you,' Mauve complained.

'He might have mentioned it,' Charlie said. 'I'll be seeing you in Cumbria. I meant what I told you earlier. If you won't come back to London, I intend to come to you.'

'It's really not necessary.' Though protesting, Mauve felt a sense of relief that she would be seeing him soon.

'You'll tell me everything then. Let me in…'

'Yes.'

'Promise?'

'I promise.'

'Are we all sorted?' Veronica asked when Mauve came downstairs. 'The bags are in the car, parked by the back gate.'

'Good,' Mauve said. 'Charlie is driving up, he'll meet us there. He wouldn't take no for an answer.'

Veronica did not reply.

Mauve noted the lack of surprise. She remembered all the times Kit had been on the phone. It was clear Charlie had been kept in the loop from the start and every step of the way.

'While I have you on your own,' Mauve said, 'is Eliza going back to London? She's been with us far too long. She must have friends to see, commitments – a lot to get on with.'

'No.' Veronica's lips tightened. 'Eliza has been amazing, so supportive. She's put her life in London on hold to help you. I hate to say this, but you are the most ungrateful, pathetically selfish person I have ever met.'

'I don't trust her.' Mauve, feeling her lips quiver, turned away so her nearness to tears could be hidden. The comment had cut, but she would not let it show how deep.

'Get over it, Mauve. Eliza is part of the crew.'

What exactly did that mean, the crew? Inwardly, Mauve boiled. Then a small pretty blond dog, with a jacket covered in pink hearts and the hair on his head gathered to be secured by a floppy pink bow, butted her legs.

'Timothy!' Mauve said with surprise.

'How could you even tell!' Veronica smiled, her eyes adoringly fixed on Timothy before scooping the dog up.

'He's still cross-eyed, with crooked, sticking-out teeth,' Mauve snapped. Immediately, the words were out she felt ashamed. It was a way of hurting back for being called selfish and ungrateful.

Veronica lifted her head with an air of disdain.

'I'm sorry,' Mauve said. 'I didn't mean it.'

'Yes, you did.' Her voice was cold. 'Get in the car, Mauve.'

After leaving the house keys on the table and dropping the latch to the back door, Veronica followed Mauve out to take the driver's seat next to Eliza.

Eliza tapped the postcode for Flookburgh, Cumbria, into the satnav.

'It's three and a half hours.' Eliza spoke over her shoulder as the car pulled away from the kerb.

'OK,' said Mauve. Timothy had put his head into her lap, and she absentmindedly rubbed her fingers up and down under his chin. She realised the joy of her caresses was causing him to dribble, making her trousers damp, but she didn't care anymore. She determined, in order not to further upset Veronica, to keep silent.

Mauve listened to the chatter between the driver

and front-seat passenger as they followed the satnav instructions to head back to towards Lincoln.

'Look, we're passing the end of Robin's street, where we went yesterday,' Eliza remarked. 'We could turn in there and check that Robin's car is not outside his bungalow.'

'No.' Mauve leaned forward. 'Keep going. We don't want to go there.'

'That's a bit of a turnaround,' Veronica said. 'The whole bloody point of you coming here was to see Robin.'

It's tit for tat, Mauve mused, glowering at Veronica. *Because I was nasty about Timothy.*

'But Eliza told us he's not even in the country.' Mauve felt again the rising of nausea. Her stomach twisted. 'I don't want us to be seen there.'

'Mauve, nobody is going to recognise you,' Veronica said.

'I'm just thinking,' Eliza said. 'It won't take us out of our way to look. Neither of the two properties has a garage, which means if there's a car outside it would have to be Robin's. It is the only place to park and I don't imagine the old bloke, the next-door neighbour, would have a car.'

'We can just look then,' Veronica said as he indicated and turned the corner.

The tyre company was busy. A queue of cars lined up alongside the driveway, with others parked, as previously, on an area of concrete to one side. Again, the noise of the machinery was relentless. Groups of people gathered waiting. The printing company on the opposite side of the road also had cars outside, indicating they were open for business.

Clouds blocked the sunshine to make the day feel dull and gloomy.

Pulling past the row of cars, the bungalows came into sight. Veronica parked on the printing company forecourt.

'Well.' Eliza was the first to speak. 'How many cars?'

'Three, all police,' Veronica said.

'What the hell!' Mauve eyes became fixed; unable to look away, she stared nervously at the vehicles.

'Wait a moment.' Eliza opened the car door.

'Don't go there!' Mauve's voice raised in alarm.

'Trust her,' Veronica said. 'And remember if you get overexcited, you'll bring on another panic attack.'

Mauve leaned back, watching her niece as she walked purposefully across the road to attach herself to a group of three men watching the police cars.

'Rubberneckers.' Veronica spoke as if to herself. 'Go, girl. Good choice.'

The conversation with the men continued for a few minutes. It was clear that all three were flirting with the attractive young woman. Mauve remembered when her presence triggered that immediate effect on men. Then Eliza raised her hand, smiling as she broke away from the group to walk back to the car.

'Let's go,' she said.

Veronica swung the car around to return to the main road. 'Well?'

'One of those blokes is a friend of one of the coppers. He went to ask what's going on. It's not Robin's house, it's that old bloke next door. He had an accident, fell down the stairs.' Eliza looked from Veronica to Mauve. 'Landed on his head and broke his neck. He's dead.'

'Wonder if he'd been watching too much television,' Veronica said. 'And maybe recognised someone.'

'It wouldn't have gone well if he'd become greedy with Robin,' Eliza said. 'Wanting money to keep quiet about the woman the police are looking for visiting the house.' She turned towards Mauve, raising her eyebrows meaningfully.

'You said something about Robin bribing him with booze.' Veronica's mean eyes met Mauve's in the rear-view mirror. 'It didn't make much sense at the time, but I think you owe us an explanation.'

Mauve shrank down into the seat. If Robin could kill the neighbour so casually to keep his mouth shut, there wouldn't be much hope for her. Then, who had been the one to suggest stopping here to look for a car? Eliza.

22

Apart from the disjointed satnav voice guiding them out of Lincoln towards Leeds, the journey began again in silence. Later, Veronica spoke quietly to Eliza, and a conversation ensued. Mauve, leaning back with her eyes closed, feigning sleep, was curious, but the voices were too low to pick up the exchange. Timothy snored contentedly, oblivious to the frosty atmosphere between the front-seat passengers and the one with him in the back.

After they'd bypassed Leeds, Veronica glanced to the back and then to Eliza. 'I'm stopping at the next service station. I think Timothy might need to have a walk and a pee.'

'Good idea, me too.' Eliza stretched her arms.

Veronica tailed behind cars and trucks to enter the busy service station and find a place in the crowded car park. Timothy sat up yawning, looking around with expectation as Veronica came around to put him on his lead before lifting him from the car. Mauve followed with Eliza.

'I'll find some grass,' Veronica said as she peeled away from the group. 'Timothy is discerning about where he'll pee.'

Continuing to the main building with Eliza, Mauve cast sneaky looks at other travellers from behind her sunglasses. Nobody noticed or appeared interested in a forty-something woman, possibly with her daughter. Although she could not stop thinking about the photographs and stories in the newspapers, she realised she was inconspicuous. No one gave her a second glance. The duplicity made her feel momentarily light-headed with relief. Was this how bank robbers and thieves felt as they embarked on something with nefarious intent? Mauve Gilcrest had become invisible, and the moment passed as she ruminated again upon Robin's dead elderly neighbour. There was not even the slightest doubt in her mind that he'd been murdered and Robin Kelly was the killer.

The day had become warm, with the sun high in a clear, blue, cloudless sky. After passing the rows of parked vehicles, they moved beyond the pumps area with the smells of petrol and diesel, past the bright lights of the fuel pay station, to reach the coffee shop, mini supermarket and fast-food outlets. Inside was a queue to buy coffee in cardboard cups from a wagon near the entrance, and family groups massed together outside the burger and pizza joints, with the shrill demanding voices of children piercing the last of her equilibrium.

'I'm going in here,' Mauve said to Eliza as she turned into the area that sold newspapers and books, seeking distraction.

'I need the loo.' Eliza nodded. 'Back in a minute.'

Mauve felt both relieved and anxious as she watched her niece walk away. Still convinced that Eliza was playing a double game, it felt good to be free of her for a few minutes. She was, after all, Lena's daughter, a Kelly, but there seemed little point in talking further to Kit about Eliza, and it appeared from her short conversations with Charlie that he would also take Eliza's side. Then, after explaining what had happened and putting him in the picture, he might be more open to listening to her suspicions. Resisting the temptation to pick up and open the same newspapers she'd seen earlier, Mauve pushed her sunglasses onto her head before plucking novels at random from the shelves. Drained and unable to focus long enough to read, she gave the impression of interest in the blurb on the back cover before returning each book.

'What kind of sarnie do you want?' Eliza was suddenly next to her. 'I'm buying sandwiches for the car.'

'Whatever.' Mauve shrugged. She had little appetite. 'Cheese and salad, or cheese with pickle,' she suggested.

Eliza nodded and, in a moment, was gone again.

Her picture was across every newspaper, a man was dead – murdered – and she was unrecognisable, even to herself, yet Eliza was wittering about sandwich fillings! Mauve did not consider herself violent, but at that moment she could easily have grasped her niece by the throat and throttled her. There was so much bottled-up emotion waiting to be uncorked. She remembered how Kit had warned her she mustn't get too emotional or it might trigger another panic attack. She went outside to find a spot near the door to watch the flow of people. Their boring normality drew her to look at faces within the crowds. Couples, business people, all ordinary folk who, judging by their clothes, were not well off. They probably got excited over a second-hand car or a cheap night out, and it was doubtful that any of these people were murderers running from the police. She envied their safe, dull normality, little friendship groups, partners and family. She had again a sense of being detached and alone; on the outside looking in. She was not a part of and did not belong to something or someone. Might that change when Charlie arrived in Cumbria? She hoped so.

Eliza broke into her thoughts, returning with a carrier bag in one hand and the dog lead in the other, Timothy trotting beside her.

'Veronica's gone to the loo.' Eliza smiled, holding up the bag. 'I've got a selection of sandwiches and fruit.'

'I'd better go before we set off,' Mauve said.

The image of the woman reflected from the wall mirrors in the toilets still caused her surprise. The different skin tone, unfamiliar make-up, and brunette hair colour had transformed her appearance. However, the area was busy, and while waiting, Mauve avoided eye contact, keeping her head down.

Outside again, she searched the faces, failing to see Eliza or Kit. Deciding they must have returned to the car, she set herself in the direction she'd come earlier, trying to remember if it had been the third row in the second block of cars or the second row in the third block, when finding herself back at the start, she realised she had gone in a circle.

The sun was high in the sky, and the afternoon felt suddenly far too hot. Her T-shirt was sticking to her back, her face and underarms were sweaty, and her head under the wig was itchy. She resisted the temptation to poke her fingers under it and scratch. Trying to work methodically, Mauve counted the point at which she had turned, then walked along each row; getting to the end, she turned into the next one studying the cars. She could feel a wave of annoyance building. Why hadn't Eliza waited for her? Yes, she had wanted time alone and might have seemed dismissive, but they were travelling together. Her niece was not shy to ask for money and, knowing the state her aunt was in, could have waited! Mauve knew her thoughts were irrational and ridiculous, but she felt alone and on the point of tears. 'Pull yourself together, woman.' She said the words out loud before turning to the next row. Walking past the parked cars, she glanced from left to right. Then, over the top of the vehicles, she saw Veronica. Overwhelmed with relief, she began to cut across to make her way over.

Veronica and Eliza stood close, talking as they drank from water bottles. Timothy was doubtless on the ground between them. She cursed Eliza again. Mauve would not have become so lost if only her niece had waited. She was one row from the car when she caught sight of the man. She immediately recognised him. Today he wore brown trousers and a black shirt, plus the dirty trainers. The wraparound sunglasses and peak of the cap hid the upper half of his face. Then, side on in the bright sunshine, she saw the shape of his jaw and his nose. An image returned: remembering Robin's profile at the moment she realised he'd been there on the night Paulette was murdered. She had no doubt now about the man's identity. He turned, his back to her, his attention fixed on the Veronica and Eliza. Stationary, Mauve rested her hand on the nearest car, then, surprised by the heat, she pulled it back. At that exact moment, she felt the familiar gasp as her breath caught, and the world stood still. Automatically, she began to count in her head, trying to regulate her breathing. The thought registered that the attacks were coming more often. She closed her eyes, continuing with the breathing exercise, determined not to go into a panic meltdown.

'Mauve!' Veronica called as she approached. 'Are you all right?'

Mauve, eyes wide open, searched about her. The man had gone.

'He was here,' she said.

'Who?' Veronica searched the area with her eyes.

'Robin. He was watching you and Eliza. He was standing just there.'

'Nobody there now,' Veronica said. 'Are you having an attack? Come back to the car.'

'*He was there.*' Following behind her back to the car, Mauve's voice rose, becoming shrill, and she sensed Veronica's dismissive disbelief.

'OK, Mauve?' Eliza smiled.

'She saw the man again. She thinks it's Robin,' Veronica said as she opened the car to bring out a small plastic bottle of water, passing it to Mauve.

'What man?' Eliza asked. 'The one from the street looking into your car?'

Veronica nodded. 'He's gone.'

Mauve looked from one to the other. They were humouring her and she felt tearful again. Biting the inside of her lip, she took a swig of water before returning to the back seat of the car. After putting Timothy into the back to join her, Veronica and Eliza took their places in the front before exchanging a look. Both turned to Mauve with expectation.

Mauve leaned back, not meeting the gaze of either. 'Let's go.'

The front-seat passengers snapped their seat belts together and Veronica pressed the starter. Nothing happened.

23

The expression on Mauve's face when the car wouldn't start was priceless, Eliza thought, catching a glimpse in the rear-view mirror. Immobilising the vehicle had been a doddle. Eliza hadn't wasted her time while going out with Sean, the mechanic, who had been the boyfriend before the boyfriend before Russ. He had been a good teacher. As well as being able to stop a car from starting, she'd also learnt how to start one, hotwiring an older model or using an amplifier and transmitter with keyless types.

The upset had not only been the car not starting. There was Mauve wittering on about the man with dirty trainers. She was wired, mentally spinning. How many men might that description fit? Hundreds, thousands maybe? Kit had said nothing about his fear of another panic attack, but it must have again been the greatest concern.

Leaving Mauve and Veronica in the car, Eliza had returned to the service station; the reception for her mobile phone, she'd told them, was better from there. She was organising a car and accommodation for the night, somewhere to fit in with the route they'd been following. Sitting inside the Happy Burger with a coffee, Eliza worked out they would expect it to take some time, and she wanted to give satisfaction. Before immobilising the car, she'd already done her research. Eliza liked to feel a step ahead of the game. She'd found the nearest taxi company that had a people carrier because of the amount of baggage that Kit travelled with, which he would not leave behind in the vehicle. Organising somewhere to stay with a dog in early July, when the schools were already on holiday, was a bit of a feat. A fourth person would join them later in the evening, a pleasant surprise for Mauve. Eliza had found a hotel with a cancellation in Blackpool, a place where they could stop overnight. She found herself chuckling; Blackpool would be Mauve's idea of hell: kiss-me-quick hats, bare-chested men walking around eating chips and donkey rides on the beach. Even worse, four people all sharing the bedroom. Eliza felt her chuckle turning into a cackle. It was a good hotel and expensive, which didn't bother her. Kit had given her his plastic to use for the advance payment. Cost was not an issue.

Eliza's thoughts drifted, as they often did, to her mother. Lena had never been an ordinary mother. Once, with maternal pride, she'd told Eliza she was *a Kelly*, as if conferring a badge of honour for the skills she'd acquired. With each boyfriend, she'd attained a new skill. It was not what she set out to do; she found it infectious when someone had a passion. With Sean it was cars, with Russ it had been martial arts and Jimmy had taught her all about computers and how to hack into them; he'd also passed on the art of lock-picking. The problem was the relationships never survived beyond six months. Once Eliza had developed each new skill, the dynamics of the relationships changed. Lena could only see her daughter as using the men, but Eliza didn't see it that way. While her mother knew every trick in the book to gain advantages and take from her victims, and the act of taking brought pleasure. For Eliza, everything she'd learnt was to help her survive. Why not take a dodgy detour if the straight route didn't work? She was all alone; her dad dead, and a mother who had never looked out for her. Aunt Mauve had more money than she could ever spend but wasn't going to pass on any of it to her any time soon. Years earlier, Lena told her that she saw getting money from her half-sister as being a bit like bear-baiting. The chains that held Mauve had been her gullibility. It had been when they were younger, when Lena reminded Mauve of her much-loved father. Despite having ripped her off numerous times, once she'd played the sister card, it had always worked. That was no longer the case. What had happened between the two eight years ago? Whatever the scam, Mauve had stumped up the money to buy the flat in Camden Town, with extra cash on top.

The only thing Eliza learnt for certain was that Mauve considered it a final payment, and the relationship had ended. The cash cow had finally dried. Eliza marvelled that anyone could be so naïve as to believe, when dealing with Lena, that there could be one final payment and she would be free. It was akin to paying a blackmailer. The latest game was afoot, something twisted, even by Lena's standard. It was where she'd come in. It had been a shock to find the flat that had been her home sold and empty of furnishings. What sort of mother moves without telling her only child? Then, if she'd believed the Friday-afternoon visit to the flat had been hell, the next day, after her split with Russ and the police interview, it had become ten times worse.

Eliza fiddled absentmindedly with the locket hanging from a gold chain around her neck, a fourteenth birthday present from her dad. When he'd died, she'd taken a lock of his hair to put inside. It warmed her to feel he was close.

After her police interview had finished, Eliza had been allowed to leave. It was clear DS Sue Teller, the police sergeant on Mauve's case, with as much charm as a rattlesnake, had developed a deep dislike for Mauve. Eliza suspected the DS had had a challenging upbringing, and someone born with the most oversized silver spoon imaginable would never be in favour with her. She would be determined to bring down her aunt.

Leaving the police station, Eliza's brain had been in a fug as she made her way back to Beatrice's flat. She intended to contact her cousin Kit, but he'd beaten her to it. Within ten minutes of her return, Kit had phoned to pour his heart out about his mother. He'd told her that after Mauve's police interview, she'd done a bunk. Kit was on his way to Norfolk in the hope of catching up. Both having screwed-up mothers somehow worked to bond their relationship, and both were artistic. While growing up, they'd each longed for a sibling and agreed their relationship felt more like that of a brother and sister than cousins. Then, as only children, neither had experience of siblings, so how would they know? The feeling was purely fantasy.

Eliza looked at her watch. She'd finished her coffee, and it was time to wander back. As she pushed her cup away, her eyeline moved from the door to a pair of brown trousers above a grubby pair of once-white trainers. They were making a beeline for her table. Her gaze continued upwards to take in the fifty-something man with the peak of his cap partly hiding his pale, lined face. Approaching her, he pulled away the wraparound sunglasses, revealing his strong facial features, a square jaw and arched nose, before stopping at the table to glance at her empty coffee cup.

'Hi, Eliza,' he said, his voice clipped. 'I'm getting a coffee. Would my favourite niece like a top-up?'

'Your only niece!' Eliza's tone was sardonic. Her uncle wouldn't reveal the end game… yet. He worked on a need-to-know basis, meaning she couldn't accidentally reveal something important to Kit or Mauve.

She pushed her cup towards him. 'Don't mind if I do.'

24

Mauve surveyed the hotel foyer. The colour scheme, furnishings and décor were dark plum and beige, and the walls hung with reproductions of landscapes by artists such as Constable and Turner. Children, using the lobby's centre as a racing track, sped back and forth while large, tattooed adults with body piercings did their utmost to ignore their offspring and huddled, gossiping, waiting to be dealt with at the front desk.

She had never imagined there would be a reason to visit Blackpool. Then, each day since the Friday of her visit to Lena's flat, her life had spiralled downwards, getting worse by the day. She was tired, thirsty and confused. Everything she did felt in slow motion, with a dreamlike quality, like wading through a mud slurry. Perhaps she wasn't in Blackpool, maybe she'd died, and this was what hell looked like.

Mauve had taken a seat on one side of the lobby. Next to her, she felt Timothy's body gently tremble against her legs. He had never been a lover of small children. He especially hated the high-pitched noises they made when they became overexcited. Through half-closed eyes, he was fixed and watchful. If a screeching child came too near, there was a deceptively small warning rumble.

Mauve was aware of what was going on and felt powerless to change anything. She could pick the dog onto her lap, if only she had the energy.

Veronica and Eliza, next to the pile of luggage brought with them by taxi from the service station, were in an endless discussion with a small, red-faced man at the reception desk. His gaze drifted back and forth between the two; head and shoulders taller than him. Eventually, they finished and returned with room cards to join Mauve.

Veronica, assessing the situation, swiftly picked Timothy up. 'Mauve,' she chided her, 'if Timothy bites one of those brats, we'll be in deep shit.'

Mauve said nothing but trailed sluggishly behind as the party moved to the lift.

'Is this it?' Mauve asked when they found themselves in the bedroom. Her lips drooped like a spoilt child. 'Have we all got to share?'

'It is the holiday season,' Veronica reminded her. 'We were lucky to get it. One double and two single beds.'

'A family room. It's got a bathroom,' Eliza said. 'It was all I could get at such short notice.'

Mauve flopped down onto the double bed. 'How long will it be before we can move on?'

'Tomorrow morning. We should have the car back by then,' Veronica said, looking at her watch and up at the ceiling. 'I need a very large drink.'

'Me too,' Eliza agreed. 'Do you want to bring the rest of your stuff up first?'

'Yes,' Veronica said, heading for the door. 'I don't want anything getting nicked.'

'Don't forget my brown overnight bag,' Mauve interrupted. 'It's got my pyjamas.'

After they'd gone, Mauve went to open the window. It felt cool in the room but also airless and stuffy. Noises and smells drifted through the open window, the salty smell of the sea and holidaymakers chattering, shouting and laughing. The sounds of others enjoying themselves added a feeling of desperation to her loneliness. She wondered what Zack might be doing, then wondered why the thought had come. That relationship had been dead for a very long time. Had she stayed with him for so long because she couldn't bear the prospect of being on her own? With Kit away at university there were only her drinking buddies, the fair-weather friends. It was a thought she'd had before and pushed away, but in that moment she accepted it to be true.

Mauve went to a wicker basket Veronica had left on the floor. It had all Timothy's requirements, but she had spotted at least one bottle of red wine. There were two. She took one out and then noticed Timothy was watching her expectantly.

After filling his water bowl from the bathroom tap, Mauve opened a tin to spoon dog food into a dish. She watched Timothy eating and then having a long drink of water.

'Cheers.' Mauve spoke to Timothy as she held up the

chunky water glass she'd found in the room, now filled with wine. Having removed her shoes, she piled the four pillows together on the double bed and nestled in the centre. Timothy wagged his tail before jumping up to join her. Replete, he happily wiped his whiskers across the duvet. Half an hour later, when Veronica and Eliza returned, Mauve, having already drunk over half of the bottle, was topping her glass up.

'Mauve,' Veronica dumped her luggage onto the floor, 'you could have waited for us.'

'I fed Timothy.' Mauve waved her glass at the dog.

'You know you can't hold your booze. You only need to sniff the cork to be pissed… Two glasses are your absolute limit.'

'I don't need you to tell me what I'm allowed to drink. How do you always manage to make me feel I'm in the wrong?' Mauve glowered at them, belligerent. 'You two – the sour-faced/best-buddies gang – you believe yourselves to be so clever and so bloody perfect.'

'Mauve… please,' Veronica said. 'Name-calling is not helping.'

She exchanged a knowing look with Eliza. Mauve read it as them agreeing that she was again in the wrong, misbehaving.

'What's happened with the car?' Mauve changed the subject.

'I'm going now to meet with the garage bloke who'll look at it for us,' Eliza said. 'The plan is to get it working. I'll bring it here to the hotel car park, and we can move on tomorrow morning.'

'And I'm going to have a shower,' Veronica said as she collected a toilet bag from her luggage. 'A nice long, hot shower.'

A few minutes later, Mauve was alone again. She could hear the shower running. Timothy had placed himself across the closed bathroom door to wait. Mauve slid from the bed to go back to the open window. She was annoyed. It seemed that both Veronica and Eliza saw her as something of a burden. They had no respect for her; she fumed. It felt like school. She was thirteen again, with a couple of nasty girls getting together to bully her. What was to stop her from going out? She'd show them; go out, have a walk and let go of her annoyance. Grabbing her bag, Mauve rooted in her case and found the only dress she'd brought on the trip, her current favourite. It was blue and tight, showing just the right amount of cleavage. She slipped her feet back into her shoes and headed to the door.

Outside, the crowds of holidaymakers moved like a rising tide. It seemed much busier than when she'd glanced out through the window, and she felt herself becoming part of it, pulled along to the seafront. There were the usual shops selling tat, including hats, candyfloss and sticks of rock. The mixed smells of the sea, sweaty bodies, suncreams and fish and chips combined to assail her senses. All around was noise. People were talking, cackling with laughter, shrieking even. Music thumped from a pub at the end of the pier, and overhead there was the raucous cry of gulls.

Mauve suddenly felt free, the happiest she'd been in

days. Through her drunken haze, she remembered that she was invisible and giggled, patting her wig as she turned into a bar. 'Adults only', a sign promised, 'Family area at the back'.

'Perfect,' Mauve muttered, heading to the bar.

Two drinks later, Mauve, perched on a high stool, and leaning into the shiny polished bar, felt she had left all her cares behind. The world seemed sweeter as she sat detached, watching other drinkers from a distance. What did it matter if the pair were ganging up on her? She wasn't thirteen anymore, they wouldn't get to her. She had lost track of the time. She would have a couple more drinks, then head back to the hotel.

A man in his mid-thirties, dressed all in denim, his shirt open at the top to reveal an expanse of chest hair, sidling past gave her a look that took her in from head to toe. 'All right, princess?' His smile was sly.

Mauve returned the smile. To her surprise, he didn't stop; instead, he walked to the exit. *Mr Denim*. After giving him a nickname, Mauve smirked as she watched his departure.

'Let me buy you one.' A second man balanced on the stool next to her took her attention. In his mid-fifties, with little hair, his once-white shirt had sweat stains spreading from under the arms and was a size too small. There were gaps between the buttons where the garment strained, showing the white of his large belly.

'No, no, thank you,' Mauve mumbled. 'I'm going in a minute.' Why did someone have to spoil her newly found equilibrium? Looking at him, she imagined a baboon perching on a tiny rock, although an ape would have had more hair. She let out a snort, then a giggle.

The baboon misunderstood, believing Mauve was flirting. He smiled, leaning in, showing yellow, nicotine-stained teeth.

'Well, you'll just have time for *just* one more. It's holiday time and Blackpool, *enjoy*.' He nodded to the young dark-haired barman. 'Tony.' He addressed the barman. 'Whatever the lady is drinking, and a large whisky for me.'

'No, really.' Mauve moved to get down from the stool to find the world spinning. '*I think I'm going to be sick,*' she said to herself as Tony whisked away the empty glass to replace it in a moment with another large glass of red wine.

'There you go.' The man lifted his glass. His eyes raked her body, moving upward from her legs to her breasts. Sitting on the barstool, the skirt of the blue dress had ridden high up her thighs, while the neckline seemed to have dropped down to reveal more bosom.

'Cheers!' he said, his eyes fixed on her breasts.

Mauve put her feet on the floor, standing up and, clutching the edge of the bar, pulled the skirt back down. The world continued to spin. She attempted a step and wobbled before stepping back to the bar.

'That's it.' The baboon bared his yellow teeth again while continuing to stare intently at her breasts. 'I'm Bobby.'

Mauve felt steadier, resting against the bar. Having given her his name, he waited, expecting to hear hers.

'Susan,' Mauve said, the first name that popped into her head. She didn't even like the name, and anyway, his name was probably also made up. There was a white band on his wedding finger where once there must have been a ring.

'Suzie-woozy, lovely name,' Bobby said. He smiled again, but stared at her oddly, his head at an angle.

Mauve felt suddenly bilious.

'Have we met before?' he said. 'Your face looks so familiar.'

The words wreaked a terrible reaction. The photograph in the newspapers instantly exploded into Mauve's mind while, at the exact moment, deep in her belly, she felt a volcanic response of something rising: the wine. She clamped a hand across her mouth in a futile attempt to keep it in. It all happened in seconds. The wine, like the red lava of a volcano, erupted, spewing forth. The baboon jerked back but not fast enough, as the jet of red hit his chest, instantly turning his shirt pink.

'I'm so sorry,' Mauve muttered.

'*You dirty cow!*' The baboon stood up to look down at his shirt as he struggled in shock to get the words out before repeating, '*You, dirty, dirty cow.*'

Mauve felt the rising before the eruption happened again. There was a part of her mind that felt detached, as if standing at a distance watching. Another part was pure panic meltdown. The second jet discharged itself. The baboon was quicker this time, jumping back. Mauve knew that Tony, the barman, had come around from the other side of the bar.

'You need to go outside. *Now!*' Tony snapped. 'This bar is open all evening. We lose customers when drunks throw up.'

Mauve gripped the edge of the bar, waiting for another rising.

'*Out, now!*' the barman ordered. He gripped Mauve by the arm.

A small group had gathered, with people drifting to the bar to take in the free entertainment. Mauve heard laughter and felt a pain in her arm as the hand holding it tightened.

'Come on.' The man pulled Mauve and she tottered forward.

'Let go of her!' The voice was cold and hard. Eliza.

'What you gonna do about it?' The barman squared up to her.

'Look what she's done to me!' the baboon joined in.

'Let her go or lose your teeth!' Eliza snarled. 'Then, as well as the wine, you'll have your blood and guts to clean up.'

There was something in Eliza's tone that made the barman let go and move away, but he wasn't finished.

Mauve looked at her niece, who'd changed her attire and was dressed entirely in black, wearing strappy biker's boots, tight jeans and a short leather jacket. Her eyes were cold and her stance menacing, feet apart and fists clenched. It was an Eliza she didn't know, someone scary. Lena's daughter, a Kelly.

'This is my bar. I'm within my rights to throw you both out.' Tony lifted his arm as if to grab Eliza. What happened next was so quick that it took not only Tony by surprise but also Mauve. As the hand approached her, Eliza grabbed the arm, twisting her body to bring Tony's body up and over her shoulder. He ended up on his back on the floor with a loud thud, his face filled with shock.

'Want another pop?' Eliza bent towards him, flicking her fingers to beckon him to her.

'Just sod off.' Tony got up but kept his distance. 'Get out of my bar.'

'That's what I intend,' Eliza said. She put her arm around her aunt and steered her towards the door.

'What about me?' The baboon held his arms up.

'*Get over it.*' Eliza threw the words at him as she took Mauve out into the street.

'What the hell?' Kit said. He was changed after the shower and dressed in chinos and a T-shirt. A white sunhat hid his hair, while sunglasses concealed his eyes and most of his face.

'Where did Veronica go?' Mauve slurred.

'*Mother!*' Kit looked from her to his cousin. 'Words fail me…'

With Eliza on one side, and him on the other, together they shuffled back to the hotel.

25

Despite the bath water being barely warm, Mauve felt refreshed. After three hours of sleep and drinking a litre of water, followed by the bath, the stench of wine had finally receded. Despite taking aspirin, her head still thumped and she silently admonished herself. Although she would never admit Kit was right, she was a lightweight when it came to alcohol.

On the way back to the hotel, the group had stopped while Mauve was sick for a third and fourth time. Kit and Eliza teased that she'd vomited more than her body weighed in wine, there surely could be nothing left.

She'd tried but couldn't remember returning to the hotel, entering the bedroom or getting into bed. It was a blur. When she'd woken, Eliza said, once in bed, she'd instantly fallen into a deep sleep.

Kit was less kind. 'After the drunken binge, you passed out!'

'You didn't bring my bag from the car.' Mauve, dressed in a sweatshirt and jeans, rubbed her damp hair with a towel as she emerged from the bathroom.

'With your pyjamas? You're surely not thinking of going to bed yet?' Kit said. 'The problem with getting pissed in the afternoon is that it screws up the rest of the day. It is only just gone 6.00p.m.'

'I know.' Mauve bounced on the double bed. Kit and Eliza had put their bags onto the single beds. It seemed by unspoken agreement she had bagged the double. 'Where's Eliza?'

'She needed some things from the shops. She'll be back soon.' Kit nodded to the car keys on the table next to Eliza's bed. 'She had the car put in the hotel car park. It's in the basement.'

'What was wrong with the car?' Mauve asked. 'Why wouldn't it start?'

'Ask Eliza when she gets back.' Kit yawned. 'She did explain what the mechanic had told her, but I'm not on that wavelength. I need help understanding car talk or terminology.'

'And Eliza does?'

'Probably,' Kit said. 'She had a boyfriend once who was a mechanic, the car language rubbed off on her. She knows more than me, but anyone and everyone knows more than me. Car engines are boring.'

Mauve felt a physical sensation of goosebumps across her back and up her arms and legs. Eliza knew about car engines, what made them go and, more importantly, stop. She watched her son going around the room and finding Timothy's lead. He was innocent, he'd not worked out the connection. Then, was she being mean? Eliza had saved her from that awful barman and the baboon. Mauve sank back into the pillows, thinking.

'I'm walking with Timothy to the beach that allows dogs. He loves running into the sea,' Kit said. 'Summer holidays mean dogs aren't allowed on the main beach here.'

'He'll think he's back in Norfolk.' Mauve smiled fondly at the dog.

'While we're alone, Mother, before I go,' Kit squared up to stand directly before her, 'tell me what you meant about Robin's neighbour. The man who fell down the stairs. How do you know there was a connection with Robin? What did you mean?'

'Nothing, nothing at all,' Mauve said. Her voice rose, and the rebuttal sounded hollow.

'I don't believe you,' Kit said.

'Believe what you want.' Mauve opened her arms towards him. '*Darling*, I was talking gibberish, then getting drunk…' She threw her head back dramatically. 'I'm all over the place. It's after what happened, going into Lena's flat, the police …. everything.'

'Mmm.' Kit stared at his mother. Mauve dropped her eyes first.

'OK. I know the last few days have been awful for you,' Kit said, pulling his hat over his hair and putting on sunglasses. He clipped the lead onto Timothy's collar. 'I may be some time. Tell Eliza I've gone to walk Timothy.'

Mauve nodded.

'And, Mother, be nice to her.' Kit paused at the door, his tone admonishing. 'Remember, she saved your bacon today.'

'I will.' She gave her sweetest smile.

Mauve felt suddenly very alone. Had Kit believed her? Probably not. She got up to wander about the room before returning to her position on the bed.

It was odd that she now craved company after wanting so desperately to have time to herself. Shuddering while remembering the confrontation in the bar, she slid down, spreading out flat on her back, and for a while played snow angels, bringing her arms up and down and opening and closing her legs. After having made a complete tit of herself, she felt lonely again.

'Lonely, confused and frightened.' Mauve spoke out loud.

It might be an excellent opportunity to take another look at the two memory sticks. As the thought drifted through her mind, her body shuddered, remembering the stop at Robin's house and the dead neighbour. She sat upright again. The bag, with her pyjamas; collecting it would give her something to do. She went to find the wig and, back in the bathroom, looking at her reflection in the mirror, she pulled it over the damp hair. Without make-up, she'd reverted to looking like a fifteen-year-old. Not Mauve Gilcrest, the lovely blonde portrayed in the newspapers.

She picked up the car key and room card and turned over a white card. It was the hotel card needed to enter and exit the car park. She left it and headed out to take the lift to the basement.

It was quiet when Mauve came out of the lift and entered the semi-darkness of the car park. She glanced around, taking in the dark hidden corners and spaces, places a watcher might unexpectedly jump from. With a feeling of trepidation, she began working methodically along each line, searching for the car. She imagined holidaymakers, having moved their luggage from the vehicles, were now out on the town looking for places to eat. The car was further down, at the end of a row on the same side as the lifts. They'd missed the bag when they emptied the car because she'd put it on the floor beneath where Timothy had been sitting. Kit and Veronica's luggage had taken up all the spare space in the car. Opening the doors, she got into the back, ran her hand along the floor to find the bag, and pulled it onto the seat with her.

As Mauve turned to the door, she froze. Strolling towards the exit was the man she'd believed to be Robin. The fourth time she'd seen him, she now would recognise him, even with a change of clothes. There had been too many encounters for the sightings to be a coincidence. In the semi-darkness of the car park, there was something stealthy about his movement. She imagined his footsteps to be silent and him sneaking up without anyone knowing his presence. Then, near the exit, she saw a woman with her head forward, a phone clamped to her ear. Mauve recognised the leather jacket, black jeans and biker's boots. With her back to the man and distracted by her phone, Eliza seemed unaware of him as he moved soundlessly and swiftly nearer.

Mauve threw herself sideways, pushing open the car door and coming around the car, ready to shout a warning. Too late. The man had reached Eliza and had put his hand to rest on her shoulder. Remembering her niece's speedy reaction to Tony's aggression in the bar, Mauve waited for her to twist around and throw the man down.

Eliza turned as the hand reached her shoulder; her face creased into a smile, and she opened her arms to accept a hug.

Mauve moved with alacrity. The pair walked away, leaving the car park. Once out of sight, she sprinted back to the lift and upstairs. After letting herself into the bedroom, she pulled open her bags and dumped them on the bed before grabbing clothes and toiletries from the bedroom and bathroom to stuff into the bags. Picking up the car park exit card, she tucked the card into her back pocket, and in doing so, her fingers encountered the shape of the two memory sticks. Her stomach lurched.

Back in the car park she checked her watch; she'd been gone from the car for twelve minutes. After pressing the ignition, she selected the postcode already entered in the satnav for Cumbria. The journey was less than an hour and a half. If the car had started, as it should have done at the service station, she would now be in Cumbria.

'Bloody Eliza!' Mauve cursed.

Going out of the car park into the light, Mauve swung the wheel to take a tight bend before joining the traffic. A woman dressed in black watched the speeding motor leaving. Eliza's face went from peaceful to shocked as she took in the driver.

Glancing in the rear-view mirror, Mauve remembered Kit doing starbursts in the road in London when she'd bolted for Norfolk. Although he was not there today, Mauve had a sense of déjà vu.

After passing Blackpool tower, Mauve followed the main exit routes from the town, gunning the engine to build up speed once she was out of the built-up area.

26

Hearing the car approaching from behind, Eliza had stepped swiftly back. It was Mauve behind the wheel. Her cold gaze focused on the road ahead.

What had happened to skitter her, sending her away in a panic?

Heading back at a run to the lift inside the car park, Eliza tried to work through what had happened. She'd left the car park card and key in the bedroom. Kit was going to the beach to walk with Timothy. Could Mauve have witnessed her meeting a short time ago in the car park? Then why would she be here? After the drinking incident, she seemed tired, content to sleep it off. Had something else happened?

Kit was not in the bedroom, so she phoned him and left a message. He responded within a minute.

'I couldn't get my phone out in time. What's happened? You said Mum's done another runner. Why?' Kit's voice was high with concern.

Eliza told him what she'd witnessed. 'I'm in the

bedroom. The car park exit card, the key and all Mauve's bags have gone.'

'*Shit, shit, shit!*' Kit shouted. 'She'll still be loads over the drink-drive limit.'

'I'm worried in case she has an accident,' Eliza said. 'The police would throw the book at her. Leaving London after she'd agreed to stay, then caught drink driving.'

'What could have made her run again?' Kit asked, puzzled.

'I don't know.' Eliza felt uncomfortable with the lie. 'Of course, she's been trying to escape, dump us, and move on alone since we were at the holiday cottage. She doesn't want you with her and sure as hell doesn't want me…'

'I'm on my way back. I'll see you in ten minutes,' Kit said, and then he was gone.

Eliza sat on the bed, nursing the mobile phone for a moment before making a second call. 'She did a runner.'

There was a pause before the response. 'We know where she's running to. Change of plan. You'll need to get another car with Kit. Make your way to Flookburgh as soon as you can. I'll see you there. I'll make a couple of calls to have someone with me. I don't want it all to go pear-shaped. Kit's still in the dark?'

'Yes,' Eliza said.

'Keep it that way. He'll find out what's going down soon enough. Has she taken her laptop?'

'Everything's gone. She'll have the laptop in the car. Surely she can use any laptop, though?'

'For transferring the amount in question, Mauve will want to use her own computer. The codes are in her head but the offshore bank will require something else; eye, or fingerprint recognition. What about Charlie?'

'Kit phoned him to let him know we were here. I imagine Kit phoned him again immediately after I told him Mauve had done another runner, taking the car.'

'So he'll go be going straight to Cumbria too. It's going to be quite a party.' The man paused again. 'I'll see you there.'

'I'm feeling bad, and I'm frightened things are going to get messy at Paulette's house.' Eliza found her voice breaking with emotion. 'I couldn't bear it if Kit got hurt, Uncle—'

The line was dead. He'd gone.

27

Mauve thought about the alcohol level in her blood. She didn't feel drunk, just woozy, but the level must have been off the scale. Doubtless, if stopped and breathalysed, it would be journey's end, game over. They would arrest her and lock her up. Her driving, reflecting her considerations, was cautious. Rather than carving between the ongoing flow, she stuck to the inside lane and kept well below the speed limit.

Audible from the bottom of her bag, the ringing of the new phone took her mind back to her journey from London to Norfolk. It had been Kit then and doubtless would be him again now; apart from him, only Eliza and Charlie had the new number. She wondered what Charlie would make of all this. She hoped he would be on her side. After seeing Eliza fraternising with the enemy, there had been no other course of action. Perhaps Eliza was being paid by Robin, and this could only mean she was working with her uncle and had been in cahoots with him from the start. But what if Charlie was also a traitor?

With a headache and dry throat, Mauve craved fluids; although the water in the small plastic bottles left in the car was warm, she was desperately thirsty, so, not wanting to stop before reaching Cumbria, by squeezing the bottles between her thighs she managed to remove the screw caps and drink three.

While driving, she anticipated how much the landscape would change once she reached Cumbria. On London visits, Paulette's love of the area had been transparent, as she'd often talked about the Lake District's wonders: the lakes, waterfalls and mountains.

Disappointingly, crossing the boundary into the county, the expected uplift with the wonderous vista didn't happen. Her mind was too sour and clogged with ugliness to care, and what did such splendour matter if she was going to end up in prison for the rest of her life? She considered the competition Kit had entered, wondering if, while navigating his way through a new life with her no longer a part of it, he might spare a thought for her, rotting in some prison cell. However, in fairness to Kit, he hadn't even mentioned the competition.

As Mauve entered Flookburgh, she tried to fix her mind back to the fateful day she'd been here with Lena, but her thoughts, like a ball of string, had unravelled and become tangled. From the arrival here with Lena to the images on the memory sticks, it all felt weird and unreal.

Yet everything seemed unchanged, like a familiar face. The word 'fish' kept coming to her; she recalled it from a childhood conversation with her aunt. Some said the name Flookburgh came from flook, a flatfish found in the area. Then, Paulette had said it was not certain, it may have been the other way around, with the fish taking its name from the town. Mauve smiled briefly at the memory. What she'd liked most as a child about Paulette was that she never patronised or talked down to her, and she enjoyed nothing more than setting puzzles or riddles for Mauve. It felt like they were two adults talking; equals having a discussion. Dear Aunt Paulette. Her dry eyes hurt with unshed tears. Then, clammy and tired, her face instantly switched to a scowl. Irritated by the automated voice from the satnav giving directions, Mauve switched it off. She knew the last part of the route so well she might have driven it blindfolded.

Paulette Franklin's funeral had been a cremation. After which her ashes were transported and scattered in her Cumbrian rose garden. The instruction had been in her will. Undoubtedly, the duty had been undertaken by some minion employed by her lawyers. Mauve felt a stab of pain in her chest: guilt. It should have been her, someone who'd loved Paulette, scattering her ashes, but remorse had made it impossible. The funeral had been a sombre affair. It had taken hours of pacing her bedroom to screw up the courage to attend. She had murdered Paulette, and then she was going to attend her funeral and shed crocodile tears. It felt strange, but her instinct and every part of her being knew she must be there. At the final hour, she'd wavered, nearly changing her mind. Given the press were aware of the bad blood between Paulette and her mother, Charlie told her she'd be mad to go, although once he realised how important it was to Mauve, he'd insisted on accompanying her.

They'd sat on the back row of the cold London church near Paulette's main home in St John's Wood. There was just a small number in attendance. Her aunt had had many acquaintances but a dearth of true friends, and apart from a few recognisable faces, Mauve didn't know any of the other attendees. Charlie pointed out three women and a man, sitting separately, all wearing dark clothing as befitted a funeral, all police officers. Then, as anticipated, there were also reporters from the press. In the closing moments of the service, before anyone moved, Charlie took her arm and swiftly guided her from the church to the car, forgoing the possibility of talking to anyone on the way out.

On the north side of Flookburgh, Mauve slowed to turn into a quiet street; at the lane end, the countryside opened up. On either side of the lane were softly undulating hills, a copse of trees, and a meadow with sheep grazing. Ten minutes later, she spotted the tall trees and high stone wall that signified the arrival at what was known locally as the Franklin Estate. The height of the wall made it impenetrable. Above, unmoving on a windless day, the green tops of tall pines. The road curved gently with the wall on her left, as if taking her in a circle. It felt an eternity before she came to the green metal gate, only a foot shorter than the wall. It was attached to square solid pillars on either side. The art nouveau design of the gate had linear struts from the bottom to halfway; the metal then twisted and interweaved to the top. It was rust-free, freshly painted in the dark green Paulette had always favoured.

Putting her hand into the side pocket of her bag, Mauve

realised that since stopping she'd been holding her breath. Her fingers found the bunch of keys hastily collected from her Norwich home. Further along the curve of the wall, on the opposite side of the estate, where there was no wall, the trees parted with a mud track wide enough to allow entry to a tractor; no need for keys there.

Leaving the engine to idle, she unlocked the gate with trembling hands while glancing furtively around. Who was she afraid of more, the police or Robin? It was undoubtedly Robin. The police would take her liberty, not her life. Lena was dead, and Mauve had no doubt who had been responsible. It was Robin who had killed his sister and the neighbour in Lincoln.

Driving in, Mauve, her eyes again feeling the sting of unshed tears, tried to focus on her arrival here with Lena eight years earlier. The gates had not been locked but left open as usual when the mistress of the house was in residence.

The pathway, as straight as the line of an arrow, was almost one mile in length, leading directly to the house. On either side of the drive, the trees formed an umbrella-like canopy, and occasional gaps gave glimpses of the pale-blue sky amongst the varying shades of green and twinkling diamond sparkles of sunshine.

The pathway had been well maintained and pruned neatly back. Nearing the end of the tunnel of trees, Mauve saw the lawn stretching out in front of the house and the back of her neck prickled, as, slowing the car to a crawl, she shuddered as she began to regulate her breathing, using the counting exercise.

The lawn in front was a sea of green, a barrier between her and the house. In the video, in the semi-darkness of the moonlit garden, she appeared to have been dancing or pulled around by Lena. The blackness and the knife built up the horror, but now, at 8.00p.m on a summer's evening, it was light, and the perfectly manicured striped lawn stretched before her without menace.

To one side was what had once been a stable block, and to the other, the glass of a conservatory, built against the house, sparkled in the sunshine. Between the two, in the centre, was a handsome stone-built seventeenth-century country house with two main floors and, above the second floor, small attic windows from the sloping roof for rooms once used by servants. The house had leaded casement windows and inside high ceilings and open fireplaces.

She moved the car forward to stop and cut the engine outside the oak doors of the main entrance. On that fateful night eight years ago, they had entered using the back door. A new memory. Mauve blinked and wrapped her arms around herself, squeezing her shoulders with her fingers. What else might she remember?

The house had been a nursing home during the First World War; apart from that, it had always been owned privately by a family, with Paulette the last in a long line of owners. Thus, the property had avoided going the way of many extensive residences in becoming a hotel or nursing home. In fact, not quite the last. To her surprise, it had been bequeathed in Paulette's will. '*To Mauve, the daughter I always wished I'd had.*' The second reason she'd had to go to the funeral, the first being guilt. When Charlie later asked what she would do with the house, she'd told him she'd found a buyer. It stopped him from asking the question again.

The maintenance of the Franklins' house had cost her much over the years, plus employing a part-time gardener. It was an expensive guilt trip, keeping it as she imagined Paulette would have wanted. Although Mauve had never returned after Paulette's death, she'd received photographs of the house and garden every six months, sent by a management agency. The standard of upkeep meant someone could move in immediately if required.

Getting out of the car, Mauve took the last bottle of the warm water, unscrewed the top, and drank it before throwing the empty bottle to join the others in the passenger footwell.

Passing the broad, squat stone steps leading to the front door, she went to the corner of the house to walk around to the back.

The rose garden was everything she'd hoped for. The natural beige-grey stone wall enclosed and separated it from the rest of the estate. Inside, a private scented heaven. Around the interior boundary walls were stone benches, and at the centre of the garden an ornate fountain with carved sturdy cherubs dancing, trumpets raised to their lips. It had a regular check to keep it in good order but had not been regularly used since Paulette's death.

Mauve closed her eyes, feeling the sun on her face as she breathed in the perfumed smell of the roses to recall Paulette walking between the different varieties carrying a sharp pair of cutting shears for deadheading. A moment later, the leaves and prickly branches brushed against her jeans as she made her way forward to the centre of the quarter of an acre plot. In peaceful dreams, this was the place she'd most often returned to. Here, she and Paulette had been at ease as one single mind. Celia, her mother, found gardening a dull occupation, a waste of time. Mauve stopped to turn a full circle, absentmindedly pulling the wig from her head to discard it and speak aloud the names of each of the rose plants, copied into her garden in Norfolk.

As she reached the centre, she rested her hand on one of the ornate carved cherubs of the fountain. A tightening came again to her throat, and like a river bursting its banks, the burden Mauve had carried for so long could no longer be contained. She turned her face to the sky, opened her mouth, and bawled.

28

The key to the kitchen door turned easily, and in a moment Mauve was inside. The house was completely silent and cool, but despite the low temperature, she felt clammy. A trickle of perspiration ran down the side of her face as she felt the familiar tightening of her chest. Standing perfectly still for a moment, she counted again to regulate her breathing. Then, going to a shoulder-high corner cupboard, she opened it to find and then flick the switch to turn on the electricity for the house. Under the sink, she turned the tap for the water supply.

The kitchen, with its cream walls and rust-coloured units, was rectangular. There was a cream Aga cooker and a deep butler sink. Along the surface of one of the units was a row of eight bottle-green plastic-lidded boxes. Paulette had brought them home from one of her American trips, and in Mauve's childhood they had held delights and goodies, dried fruit, nuts and Turkish delight. A solid pine table stood in the centre of the kitchen, eight mismatched chairs tucked under it. Mauve couldn't see them, but knew on each hard seat would be a brightly coloured embroidered cushion. It was where she'd sat as a child with Auntie Paulette looking on as she dipped her buttered Marmite soldiers and ate her boiled eggs. Pausing by the table, her mind locked into her movement through the kitchen eight years earlier. Lena had been in front, leading, turning her head to throw words over her shoulder.

'We should have gone through the main door. Paulette won't know we've arrived and might not like us coming this way.' Mauve had heard the words in her head, but they would not come out aloud. Her mouth had ceased to function. She'd stopped in the doorway to look along the hall.

Remembering, Mauve repeated the action, resting her hand on the door frame. Where had the bottle gone? Eight years ago, it had been in her hand when she'd left the car, but not inside the house. Stroking the white paint of the door frame, she suddenly recalled the trembling of her hands all those years ago.

'Come on, slow coach.' Lena had spoken as she went behind her to push, propelling Mauve forward.

Now, Mauve stepped forward into the hall, onto the walnut parquet flooring, imagining Lena was behind her again, pushing.

The lobby ran through the house, passing the grand staircase to the main entrance. Framed photographs hung on either side of the green-painted walls, documenting Paulette's busy life. Husbands, weddings, cruises, fashion show openings, parties and some with royalty and famous faces. The ones that included Celia and Henry Gilcrest had been removed after the relationship soured when Celia discovered her husband's adultery. Halfway along, there had been a group of four, with Paulette and Mauve, aged about five, in the rose garden. Mauve did not turn that way; instead, imagining Lena still behind her, she went forward into the sitting room.

'Hello, Mauve. What a delightful surprise!' Paulette had suddenly been standing in front of her. Tall, unbending and elegant. Mauve opened her mouth to speak, but nothing had come out. Then, Paulette came forward to envelop her in her arms. The musky fragrance of her perfume enfolding them. It was here the memory abruptly ended, but the look of surprise on Paulette's face stayed in her mind. Lena had lied. Paulette had not been anticipating her visit.

The air in the room was still, scented by the lingering artificial smells of furniture polish and cleaning agents. Apart from its quarterly year clean, the room was not used, and the windows were never opened to allow air inside to circulate. There were two four-seater red fabric Chesterfield sofas opposite each other, separated in the centre by a low coffee table with a marble top. Around the room were side tables with period chairs with individually handcrafted tapestry seat covers. Stopping at one of the chairs while she gripped the small side table, Mauve allowed her knees to give way and sink. She felt sweaty and limp, as if she might, at any moment, be liquefied and spill from the seat to the floor.

Paulette's favourite Persian rugs were no longer on the mahogany floor. On Mauve's instruction, they had been removed and burnt. It was in this room that Paulette had died; the blood had been copious. An expert cleaner had been engaged to remove all traces of the event. But Mauve had the memory still fixed and alive, more so since viewing the USB memory sticks she'd found in Robin's house, and the thoughts recalling again the flat in Camden Town and Lena's blood.

'I'm here.' Mauve spoke aloud, surprised by the strength of her voice. 'You've got what you wanted, Robin. I'm here, come and find me.'

There was silence; nothing moved.

Getting up, Mauve walked to the stand in front of the fireplace to kneel on the spot in the position displayed on the USB stick. She stared forward at the bare floorboards to the place where Paulette's bloody corpse had lain. The perspiration down her back and under her armpits made the cotton T-shirt cling to her body like a second skin, and a small voice in her head willed her to get up and run. She didn't – couldn't – move. Her knees hurt on the hard wooden floor while her body trembled. With her eyes tightly closed, she tried to remember being here before, but there was nothing. Her mind was blank.

'*What the hell… Mauve!*'

Mauve gasped, swinging on her haunches to turn and look in the direction of the voice.

'Charlie.'

He made long strides to cross the room swiftly. Reaching down, he grasped Mauve's hands to pull her up. Once upright, she leaned against him, and he held her in his arms until the trembling in her body had stopped.

'Let's sit down,' he said.

'Not in here.' Mauve nodded to the door. 'In the kitchen.'

They went into the kitchen without further discussion to sit at the table.

'Well,' Charlie said. 'You told me you'd sold this place. You lied.'

'It made it easier,' Mauve said. 'To stop you asking questions.'

He looked at her, not saying anything further, as if he were waiting, willing her to begin. To open-up and tell him all that she'd kept hidden, locked away. The silence lasted only a few minutes, but it felt longer. Then, once she started talking, she couldn't stop. Like the contents of an upended shaken ketchup bottle with nothing coming forth until, suddenly, the whole of the contents spewed out in an uncontrolled abundance. She couldn't hold anything back, and sitting side by side at the pine table, Mauve spoke without pausing. Everything she could remember from eight years earlier, bringing him to the present day.

Charlie didn't interrupt. It helped that he was sitting next to her; if he had been directly opposite, looking at her face, Mauve doubted she'd have been able even to begin. When she finished, they again became silent. Eventually, Mauve glanced sideways. Charlie's shoulders drooped, his face sullen and ashen.

'Mauve.' He put his arm around her shoulder. 'Why the hell didn't you tell me all this? You've been carrying it around for years, you alone.'

'I couldn't tell you, not then. I was ashamed,' Mauve said, her shoulders rising upwards defensively.

Charlie tightened his grip. 'I realised there had to be some significance in you going to Norfolk, Lincoln and then here. It was when the police made the connection between you and Paulette; your DNA was on the doll.'

Mauve nodded.

'One of my police contacts told me, off the record.'

'It wouldn't be DS Teller.' Mauve sniffed with derision.

'No way. She's a tough nut. She wouldn't give anything away.'

It felt that a weight had been lifted from her. She began to cry again. Not loudly, as she had in the rose garden, but with her head against Charlie's chest, a low sobbing. When she stopped, she could feel the slow, gentle strokes of Charlie's fingers on her hair.

'Do you have the memory sticks?' Charlie asked while she wiped her eyes with the backs of her hands. 'I'd like to see them for myself. My laptop's in the car.'

Mauve stood and brought the two sticks from her back pocket.

'Let's keep together.' Charlie was on his feet instantly. 'If you believe Robin intended to get you here, we must be on guard. He's killed twice that we know about. He's nothing to lose in killing again.'

They walked outside to his car, returning immediately to the kitchen with the laptop.

Charlie opened the cupboard doors to find glasses. 'Is the water on?'

Mauve nodded.

After filling two glasses with water and giving one to Mauve, he turned his laptop on and inserted the first of the two memory sticks Mauve had discovered at Robin's house. He watched it twice, making few comments, only observing, as Mauve had done, that the sequence of events was out of order. Charlie then watched the second. When that had finished he turned off the computer.

'They are out of sequence, but someone has gone to a lot of trouble to put these together,' he said. 'And I get your point about Lena, in the darkness appearing frightened of you. That could have been recorded anywhere.'

Mauve nodded again.

'You say this is Robin, but how do you think he intends to get money from you?' Charlie waved his hand around to include the whole room. 'It makes no sense.'

'I guess he would make me transfer it to his account,' Mauve said.

'A few thousand, if that,' Charlie said. 'Banks are very alert to unusual large transfers these days. It wouldn't be the figure Robin would be after. Anyway, the police have frozen your bank accounts; you're a person of interest on the run.'

'They won't know about or have access to the overseas account. It's in the Cayman Islands,' Mauve said. 'I have several ways to get in, to prove it's me, including an eye scan. I have access to millions through that account.'

'Money you've been hiding?' Charlie said, unsmiling. 'Something illegal, or you wouldn't need to hide it.'

'It's not illegal.' Mauve shrugged. 'It's my money. I can put it where I want.'

'It sounds dubious. And Lena knew you had that sort of money and easy access to it.' Charlie threw up his hands in horror. 'Are you mad? You know what Lena's like. You're her golden goose.'

'It only happened once. I was a bit...' Mauve trailed off.

The tension rose suddenly to hang between them like an impenetrable mist.

'*Pissed*. You were drunk and showing off. That was something else she'd never have.' Charlie glared at her. 'Your father full-time, a mother who cared about you, and Paulette, who'd always loved you.'

Mauve's body drooped as she put her head down and covered her face with her hands.

'I'm sorry, I shouldn't have said that,' Charlie's said gently.

'I agree with you.' Tears ran down her face. 'And I'm surprised it's taken so long. Lena must have told Robin about the account, and he killed her, implicating me.'

'The blood at the flat was Lena's, so it does seem probable Robin is the murderer. The fact that the two USB sticks were left on separate days indicates he must have been around. He might have been next door at his neighbour's house, watching.'

'He couldn't have been there waiting!' Mauve said. 'No... I'm sure it was him in the street.'

'The man you kept seeing with the dirty trainers?'

'I didn't get close enough to see him properly, but he had the Kelly profile, the jaw and nose.'

'He would have needed to know you were on your way. He wouldn't just be hanging around,' Charlie mused.

'Eliza?' Mauve said.

'Possibly, but I don't think Kit would trust her if she was a wrong'un. Kit has such good sense.' Charlie thought for a moment. 'But it does makes sense if Eliza is working with this bloke who's been following you.'

'It was him, and I saw them together. I saw Eliza put her arms out to hug him!'

'We need to speak to her.' Charlie ran his fingers through his hair. 'You've come all this way, was it worth it? What have you remembered? That you weren't carrying a bottle of booze when you came inside the house, and Paulette came to you, but you couldn't speak?'

'It's important.'

'Yes,' Charlie said. 'But I think you know what happened. You touched on it earlier when you talked about being dragged around by Lena in the garden: the video. You were drugged, Mauve. They set you up. I don't think for one moment that you killed Paulette.'

Mauve nodded. 'Yes, I now think that's what happened.'

'It's getting late. What do you want to do tonight? I suggest phoning the police as the best option.'

Mauve shook her head in despair. 'I don't know.'

'Everything you've told me about Robin suggests that he is dangerous. It would be best if you didn't stay here. Shall we find a hotel or pub that does B & B for the night? Think about going to the police tomorrow?'

'I need to stay just a little longer,' Mauve said. 'I want to go into all the rooms.'

'You're still hoping that going around this place might jog your memory?'

'The last chance to remember before I speak to the police.'

'Yes. I'll hang on to these.' Charlie slipped the memory sticks into his jacket pocket. 'For the police. Ten minutes Mauve, then we go.'

Thank God, Mauve thought, *that I am no longer alone.*

29

Charlie got up to trail behind her as she wandered from room to room.

'Have you checked your phone? Any calls from Kit?' he asked.

'No.' Mauve glanced over her shoulder. 'I couldn't face being given another lecture from my son.'

'Don't you think you might deserve it? That's twice now you've done a runner. He loves you more than anyone else on the planet... Well, maybe apart from Timothy. He's worried about you.'

'I know.' Mauve remembered her unkind words about Kit's beloved dog. 'I'll phone him once we've finished looking around here.'

'This is a terrible idea.' Charlie spoke to the back of Mauve's head as she entered the storage room.

Little had changed. Paulette had always used it as a dumping ground. It was here, on that fateful night, where Mauve had been carrying the wooden doll.

'This room was in the recording,' she said.

'I recognise it,' Charlie said. 'But we should leave now, immediately. What are you not getting, Mauve? It's dangerous to stay here.'

Mauve nodded, distracted as her eyes searched the room. 'I remember the smell in this room.'

'Old things rotting: newspapers, fabric.' Charlie rolled his eyes. 'It's good you've remembered, but—'

'Another ten minutes,' Mauve said, looking at her watch. 'I promise to go around quickly; please just give me that.' She realised how much his opinion and presence meant. 'Once the police arrive, I won't have the opportunity to work over my memories of that night. It's the first time I've been here for eight years.'

'Eight years of hell,' Charlie said.

Mauve nodded in agreement. 'But my memories of this place are mixed. I loved being here as a kid with Paulette. She always made me feel grown up and special. That feeling disappeared when she died in this house.'

'Understandably,' Charlie said. 'I'd prefer we left now, but if that is the only way...' He checked his watch. 'Ten minutes. I'll keep you to that.'

'OK,' Mauve said.

Much like the photographs in the hall, this room gave glimpses of Paulette's past life. A pile of suitcases reflected styles from different decades. Two pairs of skis stood propped in a corner. Paulette's second husband, Walter, had been Swiss, an expert at navigating the slopes of St Moritz. On a table, what seemed to be a complete eighteenth-century Limoges porcelain dinner service, piles of varying heights of plates, dishes and platters. A reminder of the time she'd spent at her home in France. As in the kitchen, there were a lot of odd chairs, although not in such good condition.

Charlie sneezed loudly. 'A hell of a lot of dust in here,' he commented, rubbing his nose with the back of his hand.

'Look at this.' Mauve held up a misshapen pottery cup. 'I made it for Paulette when I was about eight!'

'Very artistic, and she kept it,' Charlie said. 'Let's move on.'

'OK.' Mauve returned to the door.

In the library, the sun shone through the window like a bright arrow, splitting the long room at its centre. It had two solid armchairs and a coffee table next to the window; the bookcases from floor to ceiling were mahogany, row after row of different-coloured book spines. The deep-piled carpet and the curtains matched in a plum colour. It was in this room that the silence felt the deepest.

'Good library.' Charlie sounded impressed.

'Paulette loved reading, but it smells musty.' Mauve sniffed.

'It's the same throughout, with the rooms not being in use.' Charlie stroked the spine of a book on the shelf as he talked. 'Modern China.'

'There's something to interest most people.' Mauve glanced about before leaving. 'We didn't come in here at all eight years ago.'

'You can remember that? You are sure?'

'Yes, I don't know why, but I feel positive I didn't come here.' Mauve smiled. 'That's good, isn't it?'

As they entered what Paulette had always called the

'saloon', Charlie gave a low whistle.

'The grandest room in the house,' Mauve said. 'Only used to impress guests.'

'Well, it sure as hell impresses me,' Charlie said. He had stopped in the entrance to the large room to take in the Persian rugs, ornate chairs, mirrors with gold leaf frames, plush, buttoned velvet sofas and the grand piano. The wallpaper was handmade in yellow and blue silk. Hung against it were oil paintings of traditional country scenes. At the centre of the ceiling hung an impressive crystal chandelier. Watching Charlie, Mauve realised he might be thinking about his humble beginnings as one of three brothers in a two-bedroom terraced house. She imagined him thinking his childhood dwellings had been ordinary, while she, used to the excess that money brought, would think of this as normal.

'It's a shame the house has been empty all these years,' Charlie said, his voice almost a whisper.

'Yes,' Mauve said. 'I should have done something with it; used it or sold it. I felt I was stuck. I couldn't move on.'

'No.' Charlie returned from his trancelike state. 'I can understand that.'

Her eyes met his, to find them forlorn and momentarily unguarded. He looked away.

She wondered again about what Kit had said concerning Charlie's feelings for her.

'The only rooms I went in downstairs were the kitchen, the sitting room where Paulette died and the storage room. I can't remember going upstairs but it might come back if we go up.'

'Mauve, enough.' Charlie moved to stand in front of her. 'We've already been here too long. We need to go *now*.'

Mauve stared at him for a moment then nodded. 'You're right.'

Charlie rubbed his chin thoughtfully as he turned to move towards the door. 'There's something that's been bothering me.'

'Yes?' Mauve waited.

'This house is huge. It needed a lot of people – staff – to maintain it.' Charlie's hand wandered to his head to scratch absentmindedly. 'Why were none here eight years ago when you came here with Lena? It seems odd that an elderly wealthy lady would be alone here.'

'Lena said there would be no staff until the housekeeper and her husband, the groundsman, returned the following morning,' Mauve explained. 'The couple lived in. If we go up two flights of stairs, there is a completely self-contained flat on the top floor. I believe their son had been in a car accident and they'd rushed to the hospital to be with him.'

'A bit convenient,' Charlie said.

'What are you suggesting? Surely it must have been a coincidence?' Mauve stared at him, her face filled with horror.

Charlie stared back in silence.

'It never occurred to me.' Mauve's hand came up to cover her face as she considered the possibility that Robin and Lena had arranged the accident.

'I don't believe in convenient coincidences,' Charlie said.

'That's horrible,' Mauve said. 'Arranging an accident for the son to get his parents out of the house.'

'Unbelievable,' Charlie said. 'Another thing to bring up with the police.'

'*I think not!*'

The voice from the doorway made them both turn.

'Robin!' Mauve said.

'Hello, girl. Together at last.' Robin stepped forward, opening his arms theatrically as he entered the room. 'All those wasted visits to my sad little bungalow. We just seemed to keep missing each other.'

Mauve realised that, had he not spoken, it was only the Kelly features that allowed her to recognise him. His voice, deep and melodic, was unchanged, but not so his appearance. The cap and shades had gone. She remembered him as being thinner eight years ago, with longish brown hair. Now he was round, his belly curving out. Close to, she recognised the face of the habitual whisky drinker, reddened and jowly. His hair, mainly white, was cut short, and his attire was no longer that of the sharp man about town. He might pass for a country farmer in green corduroy trousers and a checked shirt under a waxed jacket.

'You've changed.' The words slipped out.

'It's my lifestyle.' Robin smiled. 'You might remember, I enjoy the good things, food, wine. It's possible to remain slim when younger, but middle-age spread catches us all sooner or later. Although,' he continued to hold the fixed smile, 'you have avoided it thus far.'

'I meant since I last saw you outside your bungalow and in the car park. I recognised the Kelly features. But you've lost the cap with the peak, the shades and the grubby trainers. You look like a farmer.' Mauve looked him up and down, taking in his attire.

'Interesting observation.'

His smile bordered on a smirk. Mauve felt he was playing with her. She would need to question the truth of anything he said.

'Where's Lena's body?' Mauve demanded. 'How did she die?'

'Now, now, no rush, girl. You can't know how much I've been looking forward to our get-together.'

As Robin came forward, Mauve saw a man behind him, following. She recognised him immediately.

'You…'

'Who is he?' Charlie asked.

'I don't know.' She looked at the man with the sly smile she'd christened Mr Denim. 'He was in the bar in Blackpool.'

'Changed your hair since then,' the man said.

Mauve touched her hair, thinking about the wig discarded in the rose garden.

'And had a little less to drink.'

'*Elliot!*' Robin teased. 'You're making the lady feel shy.'

'Where's Lena?' Mauve asked again.

'Who knows? In the cellar or maybe buried in the woods.' Robin lifted his shoulders in a shrug.

'We're going now.' Charlie took Mauve by the arm to guide her forward.

'Not so fast,' Robin said. 'You've given Charlie the grand tour, but have you not shown him the cellar?'

Elliot moved from behind Robin. In his right hand a gun was pointed at Charlie.

'Your man's expendable, girl. Keep that thought in your head before you do something you'll regret.'

'Is Lena here, dead or alive?' Mauve persisted.

'You'll have to wait to find out.' Robin stepped back. 'After you.' He waited as Charlie followed Mauve from the room.

'Why would you want to put us in the cellar?' Charlie asked.

'Because it has a solid lock,' Robin said. 'Shame there are no longer any fine wines. You might have enjoyed a glass or two while you're there.'

'How would you know there used to be wine? Did you go there eight years ago?' Mauve snapped.

'Still trying to remember, girl!' Robin snorted with derision. 'Keep going. You know the direction. I thought you might want to say hello to Kit before we conclude our business.'

30

Moving along the corridor to the staircase with Charlie at her side, Mauve could sense Robin and Elliot close behind. She couldn't speak; not only had she refused to leave when Charlie had urged it, but she had also drawn Kit into danger. Robin had implied Kit was in the cellar, but was that true, and was he hurt? Reaching the stairs, she gripping the rail attached to the balustrades, before sinking to sit on the bottom step with her head down while counting, tried to regulate her breathing.

'Come on, move.' Elliot poked his finger into her spine, his voice sharp.

'She's having a panic attack,' Charlie said. Mauve felt him take her hand as he sat beside her.

'Playing the wounded soldier won't work here, lady.' Elliot growled.

'No, leave her for a minute,' Robin said. 'She had one at the Camden flat when she found Lena's blood, and again at the police station.'

How the hell would he know that? Mauve continued

her breathing exercises while the name kept jangling in her mind. *Eliza, Eliza, Eliza.* It swirled around in answer to the question. She had heard Kit telling Eliza about the panic attacks when they had been staying at the holiday rental.

'OK.' A few minutes later, when Mauve was breathing normally, Robin said, 'Time to go.'

Mauve led the way. Around the side of the staircase, through the door to a back passageway. She knew well enough where the door leading to the cellar was; Paulette forbade her from going there as a child.

'Far too dangerous,' Paulette had said when Mauve wheedled to be allowed to explore. 'All those bottles, so much glass.'

Arriving outside, she stopped, and Robin walked past her to open the door. The lights were already on, but there was no noise or sign that anyone else was there.

'You found the key.' Mauve looked at the open doorway.

'It wasn't exactly hidden, girl.' Robin smirked. 'Mobile phones.' He held out his hands.

Charlie touched his pocket, hesitating.

'Do you want me to rip it out?' Robin said.

Charlie handed it over and Robin looked expectantly at Mauve.

'I left it in the kitchen.' Mauve held her hands in the air. From behind, Elliot pushed his hands over her pockets at the back and front of her jeans, nodding to Robin before he did the same to Charlie.

'Suppose I tell you I don't want to go into the cellar and I don't believe Kit is going to be there?' Mauve rested her hand on the door. She knew she was trying to buy time by talking, but for what end?

'Suppose,' Robin's voice dripped with sarcasm, 'I tell my friend Elliot to shoot your best buddy Charlie just there.' He pointed. 'Between the eyes.'

Eliott raised the gun level to Charlie's face. 'Move!'

Mauve went down the steps, followed closely by Charlie. A sour smell rose to greet them from the airless cellar. All around, built against the background of old brick walls, in the long dark room, were empty wooden wine racks, and at the end wall were ground-to-ceiling cupboards. The floor was black slate, and tiny lights in the ceiling twinkled like stars. At the centre of the room, facing one another, were two matching chaises longues, covered in grey fabric, and between them an oak table.

'Kit's not here.' Charlie stated the obvious after they'd listened to the slamming of the door followed by the scraping of the key as it turned in the lock.

'It was a way of getting me down here quickly, without making a fuss,' Mauve said. 'It's a relief, him not being here.'

'Where did you leave your bag with the laptop?' Charlie asked.

'The bag's on a chair in the kitchen, with my phone.' Mauve examined the lacy effect of spiders' webs weaving through the empty wine racks. 'My laptop's in the boot of the car.'

Charlie wandered around. 'No other way out.'

'No. When did you last speak to Kit?'

Charlie went to sit on one of the chaises longues. Mauve followed.

'I'd phoned him when I was leaving London,' Charlie said. 'Kit gave me the name of the hotel in Blackpool, and I was on my way there when I received a text to say you'd gone. I changed the route to come here.'

'I didn't know you were heading to Blackpool,' Mauve said, surprised.

'Would it have made any difference?' Charlie raised his eyebrows quizzically.

'I wouldn't have gone. I'd have waited if I'd known you were coming.'

'Kit sent a text to say you'd taken the car, so they would have to hire another one. Once that was sorted, he'd see me here. I hoped to be able to message them with the name of a local hotel or pub, if I'd managed to get you to leave.'

'I'm so sorry about that.' Mauve's shoulders drooped, and she shuddered suddenly as the coldness of the room crept through her light clothing. 'When you say "they", you mean Kit and Eliza?'

'Of course.'

'She's working with them, Charlie,' Mauve said. 'I know I keep banging on; she's been doing it from the beginning.' She went through all her doubts about Eliza. She finished with what she'd heard Robin saying about her panic attacks. 'You heard him. How would he know about those, unless someone told him?'

'Eliza?'

'Who else could it have been?'

'I don't know.' Charlie scratched his head, thinking. 'I find it hard to believe it's Eliza – I trust Kit's judgement too much – but it does look that way.'

They sat silently for a few minutes, both lost in their thoughts.

'Can I go over a couple of things?' Charlie asked. 'What you told me in the kitchen, things that didn't make much sense.'

Mauve leaned in to listen.

'You said that when you were staying at the holiday cottage near Sleaford, while you were out, someone had been in to search your room, probably looking for the memory stick?'

'Yes.' Mauve's voice was firm.

'Why?' Charlie said. 'What would be the point? If that memory stick was left at Robin's bungalow for you to find, and then the same with the second one, why would he want it back? It makes no sense.'

'I agree, but what other explanation is there?' Mauve said. 'Who else, other than Robin, would be interested in searching my belongings? And there was no sign that either door had been forced. Eliza was the last one out. She could have left the door on the latch.'

'There are only two possible reasons for the recordings.' Charlie spoke slowly, thinking it through while he talked. 'The first and most obvious was to wind you up and bring you here. Lena knew how your mind works and how you'd react... and it worked. You did what she'd expected. The second reason is they could be used as police evidence to frame you for the two deaths, Paulette's and Lena's. Robin had no need to break in to get them back. He must have copies. Lena kept saying, "Don't hurt me," as though you and she have a history of you being violent. The only thing that obviously didn't pan out is that having agreed to set you up with the recordings, Robin betrayed Lena. She could hardly have imagined he would kill her. And with the break-in, a professional could have got inside without leaving a trace.' Charlie looked thoughtful. 'What about your computer, if Robin gets his hands on it?'

'It wouldn't do him much good,' Mauve said. 'He couldn't get into my bank accounts. The information needed is here.' She tapped her head.

'And the eye scan?'

'Yes, and that.' Mauve shivered, rubbing her arms.

'Have my jacket.' Charlie stood up.

'No, there might be something in the cupboards,' Mauve said.

Following Charlie to the cupboards at the end of the cellar, they worked methodically from one side to the other. Most were empty; one contained several empty wine bottles.

'They must have been good years,' Charlie said, picking up a bottle to turn it around to read the label. 'The only reason to keep them.'

Mauve suspected he was trying to sound cheerful to keep her spirits up.

'I think Paulette would have associated them with special events, a meal with a husband.'

'Or your father,' Charlie said.

'Or him…'

'Sacks.' Charlie pulled some old dry hessian sacks from the last cupboard.

'They're a bit smelly.' Mauve wrinkled her nose as he followed her carrying the pile back to the chaise.

'It's either putting up with the smell or being cold.' Charlie draped two around her shoulders and Mauve took another to lay it across her legs.

'I guess the temperature had to be regulated.' Charlie came to resume his place beside her. 'When there were wines in here.'

'Regulated temperature, no sunlight. Not a problem in a wine cellar, and no vibration.' Mauve reeled out the list automatically. 'Paulette lost her taste for fine wines at quite a young age, when she hit fifty.' She smiled, remembering. '"Pointless filling the cellar with expensive wines when I can't drink them."' Mauve used Paulette's school teachery tone of voice. 'She did keep some in for guests, or to give as a gift, but not in the same quantity.'

'You cared about her?' Charlie said.

'Very much.' Mauve felt the tears burning behind her eyes. 'Still, it's no good thinking about Paulette now. I'm worried what Robin will do if he finds Kit.'

'Use him as a bargaining chip.'

'Yes, I think so too.' Mauve sat thinking. 'What else didn't you get from what I told you earlier, apart from the break-in to search my belongings?'

'The car not starting when you'd stopped at the service station,' Charlie said. 'You thought it was down to Eliza. But what possible benefit would there be in staying in Blackpool for the night?'

Mauve opened her mouth to respond, but Charlie cut in.

'And Denim Man, Elliot. He was obviously on your tail but how would he have found you in Blackpool?'

'Eliza again,' Mauve said. 'It has to be her.'

'There is something.' Charlie sounded hesitant. 'I don't want to start another panic attack… but…'

'I know what you're going to say,' Mauve said, her voice low.

'Once Robin has the money, we're dead meat. You and me, and Kit if he turns up.' Charlie took her hand. 'He thought nothing of killing Paulette and his next-door neighbour. It won't bother him to kill us.'

'And Lena. He killed his own sister,' Mauve felt Charlie squeeze her hand.

'We can't escape from here.' Charlie's eyes wandered around the cellar as he spoke. 'Robin knows Kit is on his way, and when he arrives, it'll be straight down to business. The only chance we've got is to drag it out as long as possible, to find an opportunity to turn the tables.'

'I know,' Mauve said. 'Once he has the money, we'll be loose ends to be tied up.'

31

They'd talked endlessly about the impossibility of the situation until Mauve felt physically and mentally drained. There was no access to water in the room; her mouth was dry, and her throat ached. When Charlie suggested she rest, Mauve stretched out on the chaise with a pile of old sacking as blankets. To sleep would have been impossible. She lay quietly chasing thoughts of escape, mentally trying to remember and cover all the areas of the house and outbuildings where she could run and hide. And then she drifted into sleep to be rudely awakened by shouting as the door opened.

Jumping up, Mauve had a blurred impression of movement, and as the door slammed, she followed Charlie to the heap at the bottom of the cellar steps, which, on closer inspection, was her son.

'Kit.' Mauve was on her knees beside him as he rolled into a sitting position. 'You've cut your head.'

'It's OK.' Kit pushed his hand across the cut on his forehead, spreading the blood around like butter on hot toast. He moved up on his knees to wrap his arms around her. 'I've been so worried about you.'

'Me too.' Mauve gripped her boy fiercely, her tears disappearing into his hair.

'What happened? Where did they find you?' Charlie knelt on the floor next to them.

'We split up when we got here,' Kit said. 'Two cars were near the back entrance to the woods. We knew Robin must have beaten us to it.'

'We?' Mauve asked. 'That's you and Eliza?'

'I don't know where she is… And that ape kicked Timothy.' Kit's lips wobbled helplessly as his voice trailed away. 'He pointed his gun, and if I hadn't thrown myself into him to push him over, he would have shot him. Timothy ran away limping. When the ape got up, he hit me across the head with the gun. Then the older one came. The ape called him Robin, and Robin introduced himself.'

'What did he say?' Mauve asked.

'"I'm Uncle Robin, but then I'm not. Your mother and I once shared a half-sister, your Aunt Lena, so that's our connection." He was sneering,' Kit said. 'And he used the past tense for Aunt Lena.'

'Oh, Kit.' Mauve felt a wave of heat run up through her body to her face. Still touching her son, her hands trembled. It was all her fault. She had tried to leave him behind in London, desperate not to get him involved, but now Robin had the three of them. This wasn't going to end well.

'We'll find Timothy when we get out,' Charlie said.

Mauve and Kit exchanged a look of surprise. '*If*,' Kit said. 'Eliza is our only hope now.'

'She's in on it, Kit.' Mauve sounded bitter. 'I ran away from the hotel in Blackpool because I saw her in the car park with him... Robin.'

'Are you absolutely sure it was Robin, Mummy?'

'Robin didn't say it wasn't him,' Mauve said.

'Neither did he say it was,' Charlie rejoined. 'He was toying with you.'

'It's impossible. There is no way Eliza would do the dirty on either me or you. There has to be a logical explanation,' Kit said. 'I'd trust Eliza with my life.' He stood up to walk around the wine cellar, almost manic as he searched the basement with his eyes. '*What is that stink?*'

'Decay and lack of air,' Charlie said. 'I hope you're right about Eliza. Looks like, trust-wise, we're all in her hands.'

'Locked in. It's like a bloody dungeon.' Kit spun around. 'We've got no chance. Robin wants money, you'll have worked that out.'

'Yes,' Charlie said. 'And the way to get it is to threaten Mauve that he'll hurt you. And when he has the money, we will all become redundant.'

'Four, if you count Eliza.' Kit remained stubborn. 'I won't be convinced she's working against us unless she tells me herself.'

Mauve looked at Charlie, then back at Kit. 'Let's not argue about Eliza,' Mauve said. 'More sensible to work on formulating a plan.'

'*What plan?*' Kit snapped. 'We've nothing to bargain with. You can't indefinitely make excuses for not transferring the money while the ape waggles a gun in my face. We're stuffed, Mother. This is down to you. Having wobbles and running this way and that like a headless chicken.'

'Nobody asked you to follow me.' Mauve pushed her hair back, indignant.

'And how would you have fared better on your own? You are so bloody ungrateful.' Kit gripped the back of the chaise as he vented his frustration.

'Don't be rude to me,' Mauve said. 'I've worked my socks off, always, to put you first, to give you a good life.'

'Mother, stop it.' Kit raised his eyes. '*Work*? You inherited your money and enjoy being in the driver's seat. You are a control freak. It's all about having everything your way. I got stuffed into doing a course at uni that I had no interest in. I was never even allowed to see my dad when I was growing up. You remember him, Thom Bradley?' Kit glowered at Mauve. 'I had to organise that myself, and he's not the monster you'd painted him. He's married to a lovely woman called Leanne, and I have two half-sisters I hadn't known existed.'

'OMG!' Mauve looked to the ceiling, raising her hands dramatically. 'You wasted time going to see that deadbeat? We'll probably die here, and in the time we've got left you think we must talk about bloody Thom Bradley. He's bringing those kids up using my money. It cost me a lot to get rid of him.'

'He's my father, and it's normal for me to want to get to know him.' Kit folded his arms and perched on the back of the chaise.

Charlie watched in silence, his head turning, as in a game of tennis, from one player to the other.

'He never worked a day in his life. He took me for as much as he could screw from me.' Mauve heard the shrillness in her voice but couldn't stop.

'Get over it, Mother. Daddy's in my life now,' Kit said, suddenly calm.

'*Daddy. Daddy!*' Mauve screwed up her face. 'He's not your bloody daddy; he's just a blood-sucking leech.'

'What do you mean?' Kit said. He stood up to stare at his mother.

'It's him.' Mauve pointed wildly at Charlie. 'He's there… if you need your daddy. Your father, it's Charlie. Thom has nothing to do with you, that's why I didn't encourage contact with him.'

The room became still and silent. Not getting a response from Kit, Mauve looked first at him and then at Charlie. Both stared at her dumbfounded.

'Charlie?' Kit said icily. 'Why did neither of you ever think to tell me?'

'I'm Kit's dad?' Charlie said. 'Why did you never say anything, Mauve?'

'You didn't know?'

Charlie shook his head.

'Mauve? Is this right?'

'I'm sorry.' Mauve walked to the chaise and flopped down onto the crumpled sacking. 'To both of you. I should have said something years ago, but it took nearly two years to get Thom out of my life, and remember you were still married to Helen back then, Charlie.'

'I would still have preferred you to have told me,' Charlie said.

'How long were you two at it?' Kit looked from one to the other.

'We were never "at it",' Charlie said wearily. 'It happened once.'

'Once... Then Thom might still have been my dad,' Kit protested.

'No,' Mauve said. 'Thom and I were living under the same roof, but there was nothing physical between us by then. And, before you ask, I wasn't sleeping with anyone else. I'm not the old slapper you imagine me to be.'

Kit stared at his mother for a few moments. 'That sounds sad, Mummy. Sort of lonely.'

'It might have been lonely, but I had you; you filled that big black empty hole. You were a lovely baby,' Mauve said. 'I think it unkind of Thom to lead you on and let you believe he's your father. I still remember his face when I told him I was pregnant. Disbelief, then amazement. We never discussed your paternity, but the lack of a sex life made it a bit bloody obvious. But Thom didn't want to rock the boat and confront me. I was his meal ticket.'

'Maybe it was awkward,' Charlie said. 'If Kit was excited to reconnect it might have put Thom on the back foot.'

Kit nodded. 'He seemed like a decent bloke. Embarrassing that I put him on the spot.'

'No,' Mauve said, 'it was my fault. There just never seemed a right time to tell you.'

'And this is it, the right time?' Kit said. 'Because very soon we're all going to be dead?'

Mauve stayed silent.

'Well... It's a bit of a surprise, but a happy one. You're

my son.' Charlie tried to smile at Kit. 'I'd always wanted to be a dad and there you were, all these years.'

'The timing might have been better,' Kit said. 'I can't think of anyone I'd rather have as my dad.' He went to Charlie to wrap his arms around him for a moment in a bear hug. Watching, Mauve noticed the similarity again: they were the same height, with long gangly limbs, and had the same shy smiles.

Charlie hugged him back, then, as they separated, turned away, his eyes glassy. As he passed Mauve, she reached out to briefly squeeze his hand.

A few minutes later, Kit returned to pacing the room again. 'We must decide what to do. How about waiting behind the door.' He looked about him. 'What could we use as a weapon?'

'We could be waiting for hours, although I doubt it. They'll want to move on now they have you,' Charlie said. 'The problem is that this room is pretty soundproof; we can't hear them approaching.'

'Until they turn the key,' Mauve added. As if mentioning it had brought the nightmare to life, a scraping sound from the door made them all turn at once.

As the door opened and Robin stepped inside, the trio remained stationary, frozen with fear.

'Mauve, my dear.' Robin made a mock bow to step aside from the door and extend his hand towards Mauve. 'Would you do me the courtesy of coming this way to join me?'

32

'Bugger off!'

Mauve's response took Robin by surprise. His face, as though sucking a lemon, became pinched. He glanced from Kit and Charlie back to Mauve.

'That's not a good way to restart our relationship,' Robin said. 'I think you'll find I hold all the aces. You have nothing to bargain with.'

'On the contrary, I'm the one with access to the money, the money you want to get your greedy little hands on. If you touch one hair on either of their heads,' Mauve swept her hand towards Charlie and Kit, 'you won't see one penny. Just think about all the time you've put into this venture, killing my sister and your neighbour; it would all have been for nothing.'

If Charlie and Kit were surprised by Mauve's fighting talk, they hid it, remaining poker-faced.

'What are you proposing?'

'Why don't you invite all three of us upstairs? We've had nothing to drink for hours.' Mauve turned her head to regard her surroundings. 'And it's bloody cold down here. If we come to the kitchen, we can work out terms.'

Robin paused as he appeared to consider his options. He looked back through the open doorway, then at Mauve. 'What's to stop me telling Elliot to kill Charlie now in front of you? You can watch. Then it will be his turn.' Robin nodded to indicate Kit.

'I know it'll be my turn after them once you have the money.' Mauve folded her arms defiantly. 'You want something from me, so I need something back. That's how it works.'

'What can I say?' Robin threw open his arms in an unexpected magnanimous gesture, revealing a gun. 'Come up. We'll head for the kitchen and make coffee.'

After a moment of hesitation, Charlie led the way, and Mauve and Kit followed. Up the narrow staircase, Robin stood back, allowing them to pass through the open door. While waiting in the corridor, Elliot scowled as they trooped past, with Charlie leading them back to the kitchen.

Mauve saw her bag on one of the work surfaces, its contents, minus her mobile phone, strewn across the table.

'Sit down, gentlemen, sit down,' Robin invited. He gave the impression that he was the host welcoming guests. 'Mauve, you know where everything is, the kettle, the cups. There is a jar of instant in that cupboard – not up to the fine coffee you're used to – and no milk. It probably belongs to the cleaners.'

'The gardener,' Mauve corrected him as she walked to the kettle to fill it.

'You're a generous employer allowing the gardener

to have his coffee inside the house.' Robin pulled a face. 'Dirty boots, and he might well be a thief!'

'John Williams was Paulette's gardener,' Mauve said. Charlie and Kit pulled chairs out from beneath the table to sit. 'He keeps an eye on the place and reports to the management agency. He's not a thief.'

'Where does he live?' Elliot went to the window to look outside.

'She's winding you up, Elliot,' Robin said. 'He lives in the village and comes in twice a week. Isn't that right, girl?'

Mauve glanced at Robin before bringing a glass from the cupboard and filling it with water, which she drank. Then she took a pile of cups from a cupboard to set three in a row.

'Don't be mean,' Robin said. 'There are five of us. Maybe six in a short while.'

'Who's joining us?' Mauve asked casually.

'You know very well.' Robin gave his sneaky half-smile.

'No,' Mauve said. 'I don't.'

'Auntie Mauve and Uncle Robin are looking forward to a visit from our darling niece. Eliza, of course,' Robin said.

'Eliza's nothing to do with you.' Kit glowered at Robin and Elliot. 'She wouldn't give either of you the time of day.'

'Oh, the sweet innocence of the child.' Robin sniggered. 'She grew up with Lena as her mother and Bonnie as a grandmother; you can't expect her to be a saint. Eliza is a Kelly through and through. Like seaside rock, she's pink and sugary on the outside; the Kelly name is printed on the inside.'

'Who's the one playing wind-up now?' Charlie said. 'If

you knew where Eliza was, you'd have brought her in here.'

'The girl will come in when she's good and ready,' Robin said.

Mauve glanced at Charlie as she added the boiling water to the cups and brought two to the table, returning for her own and joining the two to pull out a chair and sit. Robin went to pick up a cup and remained standing, leaning against the counter. Elliot ignored the remaining coffee and stayed where he was at the window, occasionally scanning the garden outside.

'Tell me something.' Mauve looked over her cup at Robin. 'What did you drug me with the night you killed Paulette?'

'Ha!' Robin's face danced with glee. 'Wouldn't you like to know? If you've worked out you were drugged, what difference does it make what it was?'

'Some form of GBL,' Charlie said. His eyes narrowed as he looked at Robin. 'From Mauve's reactions, it seems likely it was a date rape drug.'

'Give that man a gold star,' Robin sneered. 'And, to answer a question with a question,' Robin spoke directly to Mauve, 'whatever made you believe it was me who murdered Paulette?'

'Are you saying it was Lena? I don't believe you.' But even as she spoke, she realised she did believe him. It was the truth.

'The girl had always hated Paulette with a passion. And she had to do something to earn that delightful London flat.'

'And now you've killed her, a falling out amongst thieves.' Mauve sipped her coffee.

'Well, now.' Robin looked at Mauve with her hands cradling the cup. 'It's time to talk business. The computer we found here belongs to your man Charlie. His name is on the back. You can use that to transfer money.'

'I need my own,' Mauve said.

'I guessed you'd say that. I'm thinking yours is still in the car?'

Mauve nodded, her mind whirling as she thought how to spin this out and then how to make an escape. There might be an opportunity if she had to leave the house to go to the car.

'I need to know these two have left and are safe before I transfer any money,' she said.

'That's going to be difficult.' Robin watched Mauve's face as he talked. 'If they leave, we both know that they'll get straight on to the police.'

'I need to know they are safe,' Mauve repeated.

'I'm not playing games, girl. Time for you to do as you're told.' The charade of charm and pleasantries had finished. Robin's voice was stern as he put down the coffee cup and raised the gun.

'It's important… if you want the money.'

'I can't let them go until it's done. You know that.'

'And we both know that if they stay, once the money is transferred, you'll kill all of us.' Mauve said the words calmly, while her insides churned. 'They won't do anything to involve the police while you still have me.'

'I won't leave you here by yourself,' Charlie said, half-rising from his chair.

'Nor me,' Kit said, also standing.

'Sit down.' Elliot came behind Charlie to press him back down by the shoulders before stepping away.

A brief silence followed.

'No more crap.' Robin pointed his gun at Kit and fired.

Kit spun sideways, clasping his arm below the shoulder. As he fell to the floor, he knocked the coffee cup. It shot away from the table, spraying its contents. Mauve screamed as she ran to him.

'Stay there!' Robin shouted at Charlie as he moved to go to Kit's aid. 'Unless you want a bullet too.'

'You piece of shit!' Mauve screamed. Kit lay on the floor, his face contorted in pain. Blood ran together with the black coffee and the broken porcelain.

'I haven't got time for all this crap.' Robin had lost all pretence of civility. 'I'm a good shot. That's the top of his arm; the next one will be in his brain. Get your computer *now*. I want it done. Lena told me you always have at least two million in an offshore account that you can easily access. After the money transfer, we can all leave.'

Mauve stood up, glaring at Robin. 'Let me tie something around his arm to stop the bleeding.'

Robin straightened his arm to point the gun directly at Kit's head. Elliot smirked.

'No.' Mauve moved to stand between Robin and Kit. 'I'll get my computer.'

'Good choice,' Robin said. He moved next to her, grabbing her at the top of her arm with his free hand before waving the gun. 'Make sure these two behave,' he told Elliot, marching Mauve to the door.

'When I return, you can go and get the motor, Elliot. Bring it from the back woods. We'll get straight off after the money comes through.'

'Shouldn't we stay together?' Elliot's face was taut.

'You'll do as you're told. This is my show.' Robin jerked Mauve out of the kitchen.

It was still warm outside, and the aromatic smell of jasmine came to Mauve as they entered the shadowy garden. The kitchen lights made elongated shapes across the lawn and complete silence engulfed them. She felt a sharp pain in her upper arm as Robin squeezed hard, forcing her to move across the long the side of the house and work around to the front entrance where she'd left her car.

Glancing back to the open door as she was pulled away, Mauve thought of Charlie and Kit in the kitchen, hoping neither would try something heroic to challenge Elliot.

'A bit like old times, girl,' Robin snarled in her ear. 'It's nearly black enough; want to dance in the dark again?' His voice conveyed amusement mixed with menace.

'Think your man in there doesn't trust you.' Mauve nodded towards the house. 'Frightened you might get more than him.'

'Don't try to wind me up, girl,' Robin hissed in her ear. 'You know full well he's just the hired help.'

At the car, Mauve opened the boot and retrieved her computer. Standing beside her, Robin watched her every move, then took her upper arm again to retrace their footsteps to the open back door.

Kit, still on the floor but sitting upright, propped against a kitchen cabinet, looked pasty; his face twisted as he gripped his blood-drenched upper arm.

'OK?' Mauve said.

Kit grimaced. Charlie looked as though he might speak. Mauve shook her head.

Robin pushed Mauve towards where she'd been sitting. 'Turn it on and get into the account.' He turned to Elliot. 'Fetch the car.'

Elliot, feet set apart, his body tight, hesitated momentarily. Then, as Robin turned to face him, he left. His feet crunched on the gravel as he passed the window.

'I'm not sure we'll be able to get online here. I need a good connection.' Mauve lifted the lid on the computer.

'The Wi-Fi, as with everything else here, has been maintained,' Robin responded. 'I do my research. Because you pay people to maintain the house, grounds, and the bloody rose garden, you can fantasise that your dear Auntie Paulette never died, that she wasn't murdered in this house.' Robin waved his arms up and down dramatically. 'And, one day, like a magic fairy, she'll fly back into the house. Money is wasted on you, girl.'

Walking across the room, Robin picked something up from the surface of a kitchen unit. Bringing it back, he dropped it on the table. 'Back up. I'm sure you've used one before.' Mauve looked at the dongle. 'Just get on with it.'

Mauve moved the metal tray she'd used to transport the coffee to the table to one side in front of Charlie and pulled the dongle nearer.

As she looked down at the computer, she caught a movement from the corner of her eye. She looked up to concentrate on Robin's face as he stood close, observing again her every move. A shadow detached itself from the side of the kitchen door and came to life as a scruffy mongrel, with bleached blond fur, his belly near the ground as he crept stealthily towards them. The door had been left open; Timothy had found his way inside.

'How much am I meant to be transferring?' Mauve asked as she began to type the offshore bank's details into the computer, trying to keep Robin's attention fixed on her.

'Just get into the account. I'll take what's in there.' Robin's eyes, greedy to see the amount in the account, flicked from the screen to Kit and Charlie, who sat impassive and silent. 'Lena said there was over two million.'

'It will require eye recognition once I get into the account,' Mauve said. As the bank details came up, she continued to type. Her heart seemed to be beating so fast that it might burst out of her chest. She caught her breath. *No*, not a panic attack. *Please, not now*. She counted inside her head and tried to concentrate on the screen.

Then, as Timothy reached his target, sinking his teeth into the calf of the left leg, Robin jerked his head back and screamed.

33

Timothy stayed attached to the leg as Robin bellowed in anger and hopped on one foot as he attempted to shake the growling dog from him.

'*Get off me, I'll wring your bloody neck!*' Robin shouted, pointing the gun downwards towards Timothy.

Charlie rose from his seat in one fluid movement, grabbing the metal tray from the table to slam it into Robin's face. The sound was like a car backfiring. Blood spurted from Robin's broken nose as he fell backwards, dropping the gun. Mauve pounced to pick it up.

Robin's eyes burnt with anger. He pushed his hand across his face, smearing blood over his forehead and into his hair, then pulled himself up from the floor. As he did, two things came together. Timothy, who had momentarily lost his grip on the leg, returned to sink his teeth further down the same calf. At the same time, Robin met with Charlie's fist, a punch to the already damaged face. He fell backwards. His head met the floor with a sharp crack.

'Let me help you.' Mauve went to Kit.

'Timothy,' Kit said as the dog limped to beat Mauve to it, reaching him and pressing his body against Kit while licking his face. '*Timothy, Timothy, Timothy.*' The repetition sounded like a chant. 'You're hurt. He's got blood on his back leg.'

'That's two of you then.' Mauve knelt beside her son.

'Where are the phones?' Charlie bent to put his hand inside Robin's jacket pocket and pulled out a phone.

'Elliot, the ape, might have taken them,' Kit said.

'This one needs a security code,' Charlie said. He glanced at Robin, sprawled unconscious on the floor. 'He's never going to give us that.' He dropped it onto the table. 'You stay here.' Charlie spoke as he grabbed Robin by the arms and dragged the unconscious body across the kitchen.

'What are you doing?' Mauve asked.

'I'm sticking him in the cellar before he wakes up. We know he can't get out. He'll stay there until the police come.' Charlie lugged him towards the door. 'Mauve, lock the back door and keep hold of the gun. Ape Man might return before me.'

Mauve ran to the back door to drop the catch and push the bolts, bottom and top, across. Back in the kitchen, she flicked the light switch to darken the room instantly.

'Stay there,' Mauve said to Kit. 'If Elliot does come back and looks through the window, he won't see you.' She passed him the gun.

'Where are you going? Charlie said to stay here.' Kit's voice held panic as Mauve returned to the door. Timothy stayed close, not moving from his master.

'My car's near the front door,' Mauve said. 'I'll get the medical box from one of my bags. I can use a bandage to slow the bleeding.'

'No, Mummy,' Kit pleaded. 'Stay here with me until Charlie gets back.'

'It will only take me a minute.'

'No, please don't go out until Charlie gets back,' he implored her. 'We haven't got phones to call the police or an ambulance. When Charlie returns, we can all head straight to the car, then the hospital.'

'I'm worried about the blood loss,' Mauve said. 'There's a bandage I can tie around to stem the bleeding, and there a sling.' Stepping into the hall, she heard Kit's voice, still pleading, as she sprinted along the darkened corridor to the front door. Opening the door, Mauve looked out to the moonlit garden, suddenly trembling as she saw the lawn. A pinprick of a memory of the night eight years ago, when she had been on the lawn with Lena and Robin grew and enlarged. Closing her eyes, she could smell the roses growing around and above the door frame. Lena had laughed, a high-pitched cackle. Robin, filming them, was also laughing and giving instructions. 'Dance, dance!' Robin had shouted. Mauve had looked down to her torn top. Her hands felt sticky in the semi-darkness; she had not realised that it was blood, that Paulette was dead.

Opening her eyes, Mauve shook her head as if she might somehow dislodge the memories. It was what she'd come for, but now was the wrong time for recollections. Kit was sitting on the kitchen floor, bleeding heavily.

Leaving the door open, she ran across the gravel to the car and opened the boot. Leaning in, she pulled the bags containing her clothes to throw them one after the other onto the ground. She found the emergency first-aid kit at the bottom of the last bag. She took it out and ran, returning to the door to find it closed.

She cursed herself for not having noticed the door's slow closing motion.

Her mind went to the keys in the bag inside the house. She dashed along the pathway, to return to the back door on the west corner of the house. Charlie might have come back to the kitchen. She would knock on the window.

Before she reached the corner, lights from a car lit up the garden.

They were coming from the direction of the woods, also heading towards the back door. It must be Elliot returning. If she went further, he'd see her.

Turning back in the direction from which she'd come, she ran past the front entrance to reach the east corner of the house. Then, diving around, cut along the side, pressing herself into the darkness against the wall.

The beam from the headlights was still coming. The driver had not stopped at the back door as she'd imagined.

She continued along the side of the house until, set back from the main building, she reached the old stables. Her head hurt. She must stay safe, not risk being caught by Elliot, but she was going in the wrong direction. Kit was in the house, the other way.

The garden was entirely lit now by the headlights. Whoever was driving would be able to see the open boot of her car, with the bags she'd thrown from the back strewn haphazardly around on the gravel pathway.

The stables had been modernised and made into a private gallery by Paulette and had two doors, one on either side. Remembering a long narrow window next to the nearest door, Mauve headed towards it. She would break the window if she couldn't force her way in.

The door was unlocked and opened instantly. Inside, the immediate impression was blackness. Mauve remained stationary, allowing her eyes to attune to the darkness. The Grade Two listed building had been renovated over thirty years earlier, from designs produced by an internationally acclaimed architect who was a friend of Paulette's. Moonlight filtered overhead through the asymmetrical vaulted ceiling with its extended glass partitions. Black shapes around the room became grey as she made out plinths covered in sheeting, once used to exhibit pots, vases and other art forms displayed in the gallery. Looking around, she kept her back to the door to catch any movement. *Why has the door been unlocked?* The thought jarred. Negligence by the management company, or had someone been in? She couldn't stay here, but how could she return to Kit? Stay or go, she didn't know what to do and panic settled on her like a heavy overcoat, weighing her down. The breath caught in her throat, and her mouth felt dry. She sank onto her haunches, counting and holding her breath for five seconds. Then a pause and out. *Not now, please not now!* She remembered earlier begging some unknown God that the panic attack should not happen.

One minute passed, then another. Unsure how much

time had elapsed, she pulled herself up to press against the wall and peek through the side window. Nobody had followed her. With the headlight still on full beam, there was no movement. The car was stationary. If she tried to return that way, there would be no hiding place; it would be in the full glare of the lights. How to get back to Kit?

Then, a crack. Unmistakably, a gunshot.

Continuing the breathing exercises, and with a final glance around the gallery, Mauve slipped back outside. She was trembling and sweaty, but at least she had averted the panic attack. Who was shooting, Elliot or Kit? Or, maybe Charlie had returned from the cellar to the kitchen. *Don't let either be hurt!* The notion jangled, increasing her already fraught state.

She couldn't return to the back door; she'd have to go around the side of the building, passing the rose garden and, beyond that, the barn Paulette had used for parking.

Outside, after the gunshot, the silence felt ominous and heavy.

The moonlight spread fingers of light amongst the shadows. Crouching low and keeping close to the wall, she raced to reach the corner. As she neared the end, she paused before looking around and continuing. The aromatic scent from the roses was overpowering. She touched a stone bench, the coldness of the stone a familiar memory from childhood. Paulette would often sit here, on cushions brought from the house on warm evenings. On a small table beside the bench would stand a bottle of wine and a favourite rose-coloured wine glass. Climbing onto the bench, Mauve squatted to peer into the house to find the darkened view of the library. There was no movement, no light or sound.

Then, as she turned the corner, keeping close to the wall, the silence suddenly broke with the muffled sound of voices. Behind her, she'd left the bright light from the beam of the headlights, lighting up the area at the front of the house. There was only the moonlight here, and from here she could reach the back door.

The sound of voices came a second time from around the next corner, the back of the house. Might it be Kit and Charlie? Mauve edged further along, pressing to merge herself into the darkness of the long shadow of the wall.

Then, a figure stepped forward, to emerge into the moonlight.

It was Eliza, still in black, but now with her hair tied back. She was talking with an unseen companion, someone hidden from view. Mauve strained to listen, to catch the words, but the murmured words were unclear and formed only a jumble of sound.

As Eliza paused to turn a full circle, her eyes searching the garden, her companion remained hidden.

With her back hard up against the wall, Mauve waited. Then Eliza disappeared, returning from wherever she'd come. The voices drifted on the night air again, slowly receding, then silence.

Coming to a decision, she sprinted from the safety of the wall to the barn once used as a garage. Inside, feeling the security of the wooden walls around her, she scoured the garden with her eyes for anything. Nothing moved, and there were no further sounds. She waited again, accustoming her eyes to the semi-darkness. This building did not have the advantage of overhead windows. There was an opening at the rear and the moonlight made a thin line, illuminating a small section of the back wall. There was blackness after that point until the moonlight spilt into the doorless entrance. Moving further inside, Mauve became aware of a smell, strange – both sour and sweet – something, perhaps, that had died and was decaying. She kept her hand touching the rough wood of the wall until she got her bearings.

The barn, like the gallery, held strange, still shapes. Near the entrance, against the wooden wall, was a chair with a broken back. She imagined the gardener using it to rest between jobs. Nearby under a cover, she recognised the shape of a ride-on mower, and along one wall she could make out tools hanging in a line: spades, forks, a rake, a cordless strimmer. Further on, buckets and a wheelbarrow. She remembered this space was used by the gardener to store tools.

In the middle section of the long barn, the darkness was impenetrable, set solid as stone. Nothing moved. What might lurk unseen? Mauve shuddered, pressing further in against the wall.

She considered going further into the darkness, but then her mind wandered, darting from one notion to another. She'd hidden to get away from Eliza and her accomplice. There had been no sounds to indicate the arrival of the police or an ambulance, so it seemed likely that Charlie and Kit had not found a phone. Had Charlie stopped Kit's bleeding? And what had the shot signified?

If Eliza had gone away, might her best move be to try returning to the kitchen to tap on the window? Turning, she shuffled back towards the entrance with her hand again on the wood of the barn wall.

Then, from behind, came an infinitesimal sound.

Mauve swung to face the solid black wall. Gradually, a shadow appeared to come to life, and slowly, ghostlike, shifted towards her. A detached voice in her head questioned why her body, frozen in fear, would not move while her mind, like a frenzied bird, flapped uncontrollably.

'Hello, Mauve.' The woman's lips twisted, forming the shape of a smile. Her eyes said something altogether different. 'You took your time getting here.'

Mauve stared, opening her mouth, and then closed it, the name locked in her throat.

'What's the matter, sister? Cat got your tongue?'

'*Lena*,' Mauve said at last.

34

'What the hell?' Mauve said. 'I thought you were dead.'

'Only because that's what I wanted you to think. And so do the police.' Lena looked smug.

Little had changed. Still super skinny, her hair was shorter and spiky, and she'd had a hair colour change from blonde to auburn. Her trousered legs resembled two thin black sticks.

'You were in this with Robin!' Mauve gasped. 'All the shit you've put me through because you want money…'

'Yeah.' Lena walked closer, halving the distance between them. 'Easy for you to say, Money Bags Mauve. Some of us have no choice.'

'You have money.' Mauve backed away, widening the gap again. '*Had* money. Father left us the exact same amount. It was hardly loose change. It's you that's the problem. There's just never enough.'

'What is enough?' Lena laughed, the throaty sound an echo of the childhood half-sister. 'And anyway, dead old

Dad left treble that amount to your mother and you got it all when she died.'

'It was her money he'd used in the first place.' Mauve felt anger rising. 'Dad didn't have two pennies to rub together until he met my mother.'

'Yes... true. Your mother had inherited wealth. Then he was the one who knew how to use money to make more money, and the last person I need a lecture from is you.'

'How did you do it? The blood in the flat?' Mauve glowered. 'I was genuinely upset. I believed you were dead. There was so much of it.'

'Four pints, to be exact.'

'That's not possible, you'd be dead if they took that much.'

'If they took it in one hit, yes, I would have been,' Lena said. 'Don't forget, my darling brother was a doctor back in the day, before he was struck off. He knew what was a safe amount, over what period to take it and how it had to be stored. All those small amounts put together turned into one big amount.'

'But why, Lena?' Mauve held her hands forward beseechingly. 'If you were so desperate, why didn't you contact me? You've put me through hell.'

'You made it pretty clear after buying the flat and dropping a chunk of cash into my begging bowl it would be the last time.'

'That's not the real reason, there must be more,' Mauve snapped. 'Robin told me it was you who'd murdered Paulette, then stitched me up to make me believe it was me.'

'I did.' Lena flung her arms wide. 'I admit it. Life can

be so bloody boring. It's the crack, the buzz of it. You really haven't got me if you think watching telly every night, a few glasses of vino and a curry once a week is enough.'

'A buzz? You killed my auntie because it gave you a buzz?'

'She was never your auntie; she was our dear daddy's mistress. I did you a favour. She broke up your parents' marriage.'

'Don't be ridiculous, Lena,' Mauve said, exasperated. 'That marriage was broken years before Paulette became involved. You know our father would mount anything if it stayed still long enough. He loved Paulette, and so did I.'

'Now we're getting there.' Lena took a step closer, wagging her finger in Mauve's face, her voice teasing. 'I know you too well. All those hangers-on – so-called friends – but you don't give yourself to many people. Kit and Paulette. You thought you'd killed one of the few people you loved most in the world. It screwed you up. It made you keep your head down to plod onwards in a meaningless crap relationship. And then there are the panic attacks. Despite all the money, for eight years you couldn't live your life… I screwed you, sister.'

Mauve's face twisted as though in pain. She gaped at Lena. 'Do you hate me so much?'

'Yes,' Lena hissed. 'And then some more. It's been a pleasure to play you. You did what I knew you'd do: followed the desired route. You've always been so bloody predictable.'

'So, the plan was to get me here, get money and then kill me.'

'No, not exactly.' Lena put her head to one side, giving her a coquettish appearance. 'The plan had to be changed.'

Mauve waited.

'Kit and the lawyer... Charlie, they weren't meant to be here,' Lena said. 'You did as I expected. If the boy and the lawyer hadn't muscled in after we'd done the business and got the money, the police would have been alerted anonymously.'

Mauve shook her head, trying to understand.

'The plan was delicious, absolutely perfect.' Lena warmed to her theme. 'After the money transfer, the police would have received their tip-off. They'd find you here, completely off your head; drugs again. You'd go to jail as a double murderer: killing me and, with the doll having your DNA, Paulette's murder. The rest of your life in prison, while I'd be living my best life in Barbados.'

In the silence that followed, Mauve tried to process Lena's words.

'What about Eliza?' she asked.

'What about her?' Lena shrugged. 'She might kick off, but in the end she comes to heel and does as I tell her. She's a Kelly; she's always been a chip off the old block. Her Grandma Bonnie would be proud.'

Mauve looked to the exit, across the house, and then back to Lena. She started to move away to the open doorway.

'Stay here.' Lena raised her hand and in the half-darkness. Mauve saw the metallic gleam of a gun.

'What the hell's going on, all these bloody guns?' Mauve said.

'There's been two shots,' Lena said. 'Care to explain?'

'I assumed you were in charge, so you should know.'

'Robin and Elliot were in the house. After they'd brought you and the boys up from the cellar, you were doing the financial business.' Lena raised the gun to point it at Mauve. 'So where is Robin?'

'While I started doing the transfer, he sent Elliot for the car,' Mauve said. 'Maybe he'd been planning to leave with the money… but without you.'

'He wouldn't do that. Try again,' Lena said.

'I managed to get out while he was arguing with Elliot.' Mauve spoke in a low voice. 'There was no transfer, and my computer is still inside the house.'

'You're winding me up.'

'It's not going to be a happy retirement without any money. Barbados is expensive.'

'I might have to cut my losses.' Lena looked Mauve up and down. 'You're useless to me if you can't get at the money.'

'I can be if you get the computer; it's in the kitchen.' Mauve struggled to keep the desperation from showing in her voice.

'And just like that, you'll roll over and give me the money? What happened in the house? You're holding back. There's no way you'd leave Kit, your brat, behind.' Lena waved the gun as she spoke, her voice flat and devoid of emotion. 'Is Robin dead? Last chance.'

'How am I supposed to know what might have happened after I got away?' Mauve gave Lena a hard stare.

'Maybe if I put a bullet into you, it might jog your memory.'

Mauve drew a deep breath as panic moved up, tightening her chest.

'Now, Lena.' A voice from the entrance made her turn. 'Don't be hasty; give the poor girl a chance to transfer the money.'

The man she'd seen so many times over the previous days was standing in the doorway. He wore nothing on his head or face, revealing short brown hair speckled with grey, and the square jaw and arched nose that marked him out as a Kelly. His voice was sharp, correct and cultured. Below a lightweight jacket, his smart dark trousers had a knife-edge crease, and his black polished shoes shone like silver. It was an unexpected transformation from the scruffy man wearing dirty trainers.

'*Damien!*' Lena's voice gave away her surprise. She looked at Mauve. 'You might not remember my brother, another rat from Bonnie's litter.'

Mauve couldn't speak. It was Lena's half-brother. She hadn't recognised him. Of course, she hadn't seen him since childhood.

'A family gathering. I understand from Robin that my wayward daughter has hooked up with you,' Lena said.

'Lovely Eliza. You might say she'd been in touch. She and Robin are back there.' Damien nodded towards the house. 'Perhaps sharing stories of happier times.'

'There never were any happier times.'

'Maybe not.' Damien raised his shoulders, his face a crooked half-smile. 'Sad though it is, you're right.'

'You escaped,' Lena said, peevishly childlike. 'You got away. A decent father, one who wanted you.'

Damien looked thoughtfully at his half-sister as if assessing her. 'It wasn't fair, but then, what in life ever is? In the end, you make your own luck. I was always a Clayton. I took my father's surname and never considered myself a Kelly.' He looked from Lena to Mauve and back. 'Blaming your parents for all your woes is time-limited. Beyond thirty, you need to take responsibility for the shit life throws at you. And you did get to spend time with your father. It didn't work out because you screwed up. And you had Eliza. She's a live wire.'

'Whatever her faults,' Lena snarled, 'she is a Kelly. I've lost count of the men who've passed through her life. She hasn't hit the jackpot yet, the money load, but she will.'

There was a silence while Lena and Damien appeared to assess one another. Mauve's eyes went from one to another, one repeated word filtering through her brain – *run, run* – but in which direction? She was in the centre, and both had guns.

'She's playing games with me,' Lena said at last. 'She tells me she hasn't transferred my money yet. Let's see if a bullet in her leg brings her to her senses, makes her more cooperative.' Lena raised her gun again, pointing it directly at Mauve's legs.

In the second she pointed the gun, there was a flurry. Mauve gasped as she caught the movement of a second shadow breaking free from the blackness. While Damien had been holding Lena's attention, someone had crept in through the gap at the back of the barn. Unlike the first, this shadow moved with alacrity, one leg in the air as it leapt into the light to materialise as Eliza.

Eliza's booted foot hit Lena solidly in the back as the gun fired. Lena fell to the ground, face down. Dropping the weapon, it skittered wildly, spinning in circles on the concrete floor.

Lena rolled with a groan onto her back. She stopped moving as she looked up at her daughter standing over her sprawled body.

'I am the daughter of Lazor Jaworski.' Eliza spoke clearly, her voice filling the barn. 'I am not and never will be a Kelly.'

35

Mauve reacted to the sudden flurry of movement, falling back against the wooden wall of the old barn.

'Are you OK?' Damien raced to take her arm.

She nodded, her face sweaty and pasty with shock as she allowed him to guide her to the chair with the broken back. Sitting down, she watched him go to the gun on the floor and push it with his foot towards the door, out of Lena's reach.

'Thank God she's such a terrible shot,' he said.

Mauve looked from him to Eliza.

'My son's hurt; Robin shot him,' Mauve said. Her eyes filled like pools with tears.

'I know, my dear. And it's all going to be fine.' Damien took her hand. 'I've been in the house and put a belt around Kit's arm to stem the blood loss. Your friend Charlie is sitting with him. An ambulance is on its way.'

Mauve thought of her father, a ladies' man whose chivalrous attention had kept them spellbound. Her heart warmed to Damien, and she squeezed his hand.

'You pair of shits!' Lena hollered. 'You, my daughter, my own flesh and blood,' she pointed at Eliza, 'taking her side against me, and you, Damien…'

An indistinct sound from afar was approaching, and Mauve recognised the ambulance's siren.

'You bastard!' Lena screeched. 'It's the police. They aren't finding me here. I've got to go.'

'The police arrived a while ago,' Damien said calmly. 'It's the ambulance for Kit.'

'Where's Robin?' Lena screamed. '*Robin, Robin!*'

'He can't hear you. He's having a little nap in the house cellar. Charlie told me that a dog had savaged the poor man.' Damien winked at Mauve. 'He's not having a good day.'

'He's your brother. Are you giving him up so easily to the police… and me?' Lena's voice turned from shrill into a broken sob. 'If it's the money, there'll be plenty. We can split it three ways.'

In response, Damien walked outside into the moonlight. Lifting his arm, he waved it in a circle before stepping back.

'What are you doing?' Lena said.

The sound of boots running, crunching on gravel, grew louder and a moment later, four police officers wearing padded bulletproof jackets and carrying guns rushed into the barn.

'Brigadier.' The lead officer addressed Damien.

'There's no need for weapons now.' Damien's voice sounded official and clipped. 'Thanks to Eliza, the situation is under control.'

'I'm glad your strategy prevented more bloodshed.' The officer nodded to Damien, then Eliza.

'Lena Kelly's gun.' Damien pointed to the gun on the ground.

'Thank you. One of the men will bag it,' the lead officer said. 'Miss Kelly will be interviewed as the main suspect for the Paulette Franklin murder.'

'It's a stitch-up! You'll pay for this!' Lena shrieked at Damien.

'I'm going to take Mauve to the kitchen to see her son.' Damien ignored Lena as he put his hand under Mauve's arm to guide her from the barn.

'Thank you, sir.' The officer tipped his head in deference.

'And you…' Lena turned the force of her anger on Eliza, pointing her finger at her daughter's face. Her words trailed away as Eliza turned her back and walked out of the barn.

Mauve remembered her dismissive words to Eliza about Damien. *He left school at sixteen and joined the army as a squaddie.* Where had that come from? Damien was a brigadier; it was clear he had always been an officer. She cringed. Her words were not only incorrect; they had also revealed her snobbery.

Outside, away from the house, Mauve saw four police cars and a Land Rover moving in a convoy coming from the woods and heading towards the house. There were more officers on the lawn, two shouldering rifles.

'They didn't use the sirens,' Damien said, as if reading Mauve's mind. 'And they parked in the woods far enough away so as not to alert Lena, Robin and Elliot to their arrival.'

'Where is Elliot?' Mauve asked. 'He went to get the car.'

Mauve remembered what the police officer in the barn had said to Damien. *I'm glad your strategy prevented more bloodshed.* Might the shot she'd heard have been for Elliot?

'Don't bother about him, Auntie Mauve.' Eliza, standing at her side like an old buddy, linked arms with her. They progressed in a row, one on either side of Mauve, until they entered the kitchen. The glass panel in the door had been shattered, and inside the glass crunched under their feet.

The kitchen appeared crowded with two paramedics and two female police officers.

'*Mummy!*' Kit, stripped to the waist, tried to get past the sturdy paramedic treating his arm only to be pushed gently back down onto the seat. 'I was so worried about you.'

'Darling!' Mauve ran to embrace her son and rest her head against his.

'He's going to be fine,' Charlie said. 'The bullet went straight through. George here is seeing to him.'

'Hello.' The paramedic looked up at Mauve. 'We're going to take him to hospital now. With the shock and the blood loss, he'll need attention, but this gentleman's actions certainly helped,' he complimented Damien. 'He won't be going home tonight, though.'

'I'll go too,' Mauve said.

'The police will expect a statement later on,' Damien said. 'And no more runners,' he whispered conspiratorially to Mauve.

'I'm going with her,' Charlie said. 'I can promise you, that's not going to happen.'

Later, after the hospital visit and secure in the knowledge that Kit was not in any danger, Mauve and Charlie sat side by side on a bed in a hotel near the hospital. A side lamp brightened the semi-darkened bedroom. The police, having had a brief talk with them, agreed that they could be formally interviewed at 10.00a.m the next morning. Across the end of the bed, Timothy spread himself out to observe the pair.

'It's gone 3.00a.m now.' Charlie looked at his watch. 'There are only seven hours before the interviews. You should try to sleep.'

'I don't think that'll be possible, I'm too wired,' Mauve said, moving to lean against Charlie.

'You know Kit is going to be OK; he'll be asleep now,' Charlie said. 'And the police are aware that Lena is alive, and that she is responsible for Paulette's death.'

'Yes, thank goodness,' Mauve said. 'I told you what happened to me after I left the house.'

'About which – you leaving the house – I was furious. You put yourself in real danger.'

'That's all behind us now. Tell me everything that happened after I left, please?'

'OK.' Charlie wrapped his arm around Mauve's shoulders. 'After putting Robin in the cellar – and believe me, every fibre in my being screamed to chuck him head-first down the steps – but...'

'Being a solicitor and a considerate person, you

couldn't do it,' Mauve finished his sentence.

'That's about it,' Charlie said. 'It took an age to ease him down each step. The key was still in the door, so locking it was no problem. When I got back to the kitchen, you'd gone. I went to the front door and it was closed. I looked outside and could see that you'd gone through the bags in the car.'

'Strewn all over the driveway.'

'Yes,' Charlie agreed. 'You were nowhere to be seen, and I didn't want to leave Kit. I kept a lookout for you from the kitchen window. You'd switched off the lights, and the lawn was moonlit. Kit was still on the floor, with his back against the units, where anyone peering in wouldn't see him. He'd given me the gun. Then Elliot came back, his face against the window.'

'Could he see you?'

'I kept well away, back in the shadows,' Charlie said. 'Elliot went to try the back door, then I heard the glass breaking. I assume he intended to put his arm in to open it that way, but you'd pushed the bolts across when you locked it. It wouldn't have been possible for him to open it.'

Mauve waited. 'Then what?'

'I heard a man's voice. He said, "Put your gun down on the ground and step away." I didn't know it was the brigadier, Lena's half-brother. I assumed it must be the police.' Charlie stroked Mauve's shoulder absentmindedly. 'I could hear Elliot swearing but couldn't see what was happening. Damien repeated the instruction. Then there was a shot.'

'I guessed Elliot had been shot,' Mauve said.

'I went to the back door, and Eliza was there. She said, "Elliot's been shot. It's safe to open the door."'

'Is he dead?' Mauve asked.

'Yes. Eliza told me Elliot raised the gun to point it at Damien. Damien did have a gun, but the shot came from one of the police shooters. And that was it. The police then moved in and moved Elliot's body out of sight. They didn't know Robin was locked in the cellar, where Lena might be, or if either were armed.'

'Then Damien helped Kit?'

'Once he came into the kitchen, and I told him where Robin was,' Charlie said, 'three police officers went to the cellar. I led the way. Damien and Eliza stayed with Kit. I don't think Timothy was going to let Damien near his master. Then he realised Eliza was there, and he was fine.'

'What was Robin like? Was he conscious?'

'Yes, wide awake, swearing and cursing. The police cuffed him, and I left them to it. He wasn't being brought out until they'd found Lena. One of the men spotted her going in through the back of the barn.'

'And I went in through the front.' Mauve shuddered, recalling her encounter with her half-sister.

Charlie squeezed her shoulders.

'What about Timothy? Who put the bandage on his leg?' Mauve asked.

'It was a tea towel I found in the kitchen. I cut it into strips.'

At hearing his name, Timothy looked up.

'Good of the vet to come out so late.' Mauve smiled affectionately at the dog.

'I think that if he hadn't, Kit would have refused to go to hospital,' Charlie said.

'I'm so glad Timothy's OK. *You are my hero.*' Mauve spoke using a baby voice, and Timothy moved up the bed, pushing himself on his belly to squeeze between the pair. And, with a contented rumble, settled there.

'Kit said he didn't know about Eliza's Uncle Damien trailing me, his involvement.'

'No, Damien told Eliza it was on a need-to-know basis. The reason Eliza nobbled the car outside Blackpool was to allow us all to meet Damien. He knew I was on my way to meet up with you, Kit and Eliza. He felt he had enough knowledge and information about what was going on. You were right about someone having searched your bedroom. Eliza had left the back door on the latch. He found the first memory stick, viewed it in his car, and copied it for the police, then instructed Eliza to return it. Eliza got lucky with Timothy wanting to go out. Damien left the memory stick next to the back door.'

'So I wasn't going mad,' Mauve said. 'When Eliza came back she went straight up to use the bathroom.'

'Yes, to your bedroom to return the stick. Damien wanted to talk to you first because he was involving the police. He has a lot of high-up police contacts. He wanted them to be able to go to Paulette's house and be there to catch Lena and Robin, while at the same time trying to ensure you and Kit were protected. Then you took off, blowing the plan!'

'I'm sorry.' Mauve looked hangdog. 'If I'd only known. Is there anything else?'

Charlie nodded. 'The reason Robin had so much information, including about your panic attack in the flat, is that one of DS Sue Teller's team was on his payroll. He was being paid for information on developments.'

'I bet she's annoyed; it casts her team in a bad light.'

'Furious.'

Maeve laughed.

'There is something else.' Mauve looked down at her hands. 'What I didn't do. My head has been all over the place after what happened.'

Charlie waited.

'I didn't say anything to Eliza, I didn't thank her before she left.' Mauve found her eyes filling with tears again. 'I seem to be crying a lot today.' She wiped her eyes with the back of her hands.

'Hardly surprising after the day you've had, Mauve.' Charlie gave her another squeeze. 'There'll be plenty of time to say thank you.'

'I feel terrible,' Mauve said. 'The things I said and thought about Eliza when she's been nothing but kind and considerate. You and Kit told me to trust her, but I didn't listen.'

'She's nothing like her mother,' Charlie said.

'No, not a bit like Lena.' Mauve let the tears flow unchecked. 'That girl saved my life.'

36

'It might have been better if you'd told me about Damien. I mean, once Mummy twigged she was being shadowed,' Kit said. He walked next to Eliza through the woods to reach the lawn on the Franklin Estate.

'I'm sorry,' Eliza said. 'Uncle Damien was adamant it had to be on a need-to-know basis. I knew he wouldn't get involved if I told you or anyone else; we might have blown his cover.'

'He blew that all by himself, although he couldn't have known my mother is obsessed with dirty trainers. She can spot a pair at ten metres!'

'It's so funny; he was in character trailing your mum, trying to protect her. He doesn't normally wear trainers, let alone dirty ones. His shoes are always immaculate, polished to perfection.'

'Then,' Kit said, 'I didn't know Robin and Damien looked *so* much alike. They both have the Kelly square jaw and arched nose. With the cap pulled down over the forehead and the wraparound shades, the parts of his face Mum could see were more prominent. She became convinced it was Robin.'

'Yes, that was awful,' Eliza said. 'Knowing now what your mum went through eight years ago, it must have been scary imagining Robin was stalking her.'

'What is really funny is that my mother assumed Damien would have been a squaddie in the army.' Kit snorted. 'It never occurred to her that he would have been a high-ranking officer. I hate to say it, my mum is the biggest snob on planet Earth!'

'Hilarious,' Eliza agreed. 'But she'd had no contact with him since childhood. Although she might have worked out that his father had to be wealthy. Bonnie didn't waste her time on penniless men.'

'She wouldn't have married for love?'

'No way,' Eliza said. 'Uncle Damien told me his father had approached Bonnie to ask if he could take his son, paying Bonnie a sizable amount to drop any future legal claim. He'd been lucky, with both father and stepmother adoring him. He grew up with two younger half-brothers. When he expressed an interest in joining the army, his dad supported his ambitions. Happily, Damien was able to gain a place at Sandhurst.'

'Top drawer,' Kit said. 'I'm just so pleased he was there for Mum and came through for her. Was he SAS?'

'I've often wondered, but if I asked, he wouldn't tell me,' Eliza said. 'I know he worked undercover and in some strange places. I'm sure he wouldn't talk about it if he had been in the SAS.'

Having reached the boundary between the woods and

lawn, they paused to take in the peace of their surroundings. The sun was high in a cloudless blue sky, and there was no sound other than the cry of a song thrush. Timothy, who had been following behind, stopped to stretch and yawn.

'Has your mum decided what to do with this place yet?' Eliza asked.

'She said she'll sell it,' Kit replied.

'Do you feel sorry about that?'

'Not really. I get where she's coming from. There was the murder of Paulette, and then what happened to her here with Robin and Lena. She said she would never forget the wonderful memories of her childhood visits and time spent with Paulette at the house, but these other events have been too upsetting.'

'It is a difficult one. It was nice to suggest we visit and enjoy the house and gardens. We chose a good weekend.' Eliza waved her hand to shoo a wasp away as she looked at the expanse of green lawn that lay ahead, lit by the summer sunshine.

'And good to have my arm out of the sling,' Kit said.

'Shame what happened meant you missing out on the finals of the TV Talent Make-up Awards.'

'It would have been difficult to take part one-handed.' Kit smiled. 'Anyway, it helped being in the final three. I think that's what swung it to get the apprenticeship with the BBC.'

'And I'm enjoying my college course, thanks to your mum.'

'Good old Mummy, she came through in the end.'

Eliza looked towards the house broodingly. 'It's a

shame she lost Paulette's friendship,' Eliza said. 'Whenever she mentions her it's clear she was an important part of her childhood.'

'She never lost her love,' Kit said. 'Paulette wouldn't have left this place to her if the love wasn't still there. Mummy said Celia was cold and uninterested when she was a child. Celia didn't like children. Having a daughter interfered with her social life, and she loved the endless whirl of parties and functions, whereas Paulette always had time for Mummy. She made her feel grown-up and special. Mummy said Paulette thought of her as the daughter she'd never had.'

'Her feelings might not just have been about your mother, with Paulette being in love with Henry. I can't help but wonder if she constructed a fantasy world with Henry and his daughter, your mum, at its centre,' Eliza said.

'Yes,' Kit said, thinking. 'Mum told me it wasn't *just* an affair between Henry and Paulette; the love was reciprocated.'

'After her mother passed away, why did Mauve not contact Paulette to restart the relationship?'

'I think she felt it would be disloyal to her mother,' Kit said. 'When Lena suggested they visit Paulette, for Lena it was all about the jewellery. I think Mum thought going there with Lena would break the ice; she could reconnect with Auntie Paulette. She didn't know when she arrived at Paulette's house that she'd be completely off her head with the drugs Lena slipped into the booze. And she could never have imagined what Robin and Lena had in store for poor Paulette.'

'Shame Paulette stole the diamonds,' Eliza said. 'It screwed her relationship with Henry as much as with Celia.'

'"The Queen's Diamonds". I think she did it to hurt Celia, who, after all, was still married to the man she loved. Paulette really had believed he would divorce Celia and marry her.' Kit sighed, and they walked across the lawn. 'The diamonds are how it all started. And Lena was convinced she could make Paulette tell her where they were. That's why they brought Mummy here. If Lena and Robin's bullying couldn't convince Paulette, Lena believed seeing Mummy in that shocking state would make Paulette talk.'

'How do you know she didn't?' Reaching the side of the house, Eliza trailed her hand through the greenery of the yew hedging. 'After they killed Paulette, Mauve was out of her mind and didn't know what was going on. They could have found the diamonds and sold them on.'

'Mm. It's possible, but Mummy didn't think they got them. She said Paulette loved a riddle, and where she hid them would be somewhere Mummy would eventually discover them.'

'It'll have to be bloody quick.' Eliza grinned. 'If they're here and she's selling the place, chances are they'll never be found.'

'If they're even still here.' Kit shrugged. 'They could be anywhere. Let's look around. The rose garden first. Mummy copied a lot of the roses Paulette had into her garden in Norfolk.'

Eliza followed Kit and Timothy to the back of the house into the enclosed garden. 'Wow, the perfume is amazing.' She threw her arms out and turned a full circle, breathing in deeply.

'The smell must have been just as lovely the night we were here. I can't say that I noticed.'

'Me neither,' Eliza said. 'Then, it's hardly surprising.'

Later, after exploring the garden, they took a picnic basket from the car and sat with it on the lawn.

'Mummy's not driving you mad now you've moved in with us?' Kit gave his cousin a cheeky grin as he bit into a slice of Victoria sponge.

'No, that will never happen.'

'Ha... give it time,' Kit mocked.

'I'm thrilled she invited me to move in,' Eliza said. 'The room is massive, with an en-suite bathroom. The cherry on the cake is giving me a workroom for my sewing machine and a drawing table, and her telling me to have both rooms redecorated to my own taste, with her paying. I could never have afforded anything like that. And she's just been so sweet to me.'

'Mummy always said Lena was one extreme or the other, nothing in the middle.' Kit wiped his hands on a paper tissue before rolling onto his side to scratch Timothy behind the ear. 'It must be a family trait. As much as you could do nothing right before, you can do no wrong now. Not forgetting the small matter of you having saved her life!'

Eliza smiled, looking around at the garden. 'I can't believe how calm and perfect it is here. It's putting a few bad memories to sleep.'

'Have you,' Kit said hesitantly, 'heard any more from Lena? I know she contacted you.'

'I heard from her through her solicitor,' Eliza said. 'She asked if I would go and see her.' A shadow of sadness passed across her face. 'I'm not saying never,' she said. 'I told the solicitor to relay that I can't see her now. It's too soon. Maybe once the trial is over, maybe sometime in the future.'

'It's difficult,' Kit said.

'Absolute hell,' Eliza agreed. 'The idea that they were at the flat, hiding, when I went there. They were about to set the trap… it makes me feel sick.'

'You don't know for sure.'

'It's what Uncle Damien and the police think must have happened. Lena and Uncle Robin won't talk about it. The lock on the front door was already broken.' Eliza looked far away, remembering. 'Horrible that they hid, probably in the back garden.'

'Although it was finding the flat stripped and me telling you about Mum doing a runner that prompted you to contact Uncle Damien.'

'Yes.' Eliza nodded. 'That's when I phoned him and told him everything. He's been brilliant. I can talk and offload my feelings onto him. He knows better than anyone what Robin and Lena are like.'

'What does he say?'

'He says I shouldn't do anything I don't want to.' Eliza started to clear the debris of the picnic into a bag. 'About Lena, he says if I decide I can't bear to see her, that's OK, then if in the future I change my mind, that is also OK.'

'Good advice,' Kit said. 'Come on.' He got up, followed by Timothy, lightening the mood. 'Let's look around the house. Mummy had the agency send someone in to ensure the bedrooms were aired and there was fresh linen. The bedrooms are on the same floor facing one another, so we can leave our doors open and shout to one another if we hear creaks in the night.'

'You OK about the kitchen?' Eliza looked sideways at her cousin. 'It's where you got shot.'

'I'm not on my own,' Kit said. 'I've got my two best buddies with me.' He smiled, looking down at Timothy. 'And there is something I want to explore before the light fades.'

'What?'

'In the rose garden.' Kit raised his eyebrows.

'Tell me.'

'One of the roses… Mum has it in her garden in Norfolk. It's the Queen Elizabeth II's Diamond Jubilee Rose. Known as the Queen's Diamond Jubilee Rose.' Kit looked smug.

'You're not thinking…' Eliza stood up, staring toward the rose garden. 'Mauve said Paulette liked puzzles and quizzes. It's got "queen" and "diamond" in the description.'

'It's got to be worth a look. There are spades in the barn.'

'Very funny! Any clubs? OK, but you must be careful when transplanting a rose bush. We don't want to kill it. We'd need to dig a wide area around the base to ensure we get all the root ball.'

'Don't tell me.' Kit laughed as he put his hands on his

hips to assume a position as he faced his cousin. 'Which boyfriend taught you all about gardening, and did he last longer than six months?'

'His name was Neil, and no, he lasted just under four months.' Eliza laughed. 'Bugger going in to check out the house. While it's still light, let's go dig up that rose bush; see if anything's lurking underneath.'

37

'Small, round and dark.' Charlie described DS Sue Teller's eyes. 'Like piss holes in the snow.'

'I'm glad I'll never meet her again,' Mauve said. 'Ever.'

Damien laughed. Beside him, an attractive woman with dark, shoulder-length hair joined in.

'Grace thought it hilarious that the dirty trainers made you notice me,' Damien said, looking at his wife. 'It blew my surveillance cover.'

'Look at him.' Grace waved her hand towards to her husband's pristine shirt, smart trousers and shiny black shoes. 'He's every inch an army officer, even out of uniform. The very idea of wearing dirty shoes appals him.'

'I was in disguise.' Damien patted his wife's hand. 'Incognito. the shoes and clothes were meant to make me blend in.'

'Mauve has a similar aversion: white trainers that are grubby.' Charlie pulled a face. 'It's just something she notices.'

'There we are. I wasn't to know.' Damien put his teacup into its saucer on the marble counter before him.

In Mauve's London kitchen, the four were seated on high stools around the central marble unit, on which rested teacups, cakes and biscuits.

'You said you were hearing from the FLO, the family liaison officer, last week, right?' Damien looked at Mauve.

'Yes, she came here to see me and Charlie,' Mauve said. 'Kit and Eliza were here as well. They also wanted to know how things had progressed in the last six months.'

'I understand this house is home to both now,' Grace said.

'Yes.' Mauve's gaze moved around the spacious kitchen. 'You probably know my ex, Zack, moved out after I came home.'

'And I moved in a short time later,' Charlie said as he pushed a plate of small cakes closer to Grace and Damien.

'Strangely, Zack and I are still on friendly terms,' Mauve said. 'It came out he'd been seeing someone called Joanna. I didn't know about her. He told me after we'd sat down to put our cards on the table. It was a relief for both of us to call time on our relationship. It was easier with us never having married.'

'You made him a generous settlement.' Charlie looked at Mauve over his teacup. 'More than was strictly necessary for an ex who wasn't your husband!'

'Yes, to set him free,' Mauve said. 'I don't think I treated him well when we were together. The money will give him choices he wouldn't otherwise have.'

'The house is big, lots of space,' she went on, moving

the subject away from her ex-partner. 'It only seemed sensible for Eliza to move in here with us. She has her own en-suite bedroom. And she's taken over a room at the back to set up her drawing board and her sewing machine.'

'She likes it because it overlooks the magnolia tree in the garden,' Charlie chipped in. 'It's not much to look at now, but it was in bloom when she moved in.'

'The children won't be long. I shouldn't really call them children.' Mauve glanced at her watch. 'They're desperate to see both of you. And it's so wonderful you can stay overnight so we can all have dinner together and have a few drinks with nobody having to drive. Eliza is cooking. We take turns.'

'Kit said he'll act as Eliza's sous-chef for the evening,' Charlie added. 'Which means all the washing-up will get done as they go along.'

'Eliza phones every few weeks,' Grace said. 'She keeps in touch.'

'She's very close to the two of you,' Mauve said.

'Which is why she decided to contact me when she became concerned about you,' Damien said to Mauve. 'As you know, Kit contacted her after your visit to Lena's basement flat and you'd been put under caution by the police. If anyone is aware of what a nightmare Lena can be, it's her daughter. And, as half-siblings, I know Lena and Robin only too well. None of it good.'

'I understand your first Christmas together in the house was quite jolly,' Grace said.

'Best Christmas I've ever had.' Mauve smiled at Charlie. 'Kit making a full recovery after the shooting made it feel extra special. I don't like thinking how close I got to losing him.'

'Or him losing you,' Damien pointed out.

'Yes,' Mauve agreed, her voice shaky.

'Kit had invited his boyfriend, Jake. And Veronica made an appearance over Christmas,' Charlie said. 'She played the piano, and Eliza gave her rendition of "White Christmas". She has such a lovely voice. Eliza's latest boyfriend, Max, also joined us, so we were six.'

'It felt so old-fashioned and Christmassy with us all gathered around the piano.' Mauve shivered. 'Even now, I get happy goosebumps remembering it.'

'*Hrrrrhoo*.' Timothy emerged from under the unit, his tail wagging gently.

'Ahh. Is Timothy saying he likes a happy ending?' Grace smiled.

'He's more likely to be asking where the devil has Kit got to,' Charlie said. 'And what time is dinner.'

'Getting back to the FLO,' Damien said seriously. 'You've kept us up to date with everything that happened after that evening last year. We haven't spoken since the FLO's visit.'

'She's very good,' Mauve said. 'Calm and informative. The court case comes to trial in just over eight weeks.'

'In March,' Charlie said. 'Neither of them, as you know, was allowed bail.'

'Robin and Lena were both charged with Paulette's murder and an attempt to pervert the course of justice by setting me up to take the fall for Lena's murder,' Mauve said. 'Robin has been charged with grievous bodily harm for shooting Kit. Also, for the murder of Adam Manning. He was his next-door neighbour in Lincoln. Foolishly, Adam had tried to blackmail Robin. He watched for comings and goings at Robin's house, reporting back when I turned up there with Kit and later with Kit and Eliza. Adam saw the photograph of me in the paper and suggested he might get a better reward from the police if he were to contact them!'

'He chose the wrong person to blackmail,' Damien said.

Charlie nodded. 'And Robin and Lena rather shot themselves in the foot with the film clips left for Mauve to find in Robin's house. The intention was to get her to Paulette's house and then use the clips to convince the police of Mauve's guilt. They're now part of the evidence to be used by the prosecution team in the case against them, proof that Mauve, having been drugged, was not capable of murder. Lena and Robin were clearly playing her. She could barely stand.'

'It sounds like they will both go away for a long time,' Grace said.

'Yes,' Mauve said, her voice bitter, 'I'd like them to throw away the key.'

They sat in companionable silence as Mauve went to boil the kettle and filled the teapot with fresh teabags and hot water.

'There was some good news,' Mauve said as she rejoined them at the table.

'The Queen's Diamonds?' Damien said.

'Yes. You knew Kit and Eliza worked out where they were and dug them up?'

'Under the rose bush named, in honour of Queen Elizabeth II, the Queen's Diamond Jubilee?' Grace asked.

'It was such a whopper of a clue. I can't believe I didn't work it out.' Mauve smiled. 'Paulette loved games with clues, crosswords or anything involving mental challenges. She left me the house and I believe she imagined I'd work it out.'

'Her death, and the manner of it, put you in a bad place.' Charlie stroked Mauve's hand next to his, resting on the counter. 'Why would you have thought about it with all the horror in your life?'

'No more panic attacks?' Damien asked.

'No,' Mauve said. 'I'm doing well.'

'And,' Charlie said, 'you no doubt saw in the papers that the diamond necklace sold for two point four million.'

'Yes, we saw the press coverage. It belonged to your mother, I understand,' Damien said, looking at Mauve.

'Because the insurance company didn't pay out for the theft, the necklace still belonged to Mauve's mother,' Charlie said. 'When the value of the sale hit the newspapers, Mauve received a letter from Lena's solicitor. She believed it belonged to Henry and wanted half the money. Mauve's solicitor put him straight. After the theft, all paperwork and contact with the insurance company was in the name of the legal owner, Celia Gilcrest. On Celia's death, ownership passed from Celia to Mauve, and Lena wasn't entitled to a bean. And I can't help but think how she believed she'd enjoy spending the money from inside a prison cell.'

'I wouldn't want the bloody thing,' Mauve said.

'Mummy thought the superstition surrounding it was amusing. It's said to bring bad luck to anyone who has it or is associated with it.'

'That's true of Marie Antoinette and Paulette,' Grace put in.

'And,' Mauve added, 'look what's happened between me and Lena.'

'The papers said it had been bought by a Russian oligarch for his wife,' Grace said.

'Good luck to her,' Mauve said. 'I hope she enjoys wearing them. And…' she hesitated, 'I wanted some good to come out of it. Kit and Eliza found it. They deserved a reward. I've invested half, the other fifty per cent is split between the two of them. It's in trust funds. They have some money in the bank and a monthly allowance.'

'That is generous,' Damien said. 'Eliza did say she'd come into some money, but didn't tell us how.'

'I know you provided funds so she could take up the place she'd been offered at art college,' Grace said. 'And she lives here as a family member, rent-free. We offered her money recently, a top-up. She told us that she was sorted. We guessed it was you.'

'I told her that I didn't want her to move. But I did ask if, knowing she was financially secure, she might prefer not to live with us. I didn't want her to feel an obligation to stay. As I said before, money gives freedom of choice.' Mauve looked around at the three faces. 'She told me I wasn't getting rid of her that easily, that I'm stuck with her *whatever*! She said she's happier with us – Charlie, me and Kit – than she's ever been. We are her family now.' Mauve's lips trembled and she sniffed, determined not to cry. 'I think her childhood lacked any form of joy or happiness.'

'Yes,' Damien agreed. 'I suspect things were quite awful for the poor girl. Bonnie's influence had a long reach through the generations. It was Eliza's father who made his daughter's life worthwhile. She adored him, but she was young when he died.'

Timothy began barking, running out of the kitchen to the front door, then running back, alerting them to an arrival.

'That must be them now.' Mauve smiled as she followed Timothy out again into the hall.

'Out of interest,' Damien's voice was low and conspiratorial, 'Max – Eliza's current boyfriend – does he have a speciality, workwise?'

Charlie smiled knowingly, joining in with the joke, his voice barely above a whisper. 'Max is the head chef in a restaurant with not one, but two, Michelin stars.' He winked. 'She's only been seeing him for five months. He is such a sweet, lovely bloke; we're all hoping it will go beyond six months.'

Damien glanced at Grace and back to Charlie, all sharing the same smile. 'Wow!' he said. 'I'm so glad we came when it's Eliza was turn to cook!'

About the author

Kate High is a graduate of the Faber Academy and a contemporary metals artist. She has exhibited internationally, with her work having been displayed at the V&A, the Design Council, and sold through Liberty London. The Estonian Museum of Modern Art holds one of Kate's pieces in its private collection. Before founding Lincs-Ark, a charity dedicated to supporting older animals, Kate worked with the RSPCA.